Hustling Backwards

A Novel

By Ronald R. Hanna

<u>Special Thanks and Tribute</u>

To Lloyd Johnson, model for my front and back covers, for providing me a number of exceptional photographs for future use and authorizing me to use them, although you have long since passed on spiritually. As we so often discussed, we are physical conduits for continuous spirits, on a universal sojourn sometimes unfathomable in the present. Your untimely exit from the physical plane is a constant reminder to me of how fleeting our lives can be when we combine "hustling" with an indulgence in mind-altering chemicals in misguided efforts at celebrating our lives and accomplishments. Rest in peace always my brother, and when allowed to, arise and pass on your galactic experiences to us still struggling in the clear and present.

Dedication

To Allen Ford Jr., Darryl T. Young, Lloyd Johnson, Reginald Walter Jones, Tony Hursey, "Cisco," Ronald Holley, and all the brothers from Southeast/Garfield, Parklands, Valley Green and Barry Farm who made the 1960s, 1970s and 1980s some of the most memorable of times, and those which provided me with enough crisp memories to write about for a lifetime.

Chapter One

There were guardrails aligning both sides of the tight, two-lane road which skirted the hillside just above the Potomac River. Ellis was unfamiliar with the area, having just dropped off a new female friend at her apartment in an equally unfamiliar section of Alexandria, Virginia and taken this foreign route back to the city. They'd both had more than a few drinks earlier; it was now shortly before sunrise, and he was trying to get home to his live-in girlfriend while she remained in a deep sleep and perhaps not be aroused and take note of the early morning hour.

The guardrails reflected the lights from his late-model SUV, causing him to glance askew as he rounded curves shadowed by the lush overhanging trees. On a particularly steep section of the parkway, he lost it. The SUV seemed to dance a drunken skedaddle along one guardrail, sending sparks into the air and causing Ellis to panic. He overcorrected, sending the vehicle into the oncoming lane. He immediately regained control however, finally eased on the brakes and slow-rolled out of the heavily wooded section, glad to see the broadening road and the overhead lights before him. At a deserted gas station he pulled into a service lane, got out and inspected the damage.

"Damn!" he spat in frustration, eyeing the inch-wide scar marking the black paint the entire length of the passenger's side. "Ain't that a bitch!"

He climbed back behind the steering wheel, then headed further east. Immediately he began lambasting the young woman he'd been with earlier, reasoning that had she submitted completely to his advances he would not have been so frustrated and drowsy and would not have done the damage to his prized vehicle. The cost of repairs would cut deeply into his unsteady income, he was already estimating. During his often tumultuous twenty-five years, he'd always blamed others for his problems, and this was surely no exception. As he neared home, he mentally played over schemes to get the woman to somehow pay for this latest in a string of costly misfortunes.

"The bitch gonna have to put some of my products out there in her 'hood," he whispered to himself, pulling up before the apartment building, easing out of the car and quietly moving towards his girlfriend's unit in that awkward, be-bopping gait he'd assumed since his teenaged years.

He tried to make as little noise as possible when freeing the multiple locks on the apartment door, hoping Shantelle was in the rear bedroom, in a deep sleep. But apparently she'd spent the night on the plush living room sofa awaiting him, head planted on a pillow near the end table clock which glowed a prominent red "4:37 a.m."

"So," her drowsy voice arose from the darkness. "Who's the little skeezer had your ass out there till this time of morning?"

He moved in a practiced pattern around the coffee table, to an end table and turned on a low-wattage lamp, even then forming the toothy smile she so loved and formulating his alibi.

"You know I had to be out there handling my business, baby," he said, setting on the end of the sofa, reaching under the comforter and running a hand along a warm thigh. "Had to get my hustle on, baby. You know that."

She sat up. "I thought them young'uns you got slingin' for you were handling your shit on the streets. Thought you ain't have to bother with that kinda stuff no more. Come here."

She reached for him, and he unsuccessfully attempted to feign away the motion he knew she was trying for. She buried her nose into his chest, then as immediately recoiled. The sweet smell of an unfamiliar female fragrance pierced her nostrils, and a sharper pain rankled her brain, her heart, the very fabric of her being.

"Mother fucker!" she shouted, throwing back the comforter and maneuvering her legs around him. "You tired-ass mother fucker!"

She arose and dashed into the rear bedroom, and as he sat trying to formulate some sort of plea, he pulled on the front of his shirt himself, whiffed the fragrance Janet had virtually embedded in him and shook his head. He could hear a tumult coming from the back, but couldn't imagine what Shantelle was doing. He found out in moments, as she rushed back into the living room, arms laden with what appeared to be every bit of clothing he had in the apartment whose lease bore only Shantelle Bridgefield's name.

She tossed the mound at his feet.

"Here's all your shit! Now get the fuck back to that bitch you was with! And don't even *think* about calling me or ever coming back in here! I'm tired of your shit, Ellis! Mother fucker..."

While her tears flowed, he managed a slight smile, arose and began gathering his things. He placed them on a chair by the door, turned and moved to her.

"Baby, you know how it is," he pleaded, moving to embrace her. "I was just, you know, out there and some honey I've known for a long time gave me a hug. That's all. I smell her perfume on my shirt. That's what the problem is? Come on. You know me better than that."

"Fuck you," she said softly, twisting with little true effort to free herself from his embrace.

"You know how it is," he repeated, lips on her cheek, on an ear, lightly grazing, nibbling at her lips. "All these holidays coming up. I gots to make my bank. Come on. Let's go to bed and talk about this in the morning."

"It is morning, mother fucker...."

But he had her now, in a closeness she'd given in to first three years earlier, when they'd initially met. And he leaned back, flashed the smile which had warmed her and won her over countless times, seduced her and not for the first time made her contemplate forgiveness and again reason that she was so wrong about him, about the present charges.

"Man, I got to get ready for work in another hour or so," she relented, moving back to the bedroom and looking over her shoulder to him. "You coming?"

"I'm coming," he said, then placed a hand down the front of his pants, stroking himself and again faulting the woman he'd been with in Virginia earlier for failing to sate his always active sexual appetite.

He gathered his clothes.

"Yeah, Shantelle. I'm coming," he whispered. "Or I will be in a minute, better bet it."

* * *

There were few things Ellis Davidson wanted for besides regular sex, toking on a blunt marijuana joint with regularity, and the equally regular trips out to Sam's Car Detailing joint, the only place where the $2500.00 rims on his black SUV could be polished to the splendor they'd been when he dropped a few hours' income on them the previous spring. At a slender six-foot seven-inches tall, he towered over most of his young friends, and even more so over the young women he counted as among his regular lovers. Shantelle had a voluptuous build, nice globular rear and fine, shapely legs. But at a mere five-foot six-inches she stood barely to Ellis's muscular chest, making his nickname for her, "Shorty," even more appropriate.

They'd met at Martin's, a fine dance club in suburban Maryland not that far from either's D.C. neighborhood. She was attracting the attention of a host of young men well into their cognacs and colas, some virtually foaming at the mouth as she and her friend Lana sat at a table for two just alongside the dance floor. She'd peered through the clutch of boisterous men directly at Ellis when he walked slowly into the club and took a seat at the twenty-foot long bar. He caught her gaze, smiled, then turned his back to the dance floor, to her, and ordered a Remy. He'd sip on that for the duration of his time there, merely coming to the haunt favored by many of his age set for a prearranged meeting with his friend Mumbles.

Shantelle told Lana that she thought that the young man at the bar was "all that." She could just tell, she said, by the way he carried himself, by the way he dressed, the way he walked, the way he eased onto the barstool, giving her a glance but not appearing all that interested. She was determined to get with him from that first glance, and was sure that, should she not make a move then, he would disappear from her presence and perhaps never be seen again. So she excused herself from her friend and the leering gentlemen around her table and walked over to Ellis, introduced herself.

Of course Ellis took her approach as a green light, giving indication that a sexual dalliance was possible with little effort, and after a few drinks, an exchange of phone numbers and a cursory dismissal for that particular night, she received a call from him just over a week later, was "scooped up," treated to a minimum fast-food order and bedded within hours of their second meeting.

Now he was in a quandary, unable and unwilling to relinquish the female associates in his immediate past nor what had been a perceived blessing in his immediate presence. Sure, his love for Shantelle had grown with expedience, and was unequivocal. And he also developed feelings for her children. But Ellis cherished the admiration given by his peers when he detailed the most recent conquest, using words he would never use in the presence of women. He was hard-set on developing his "creds" among the fellas, ensuring his place in a perceived realm of male conquest and territorial domination which fit well within his current chosen profession.

Ellis was a self proclaimed "hustler." He'd been so since a stepfather put him to work selling small quantities of marijuana in his old neighborhood, a parcel of two-story seedy public housing projects set on a hillside in the furthest corner of Southeast Washington. The neighborhood was so far from the bustling and moneyed sections of the nation's capital that if one were to virtually fall out of bed, they'd likely land in an equally seedy section of Prince Georges County, Maryland which abutted this part of the District. Since quitting school in the 10th grade, he'd never even considered legal employment. His stepfather, long since carted off to do another in a string of judicial sentences in some far away federal institution, had left him with the necessary contacts to continue his illegal trade. Now, after twelve years of hustling, he held no plans in life to do anything else.

*   *   *

"You gonna take me to pick up the kids?" Shantelle asked, climbing out of the bed after their brief but satisfactory encounter.

"Yeah, I got you, babe," Ellis answered, exhausted but relieved that he'd apparently been forgiven for this latest of transgressions. He really needed some rest, but would do as Shantelle wanted, retrieve the children from her mother's and try to get some sleep while little Ebony and Derrick, hopefully, confined themselves to the rear bedroom and occupied themselves with the PlayModule system he'd bought them.

"And you got that money for my mother I promised her to watch them this weekend?"

She was standing at the bedroom door fully dressed as he struggled back into a pair of oversized jeans.

"What you tell her: Fifty?"

"A hundred, Ellis. You know she asked me for a hundred to help her with that gas bill."

"Damn! And you told her that you had it, huh?"

"Yeah, Ellis. You don't have no problem with that, do you?"

"I got it. I got it."

He arose, pulled a knot of money from a pants pocket, peeled off some twenties.

"I ain't make but a few hundred last night, baby. And then I banged up my ride a little like that, out there all drowsy and shit trying to take care of my business. Ain't make no profit out this mother fucker, you count what I'm spending and shit. Damn."

She took the money he held forth, left the room.

"What you need to do is get yourself a regular job," she shouted back from the living room. "Like you got some sense."

But Ellis only allowed her suggestion to momentarily filter into his mind. He couldn't even fathom what a "regular job" for him would consist of. He counted out seven-hundred forty dollars he'd come in with this morning, kept two-hundred in his pocket and put the remainder with a mass of bills bound with rubber bands in a shoe box under the bed.

"I got a regular job," he said, looking into the mirror and running a hair brush over his head, his light beard. "I'm a hustler, yo. And a damn good one."

Chapter Two

When the unemployment rate among black teens reached 27 percent in Washington and the national unemployment picture was bleak by half as much, depression took hold of an unprecedented segment of the general population. Psychological woes were even more pervasive among those wallowing in deep poverty, with food and shelter evasive for many even in the capital of the world's wealthiest nation. Quick fixes to remedy mental desolation only served to further deepen the state of abject poverty some were experiencing, and the ever-present liquor stores in mostly low-income sections of the District were experiencing staggering sales.

Still purveying their products on the streets of the most depressed communities, the dealers of heroin, cocaine and marijuana didn't lack business either, further serving to debilitate these communities both financially and socially. The local and national lotteries also stripped untold millions from the same communities, leaving the by now $4.00 loaves of bread at the corner store a luxury for all but a few.

Ellis didn't consider himself part of the problem, for he justified his drug associated largess with his being afforded the wherewithal to see after Shantelle's two children, whose own father had been killed in a drug-related misadventure not a year earlier. And he did contribute to the financial needs of his own two: Lauren, a year old, by Donna in the Kenilworth section of the city, and Michelle, a three-year-old, by Linda in the Barry Farm public housing project in another section of the far Southeast community.

Danger in various forms did certainly haunt such drug marketers however, and Ellis had seen his life flash before his eyes on a number of occasions. There was always the "stick-up boys," a generic term used for those marauders whose sole occupation was the robbing of individuals, groups or establishments. By the time of the most recent economic turmoil, these felonious individuals and groups numbered in the thousands, and were as common as the "original gangsters" with names such as Dillinger, the Barrow Gang, and Capone.

But unlike these historic hoodlums, the present-day miscreants lacked few mores, and would often become victims of members of their own posses when one or another felt their needs additionally pressing, or simply fell under the influence of some mind alterative themselves and, always armed, took out their frustrations on the closest presence.

Ellis trusted no one. Not even Shantelle. Not his mother. He didn't know his father, but had been told that he was being released from prison soon after serving twenty-one years. And Ellis hardly said but a few words to his own childhood associates when they returned to the streets after serving time. He didn't trust them, and his own father was surely a stranger, not to be sought out nor shown any measure of trust.

He feared the police, and especially "snitches." Ellis had never so much as generated a speeding ticket, and had an innate fear of ever getting caught up in some misdeed, convicted, and sent off to some joint for an extended period of time. To ensure he never did, he trusted no one. Not his girlfriend. Not his closest friends. Not his own mother.

A towering figure, he'd missed his chance at playing collegiate-level basketball through his insistence that he "get his hustle on," on the street corners instead of at practice when a standout on his high school squad. And dropping out in the eleventh grade didn't heighten his appeal among college recruits who'd been previously scouting him. So the lanky youth entered adulthood with little career prospects, and never well-read, opted out of even potential suitable employment ventures directed his way by family friends when he insisted on taking home required employment applications instead of filling them out at job locations. His reading and writing skills were fundamentally unsound, and he'd succeeded in hiding the fact even through the three years of high school he'd attended.

If anyone could be considered a true friend, it was Mumbles, his cohort in the drug trade and a friend since the two were pre-teens. The two comprised a team so at physical odds to one another that few who saw the two together could imagine the pair being more than casual acquaintances. Ellis towered over the short, muscular Mumbles, who'd gained his nickname as a child due to a speech impediment and whose true name remained a mystery even among those he regularly did business with. Even Ellis had only a cloudy recollection of having once spoken to Mumbles' mother years ago, and still only guessed that his cohort perhaps bore the same last name as "Mrs. Johnson."

The two met regularly, and even though Ellis formed the titular head of his drug posse, Mumbles had always been equally rewarded in their financial profits, though he was more so responsible for the least attractive segment of the venture: Intermingling with the team of underlings who ensured their products saturated the streets of particular Southeast and Northeast Washington neighborhoods. It was time for them to resupply their legions on a chilly morning midweek, just prior to the lucrative Thanksgiving holiday. They met, as usual, at Melody's Bar-b-Que Rib Shack, a flat, nondescript business on the avenue which divided Southeast Washington from Prince George's County, Maryland.

"H...h....h....hey...E...E....Ellis," Mumbles stuttered, arising and greeting his associate with a customary embrace.

"Mumbles," Ellis said, took a seat in the booth his friend occupied.

"Di....di....." He paused, a common effort abided by close friends, when he couldn't get his words out.

"Di....di....did...F...For..For...Forman...ha...h a...have the...sh....sh...shit?"

"He had it, man. And it was the bomb. I had one of them crack head bitches down on 22nd check it out. Mumbles, that shit had her choking. We gotta get this shit out by tonight. I got it diced up. In the trunk. I'm gonna put you down with a shitload. You oughta come back with about ten grand off this shit, okay?"

"O…O..ku…ku...O..ku…ku…yeah…E…Ellis."

The two could be seen through the floor-to-ceiling windows of the rib joint by the two men in the late-model Cadillac parked across the avenue, on the D.C. side of the strip. They knew Ellis's car, and knew also the battered pick-up Mumbles used when running drug transactions to appear less conspicuous.

"You might have to bust one in his ass, know what I'm saying," the man behind the wheel of the Cadillac said to his front seat passenger.

"I don't give a fuck," the passenger said. "Much shit as you say he'll be holding, I probably need to off his ass anyway. Make sure ain't no come-back. That boy Ellis ain't no bitch-ass mother fucker. His boy recognize us from around the way, they be back on our asses. Might as well cap his ass, make sure of that shit, know what I'm saying?"

"Yeah. That might be best, yo."

Chapter Three

Miss Melody, who owned the rib joint with her husband David, was acutely aware of the happenings along her neighborhood streets, and equally familiar with the mannerisms, the personalities, the events in the lives of the young black men and women who made up her primary customers. A robust woman whose generous girth was reflective of her love for the pork products she sold and a general liking of a lifetime of consuming sugary "soft" drinks, for years she'd observed her primarily youthful, black clientele, nurtured many of them and quite often provided the caring shoulder on which many of them leaned. She moved about her establishment trailed by a rear end which moved to a beat all its own.

While business was all but nonexistent as Ellis and Mumbles sat engaged in one of their regular meetings there, Miss Melody moved between preparing ribs for the afternoon rush and casually cleaning the front of the store, particularly the large windows fronting the place. She was keeping an eye on the two men in the Cadillac across the street, and although she was certain most potential miscreants in the neighborhood were well aware that the rib joint was at best a most dangerous target for robbery (both David and Miss Melody had long ago dissuaded a few attempts with fatal blast from the shotgun and pistols both were known to use with precision), she was certain that some of her customers, particularly those whom she knew were involved in the drug trade, might generate the attention of "the stick-up boys" at any given moment.

She took Windex to the windows once again, then walked slowly past the booth Ellis and Mumbles occupied.

"Some boys out there been having an eye on y'all since you showed up here," she whispered, moving further into the carry-out. "In a grey Caddy parked out across the street."

Mumbles, seated facing the window, immediately saw the car Miss Melody spoke of.

"Y...y...yeah.....E.....E.....Ellis....I... El...Ellis. I....I...I...see...I...I...I...see...I see...them."

Ellis wouldn't turn to look, but arose and moved to the counter at the far rear of the carry-out. Miss Melody pinned him with a cautious gaze, a half-smile, then cowered eyes before speaking.

"You know everybody all up in your business from here to Upper Marlboro," she said. "That's the problem with you young'uns: Business you choose require you let on to some seedy people so your business keep going. And the way money tight out here now, you know it's some people always out there gonna try you."

"I hear ya, Miss Melody. I know that car from down there off Shelter Road. Dudes always scoping out my boy Darren when I be going by his crib. I know they're up to something. Stick-up boys. Been known to raze fools they catch sleeping."

"Well," Miss Melody said, turning to the massive grill and slathering sauce on a rack of ribs, "you be careful, you hear me?"

"I hear ya."

She checked on the order he'd placed upon entering, ensuring that the ribs were well done, as he liked them. Two Styrofoam containers were filled to the brim; she struggled to close them, secured them with strips of Scotch tape. He gave her a twenty, waved away the change.

"Good lookin'out, Miss Melody," he smiled, took the containers and returned to Mumbles, who stood just inside the door eyeing the car across the street.

"They…they….they….stick-up…stick-up…boys," Mumbles said, moving out the door and holding it open for Ellis.

"I ain't worried about them fools," Ellis said. "I got my shit."

He eased the front of his NorthFace jacket up, displaying the handle of a pistol tucked within his front beltline.

"I…I…I'm…st…..strapped…t….t….too."

"Cool."

Moving to Mumbles' pick-up, Ellis put one of the containers of ribs in the passenger's side of the Ford, nodded to Mumbles and deposited a brown paper bag under the passenger's seat. Mumbles nodded back, as Ellis moved to his SUV and secured the door. He waited until Mumbles pulled out of the parking lot, watched the idling Cadillac and noticed the attention the two occupants paid to Mumbles. He caught the eye of the man behind steering wheel of the Caddy, nodded his head and cast slit eyes at the driver as if challenging him to make a move.

"Them mother fuckers on to us," the driver whispered to his cohort, not breaking eye contact with Ellis.

"Fuck 'em," the cohort whispered back. "They ain't all that."

"Yeah. But anyway, let's just cool for a minute till they out the way. Know they probably headed down Shelter Road so that boy Darren can re-up. We see what it look like over that end."

"Yeah. Okay."

Chapter Four

Ellis Davidson was among the many young black men who uttered the common reassurance, to themselves and to others, that their mothers hadn't raised any fools. And knowing that the stick-up boys were casing their pre-holiday moves had him immediately on his cellular phone raising Darren, and subsequently Mumbles, rearranging the location of their afternoon meeting. It would be foolish, he admonished both, for them to do any business along the particularly deserted stretch of Shelter Road, where Darren maintained an apartment and where, nearby, a crack strip bustled 24/7 with business. Most of the product being sold there was by Darren and his underlings, who received their supplies solely from Ellis and Mumbles.

Unbeknownst to the two, however, was that Darren, a hard-core gambler who spent many evenings on his knees in the hallway of a Shelter Road apartment building, had just recently crapped out. Literally. The money he'd earned the weekend before Thanksgiving, over three thousand dollars, had been whisked away in a dice game which included among the players the same two young men who'd been surveiling Ellis and Mumbles outside Melody's Bar-B-Que Rib Shack. Darren had left the game not only broke, but still owing one of the men, QT, four-hundred dollars he'd been fronted to remain in the continuously losing gamble. As a result, QT had been surrendered the remaining crack packages Darren had once the craps game ended, and remained unsatisfied with the debt, then chiseled down to a hundred fifty dollars.

He and his constant cohort, Lil' Marshall, had taken Darren aside and convinced him that the debt would be forgiven if Darren participated in "setting up" his suppliers, Ellis and Mumbles, for what was anticipated to be a most lucrative robbery. Darren, though holding Ellis and Mumbles in high regard, nevertheless relented, shown the business end of a 9mm pistol and convinced immediately that he had little choice in the matter. So Darren delivered in precise detail the movements, the schedule, of Ellis and Mumbles, and assured the two robbers that a large delivery was due to be made the Wednesday before Thanksgiving Day.

When Ellis called him that afternoon though, Darren reasoned that it would be best to remain faithful to his years-long suppliers rather than keep quiet, as he'd assured QT and Lil' Marshall he would under penalty of certain death. The robbers were set to "raze" Mumbles when he made the afternoon delivery on Shelter Road, Mumbles corralled and retained while Ellis would be summoned by phone to free his long-time associate, with, at minimum, five thousand dollars and an equal amount of cocaine.

Ellis stayed well behind Mumble's pick-up as they headed towards Shelter Road, peering regularly into his rearview mirror to see if the men in the Cadillac were tailing him. They had for a moment, then seemingly aware that they were being watched, took a turn onto a parkway well before the road leading to the Shelter Road apartment complex. Mumbles, apprised to do so by Ellis, neared Shelter Road then sped past the turn leading to Darren's apartment complex. Ellis followed him, a mile distant, and then pulled into the parking lot of a shopping center well away from Darren's home. Seated behind the wheel of his older model Chevy, Darren felt somewhat ill at ease when he recognized, first, Mumbles' "work truck," and then Ellis's SUV.

Both Mumbles and Ellis moved through the chill to Darren's car, Ellis climbing in the front passenger's seat, Mumbles easing into the back of the old four-door "hooptie."

"Them fools was on us, yo, like you said," Ellis began, removing gloves and blowing heated air into his hands. "What the fuck make them key on us like that, man?"

Darren, feeling particularly guilty after having been afforded food, shelter, and a considerably comfortable lifestyle during the more recent of his 22 years by Ellis and Mumbles, looked downcast, fought for words.

"I like…first like….I ain't got the cash like I'm supposed to," he stammered, peering into his lap at folded hands.

"You ain't got what?" Ellis asked slowly.

"I ain't got shit, man," Darren said.

"You…you…you…"

Mumbles tried questioning him, but was cut short by Ellis.

"You ain't got what, man?" It was both a statement and question.

"I ain't got that bank I'm supposed to, to re-up like that."

"You….you….you….you ain't…"

"What happened, dog?"

"Gambling, man…"

"You gambled up all the profits?"

"Yeah, man. And then QT and Lil' Marshall, they made me give them the rest of the shit I hadn't sold for…like…collateral or some shit…"

"Then they had you try to set our ass up, huh?"

"They….they…….try…try……..to….set…you mean…they try…try…try to…"

"Yeah man. That's about how the shit went down." Darren was almost in tears.

"That's fucked up," Ellis said, shaking his head.

"That's…that's…fu….fu….that's…fu…fucked …fucked…..up!"

"So how we gonna straighten this shit out, D?"

"I could work it off, with, like, people be copping over the weekend, Thanksgiving and shit," Darren said, mentally lost, guilt gnawing at him. "But, like, them boys gonna know I tipped y'all off. I get back to work on Shelter Road, they gonna be waiting for my ass. Raze me, at least, if not bust caps in my ass like that."

"You....you...you...man....you...you..."
Mumbles had an idea, but when pressing issues arose, it was even harder for him to get his words out. "I...I...don't...don't....worry.....about....about....their ass!"

"Yeah," Ellis, quite familiar with Mumbles' chain of thought. "We can't let them fools keep on breathing after this shit. They gotta go."

"They....th..th...they...gotta...got...got...gotta ....go!"

Chapter Five

Business was brisk around Shelter Road the Wednesday night before Thanksgiving. Darren had not returned to his usual corner, but had secreted a fresh supply to the seven teens who were in his employ around the neighborhood corners, ensuring a measure of return to him for the debt Ellis was not about to forgive. But his girlfriend maintained a one-bedroom unit smack dab in the middle of the Shelter Road apartment complex, and well aware of this, QT and Lil' Marshall had camped out in the parking lot adjoining her building, awaiting Darren's return.

What QT and Lil' Marshall didn't know though was that Darren, Ellis and Mumbles were expecting this, and had delivered complimentary doses of crack to three of the neighborhood's seasoned addicts that they might immediately call either of the men when QT and Darren were spotted. Darren, a very light skinned young man whom many considered of too mild a mannerism to be involved in the drug distribution business, certainly lacked the disposition to even be considered leveling a pistol and eliminating the two, as Mumbles and Ellis had planned. Ellis, for his part, talked a big game but was equally undependable at carrying out such an assault.

Mumbles, to the contrary, had used a gun on a number of occasions, and it was well known on the streets of Southeast Washington that the young man, short on words, was quite robust of heart. At least three murders were attributed to him, though those in the know would never have fingered Mumbles to law enforcement authorities. An uncounted number of errant dealers, users and the like had been pistol-whipped by the strong hands of the often silent, muscular man, and when Ellis and Darren agreed that the two stick-up boys would comprise a serious blockade to their continued business around Shelter Road, Mumbles immediately emitted a staccato utterance expressing his willingness to eliminate the two.

"I....I....I...bu....bu.......I.....I......bu....bu...... bu...bu....bust...they....they....ass," he'd said, and that Wednesday just before midnight, a crack head raised Ellis on his cellular, notifying him that QT and Lil' Marshall were parked in the Cadillac outside Darren's girlfriend's building.

The security lights which were affixed to the three-story apartment buildings, directed at the parking lots nights ostensibly to give reassurance to residents arriving home after dark, had been shot out repeatedly by drug dealers not wishing to do business in the bright spotlights. After a few years, the property managers stopped replacing them, and the perimeters of the buildings, additionally cast in gloom by waist-high decorative bushes, were pitch black even on moonlit nights.

QT and Lil' Marshall were passing a marijuana blunt between them, seated in the Cadillac to the rearmost parking space in the lot with a clear view of the street. They'd been reassured by two crack addicts that they'd be alerted should either Darren, Ellis or Mumbles arrive, and were nodding through creased, red eyes to a rap favorite when the shadowy figure eased up to the rear of their vehicle from the dank underbrush to the rear of the parking lot.

Crouched and murmuring to himself in a raspy voice, the gunman seemed to be reinforcing himself to commit the planned act with words to himself, as he eased up to a near standing position just a foot from the smoke-blowing head of Lil' Marshall, sputtered in a louder, chilling release.

"K…K…Kill…M…M…Mumbles! K…K…Kill!" he shouted, while directing a barrage of fatal rounds into the heads of both Lil' Marshall and QT.

Chapter Six

Shantelle wanted Ellis to join with her family for Thanksgiving dinner. But so did Donna, the mother of his year-old daughter, and Linda, the mother of his three-year-old girl. He'd come in close to three o'clock that morning, bearing his standard explanation that his "business" on the streets of Southeast Washington required a bit more of his personal attention on the eve of the holiday. He seemed somewhat shaken, Shantelle thought, and had allowed him to sleep well past the hour she was expecting to leave for her mother's with toddlers Derrick and Ebony.

But now she was growing antsy, as was two-year-old Derrick. Ebony, five and considered well beyond her years in perception and mannerisms, pouted before her mother when she bluntly asked when "that old Ellis" was getting out of bed to drive them to grandmother's house. A feisty child, not unlike her mother, Ebony paced about the living room of the apartment in a huff, shaking a head adorned with numerous small plaits festooned with a spectrum of colorful barrettes.

"Ma, that ol' Ellis gonna make us late," she said plaintively. "And how he supposed to be going to somebody's house for Thanksgiving and he come in the house at three o'clock in the morning like that?"

Shantelle, fuming herself, was surprised by her daughter's statement.

"How you know what time he come in the house?"

"Ma, I hear *everything*! Even if I am asleep. And I see the dial on the clock in my bedroom. I know what time it is."

"Well, girl, still, that ain't none of your business. You leave Ellis to me. Ain't none of your concern."

"He late," little Derrick said from his seat on the living room floor, rolling around small toys and, already showing the familial grit, not willing to be left out of the conversation.

It was nearing noon; the television was blaring the Thanksgiving's Day parade preparations, and Shantelle, still fuming, picked up the phone to try raising her friend Lana, who always lent a receptive ear when Shantelle needed to vent. But before the call was answered, Ellis, barefoot and in nothing but boxer shorts, sauntered out of their bedroom, glanced in their direction without a word and moved to the kitchen.

"Dag!" little Ebony blurted out, especially it seemed so that Ellis could hear her. "He ain't got no kinds of respect!"

Shantelle disconnected the phone and placed it on the coffee table.

"Man," she shouted. "You gonna take us over my mama's or *what*?"

He returned to the kitchen foyer, sipping from a carton of orange juice.

"Yeah, shorty. It ain't hardly noon yet. Give me a chance to get my head together, take a shower, put some food in my stomach."

"And you shouldn't be drinking out the juice carton!" Ebony said, standing, hands on hips. "Don't nobody want to be drinking behind you! Don't know where your mouth been!"

He looked down on her with cowered eyes, moved back towards the bedroom with the juice carton.

"Little girl, don't start with me this morning. Have me come back in there and spank that fresh ass of yours..."

Ebony looked to her mother with a glare of disbelief, and apparently not getting the support she expected, stepped and moved to the hallway, shouted back to the bedroom.

"You better *not* even think about putting your hands on me! Or my brother! You ain't none of our daddy!"

"Girl, get your tail back in here," Shantelle said, and welcomed Ebony as the daughter moved to her and fell into an embrace.

"Ma, I know you won't let him put his hands on us, would you?"

"Naw, baby. Ellis just talking smack. He better not lay a hand on either one of you."

"Good. 'Cause I'll call my grandfather. And you know he don't play."

Shantelle just laughed, kissed Ebony on the cheek. There was no telling whether Ebony and Derrick's "grandfather" was even accessible, as he spent regular periods of time incarcerated for either committing some usually petty crime, or violation of probation (usually turning up with a drug-stained "dirty urine" sample) after being back on the streets for little more than a few months.

Ellis meanwhile was in the bedroom raising one "baby mama" on the phone, then as quickly the second mother of another he'd fathered. Both demanded his presence, and he did the math, divided the hours, and promised both that he'd make a family showing.

"Trying to see how you gonna get to spend some time today with your skeezers?" Shantelle said from the bedroom door, shocking him.

"Naw, it ain't like that," he lied, flipping the cellular closed midsentence a petition from his three-year-old's mother.

"Well," she continued, turning her back to him. "We're ready."

"Let me wash up," he said, wishing a full, long shower but reasoning that could wait until he'd dropped off Shantelle, Ebony and Derrick at Shantelle's mother's house, not that far away.

"Damn!" he spat, on the way to the bathroom with the cell phone ringing again before he could even return an apologetic call to the name which now appeared on the caller ID: Donna, one-year-old Lauren's mother.

After a cursory going-over with soap, toothpaste and a hairbrush, Ellis donned a pair of baggy jeans, a sweater and leather jacket, walked smiling into the living room and was greeted with cold stares from Shantelle and the children.

"What y'all all grittin' on somebody like that?" he said, moved to the door while Shantelle glared between him and the large grocery bag setting in the lounge chair beside him. He seemed to become acutely aware of the unspoken communications both Shantelle *and* Ebony directed towards him, issued a little guffaw and peered into the grocery bag.

"What? Y'all taking this?"

He only received the continued cold stares, lifted the considerably weighty bag and moved out of the apartment.

"Ma, I don't know what you see in that fool, for real," little Ebony said, shaking her head and taking Derrick by the hand, leading him out the door.

"Just watch your mouth, girl," Shantelle said, exiting last and securing the multiple locks on the door. "Who you think paid for them three pair of

Timbs you just had to have, and put them games in your room. And them Air Mikes you and your girlfriends all had to have. Now you just be nice. Today's a holiday, family time."

"I know Ma. But, *dag*!"

Ellis was already in his SUV, engine running, doors closed, awaiting them. Neither Shantelle nor Ebony expected him to free the door for them, nor secure Derrick in the child seat affixed in the rear passenger's compartment. And even though the family shopping trips, the family outings, were a rarity, they knew to expect little by way of social graces from him, and mother and daughter moved out of habit to seat Derrick in the rear, secure themselves in the vehicle while Ellis looked through compact discs and primped in the driver's vanity mirror.

"After I drop y'all off, I got to make a couple of runs," he said nonchalantly, looking to ensure the children were seated, Shantelle secure before backing out of the parking slot.

"That's alright," Shantelle said. "My mother and them wasn't expecting you anyway. And my uncle will give us a ride back home, so you just go on, drop us off and go do....whatever it is...you got to do."

"Go and see your baby mamas," Ebony spat, folding her little arms across her chest with a dramatic flair.

"Girl, you better shut your mouth!" Shantelle said, but with a little smile creasing her lips.

"That's alright," Ellis said. "Her little smart ass won't be saying that when she all up in somebody's face talking about what she gonna get for Christmas."

"I don't need nothing from you!" the little girl screeched, leaning forward towards the driver's seat. "You ain't all *that*!"

Shantelle turned, reached back threateningly.

"Girl, sit your ass back and be quiet! You a mess!"

"Just like her mother," Ellis said, almost in a whisper.

"Huh?" Shantelle missed it.

"Nothing," he replied, looked into the block ahead of small, single-family homes and was relieved to see a tight line of cars parked on the street.

He pulled before Shantelle's childhood family home.

"Ain't no place to park out this joint," he said. "I would stop and holler at your peeps, but like, I have to park way around the block somewhere. I'll stop in after I make my little runs."

"Don't bother," Shantelle said, freeing her seatbelt and hurrying out of the car.

She retrieved her children, the grocery bag Ellis had placed in the far rear of the SUV. Escorting the children to the curb, she looked over a shoulder, customarily, to wave a departing hand at Ellis. But he was looking well ahead, already motoring off the street.

"Tired-ass mother fucker," she spat, then put on a pleasant façade, led the children up the long walkway to join the celebratory events with her extensive family.

Chapter Seven

Mumbles didn't have any family. Not any that he knew of, anyway. Shuttled between foster homes and government-run facilities as a child, he'd only heard inklings of who his parents were, could remember childhood references of a few brothers and sisters, but for the most part, he'd grown up a lonely child, derided for his speech impediment and, although such was long available in D.C. public schools, never enrolled in any of the myriad programs for children deemed "developmentally challenged."

He'd been afforded a one-bedroom apartment through a series of manipulations whereby a female friend of Ellis's had "fronted" for the unit, filling out the paperwork (Mumbles could barely read, and writing was a struggle he'd overcome by simple avoidance) and directing him in the methods and location for making his monthly payments. Of course, his trade in drug distribution saw him with ample funds, but any means of official banking was little more than a passing consideration. He paid his monthly bills through acquisition of money orders from the corner grocer, and usually had a female associate fill these out and either they or Ellis delivered them, or mailed them, to the appropriate payee.

Holidays additionally riled him. He was well aware of the celebratory airs among the families in his twelve-unit complex, and those evident among his peers. Ellis was never around Christmas, Thanksgiving, Memorial Day, the Fourth of July, those holidays when families nationally, and particularly in the District's black communities, made an all out effort to show some love for one another. Mumbles couldn't even name a family member, considered Ellis the closest person he could call even close to anything resembling family, and he was additionally steamed that the hours even some of his drug-addled customers gave over to family tradition during these times could have well been spent consuming his products and further padding his pockets.

More often, Mumbles ate prepared meals from the neighborhood carry-outs. He did however keep a refrigerator full of soft drinks, a few microwavable meals in the freezer, and always, bacon and eggs. He could throw together a passable, edible meal with the simplistic items he culled together in the fridge and cabinets: Plenty of canned soups and vegetables, microwavable popcorn, peanut butter and jelly. And even though his reading skills were at best rudimentary, he'd long been able to distinguish oven temperature and time indications on the cooking instructions of many of the packaged, frozen foods he bought, scanning over packages for a number, followed by the "0"-degree symbol, and another with "min." behind it.

On this day, out of consideration for the holiday, he decided to treat himself to a hot meal, a "pot pie," the crusted, small self-contained meal usually containing a meat, some undistinguishable sauce, and vegetables, fitted in an oven-ready foil dish. He retrieved two turkey boxed pies from the freezer, moved to the oven while making out the "375" indication for preheating the oven.

Someone knocked on the apartment door.

Setting the turkey pot pie boxes aside, he stepped slowly out of the kitchen, crossed the living room and inched an eye to the peephole. LaShanda, the neighborhood "head nurse," stood in the hallway, seemingly dancing on legs as if she was pressed to relieve herself.

"Wh…wha….what up…gu….gu..gurl?"

She pinned him with a awkward smile, crack addiction have long ago worn away any measure of attractiveness about chapped lips and a gaping hole where one of her centermost upper front teeth had succumbed to the blunt force of a hiking boot during a failed attempt at crack thievery.

"Can I come in?" she said, almost pleading.

He stepped back, allowed her entrance. On occasion, Mumbles, like many crack dealers in the neighborhood, would trade a considerably small dose of the rock to a female addict for oral sex. Few would venture into the vaginal depths of such a woman, however, even while wearing a sturdy condom. So "head," if any service was desirable at all, usually comprised the most any dealer would engage a female addict in. LaShanda, a crack addict for over fifteen years, was particularly expert and notably adept at delivering quick, efficient oral sex, was never known to even allow spillage on the recipient's pants, thus the designation "head nurse" among neighborhood regulars.

"Wh...wha....what.....Wha...wha...wha....w... w...what...up...Sh...Sh...Sh....Shanda?"

He secured the door and she made a show of warming herself, blowing into her ungloved hands and rubbing hands over the tattered jacket she'd worn apparently through a night where wind chills were in the single digits.

"I'm trying to do a little something-something, you know, for a couple of twenties," she said, following Mumbles as he moved back to the kitchen.

"T….t….t….two? T….t….*two*?!"

He placed the pot pies in the oven, turned and sat in a dinette chair. He motioned for her to sit, and she took a chair opposite him.

"Yeah, lover." Her ploy began, as she leaned forward and reached into his crotch with worn hands, stroking in an effort to find his penis. Again the wayward smile. "It's the holiday, baby. I need to get at least enough to hold me for a while."

"Y…y….you….." But he never finished. He was in her grip now, freed from the jeans and now erect, directed towards the depths of her throat as she deftly eased to her knees, engaged in her specialty.

"O…oh….oooh….Oh….sh….sh…..*shit*!" he uttered, and it was over.

She arose, flexing her shoulder as if some conquering athlete.

"That was worth at least a fifty," she suggested, again taking her seat before him. And he couldn't disagree.

He arose, moved to the back bedroom, returned and handed her four twenty-dollar "sacks" of crack.

"Yo...y....you...take...."

He was still trying to deliver a message to her, but actual possession of the crack didn't allow for cordialities. She was slamming the door even as Mumbles fell back into a dinette chair, momentarily exhausted. He closed his eyes, slid a hand down the front of his jeans as if to give comfort to a defeated beast.

"D....d.....d......d...d....*damn*!"

Chapter Eight

Ellis had two separate runs to make: First he'd visit the home closest to that of Shantelle's parents, the public housing unit where Linda, mother of his three-year-old daughter Michelle lived. The small home, sandwiched between two others in the Barry Farm projects, was already packed with members of the Bellamy family: Linda, her mother, grandmother, five of Linda's siblings, three of their combined children, the proverbial drunken uncle already making an inebriated fuss, two young "baby daddy's," one "baby mama." Ellis arrived at the front door bearing gifts: A pair of Thanksgiving's Day greeting cards, each stuffed with a hundred dollars in twenty dollar bills. That was the most desirous gift expected of the recipient: Linda, little Michelle's mother, and "Miss Bellamy," Linda's mother.

His arrival did little to quell the tumult already saturating the small home, a compact unit for even the family members who lived there and an overwhelmed abode with the presence of the extended familial and not-so-surely acquainted people there just after 2 p.m. on the holiday. The small kitchen, which reminded more than a few of the young men present of some prison cell they'd once occupied, teemed with women of quite generous girth and young ladies of beanpole likeness. A worn sofa in the entry living room was occupied by three men in their mid-twenties, focusing on the football game playing out on the big screen television on the wall before them, and 40-ounce malt liquors making wet rings on the coffee table.

Toddlers and pre-teens scampered about, some moving up and down the staircase to the rear of the wall where the television hung, through the compact living room and through the dining room and, some, through the kitchen, where a rear door occasionally opened to allow children to exit, or yet another visitor to enter.

After greeting Miss Bellamy and watching her joy as she secured the twenties somewhere next to generous cleavage and unceremoniously pitched the card to a countertop without so much as a read, Ellis found a corner in the dining room where he could speak with Linda above a yell, picked up little Michelle, gave her a kiss and explain away the brevity of his visit with as few words as possible.

"You know Shantelle wants me over there with her people like that," he whispered down to Linda. "I'll hit you up on your cell later, alright?"

Of course, Linda knew quite a bit, maybe too much, about Ellis's current girlfriend and living arrangements.   After all, they'd parted ways amicably, even before Linda became aware of her pregnancy. But for over a year prior the two had been heatedly engaged in a relationship which left little room for another, on either's part.   Ellis's "business," and in no uncertain way the gulf in age differences, quickly extinguished any idea by either that some sort of long-term relationship was possible. He kept in touch though, and when the baby was born lavished gifts on both mother and child.

"Ellis, I'm going to need a couple more hundred, baby." She looked up to him with pleading, doe-eyes. "I'm trying to start that Medical Tech training at SANS in January, and you know, I'm gonna have to start giving my mother something to watch Michelle while I'm in school."

Ellis gritted his teeth, peering at the intricate pattern of the cornrowed design which ended in extensive braids flowing down Linda's back, and, having another girlfriend who specialized in such braiding at a local beauty salon, knew well that

Linda's fresh hairstyle had cost at least $130.00. Nevertheless he relented, quite sure that Mumbles had placed enough of their product on the streets to generate a few thousand dollars for each of them over the weekend. He fished a knot of bills from a pocket, peeled off two-hundred dollars.

"Here you go, girl," he said, feigning disapproval. "Don't you be coming back at me no time soon for no more, you hear?"

"I'm cool with that, baby," she purred, the money an immediate salve.

"Look here," he zipped up his coat, donned his gloves. "Tell your peeps happy Thanksgiving for me. I'm gonna slid out the back so that ol' uncle of yours don't be hitting on me again for no shit on tic, or that other one for no cash."

He planted a light kiss on her lips, lifted his daughter again for a hug and kiss, handed her over to Linda and eased through the kitchen, hugging Miss Bellamy and making a hasty exit.

Just north of the Barry Farm projects the U.S. Capitol building provided a visual reminder of the diversity not two miles apart in the nation's capital. Ellis exited "The Farm" at its northernmost border, where Suitland Parkway gave way to the South

Capitol Street Bridge, a direct roadway to Capitol Hill. Before crossing the bridge however, he took a route east, 295, which would cut alongside the Kenilworth Terrace complex five miles from Barry Farm. There, Donna Short awaited him, along with a plethora of her family members, and little Lauren, his one-year-old. Before arriving in that community, which occupied a sparse parcel of land just yards within the city's northeast border, he retrieved a satchel from underneath the driver's seat, unzipped it while maintaining steering control with his knees, pulled a fold of money from it and stuffed it into an inside jacket pocket to replenish his "spending capital."

"Damn honeys and kids and their people got me spending more than I make," he said to himself, slowing the SUV to 50 for the Kenilworth exit. "Have a dude hustling his ass off and not making no headway out this joint."

Certainly, Ellis was acutely aware of every dollar he spent. If he'd of been employed in some financial institution, Ellis would have been recognized as a genius with numbers, without the need for any electronic calculation device. With mounds of cash in all denominations brought to him regularly from drug sales, he could spread a cache before him on a table, hundreds of bills, and within seconds guesstimate the total amount to within a few dollars.

But socially and in general knowledge, he was about as smart as two rocks. His mentor, or more correctly the neighborhood elder who dispensed what comprised as close to words of wisdom as Ellis had access to, was Big Mack, a wheelchair-bound man of 60 who, dressed to the nines, held court outside the Shipley Terrace Liquor Store in Ellis's childhood neighborhood. The strongest measure of advice he'd given Ellis, repeatedly, since the strapping boy was a teenager, was an admonishment that he "don't let your dick make a bum out of you." It had taken Ellis years to figure out just what that warning amounted to. But by that time, he'd already fathered two children, that he knew of, and only avoided judicial child support charges by regularly doling out considerably paltry sums of cash to the children's mothers.

The mothers for there parts were apparently not as good at mathematical calculations, for had they made Ellis legally responsible for child support payments, they'd probably not be forced to depend on D.C. government social programs for child support benefits, food stamps, and the generosity of parents.

None was willing to pursue legal actions against Ellis, even at the threatening suggestions of social workers, and with a workload teeming with teenaged mothers and thousands of children out of wedlock, the District's court system only occasionally completed action against some errant "baby daddy." And, as was common, the father was unemployed, carted off the jail for contempt, further adding to the financial constraints on a city already suffering under a mounting budget deficit.

He parked the SUV on a corner a block from the Short family home, illegally close to the stop sign pocked with the holes of test bullets. He eyed a group of young men gathered in the chill by a storefront, retrieved the 9 mm from under the car seat and the money pouch, locked the theft deterrent "club" on the steering column and moved with haste back down the street towards the Short home.

"Young bucks trying to get paid," he said to himself, mentally formulating words to escape the Short family gathering quickly and ensure that his SUV was not expediently set upon cinder blocks and that he retained his expensive tires and rims.

The Kenilworth housing units near mirrored the ones in Barry Farm, except these Northeast Washington structures had brick on the outer facings.

When the small boy answered his knock and pushed open a storm door, the blast of scented air was welcoming, although the density of bodies evident in the tight dwelling was as repulsive to him as the throng had been in Barry Farm.

"There my boo!" a compact, well-endowed young lady shouted out from across the packed living room. Donna Short, 22, sashayed through the throng, stood on tip-toes to place arms around Ellis's neck and plant a moist kiss on his lips.

Greetings were shouted out from throughout the living room. A few hands waved to him from the dining room to the unit's rear, where an adjoining kitchen was busy with women and spewing steam.

As in Barry Farm, the living room was stuffed in every available seating space with young and older men, attention focused on a panel television affixed to a wall displaying a pro football game.

"You want a beer, bro?" a man held forth a bottle to Ellis, who declined and was lead to the rear of the home by Donna.

At 22, Donna was one to get right to the point. Abandoned by a heroin-addicted mother from childhood, she'd languished in poverty throughout her teenaged years, stuffed, virtually, in the small

Kenilworth two-bedroom unit of her maternal grandmother along with five siblings, one drunken uncle who'd abused her, and another whose own drug dependency saw him in and out of jail, yet another weight upon the stooped shoulders of Sandra Short, the single matriarch of the seriously disjointed family.

"You got that little something I asked for, Ellis?" Donna said, the plastic smile no longer deemed necessary.

He reached into a jacket pocket.

"What you say, a ball fifty?"

"Yeah," she said, looking at the amount of cash in his hands which surpassed any volume she ever anticipated even being so close to. "A hunnit fifty."

The manufactured smile returned as he peeled off the amount in twenties to her. She took the money while looking up into his eyes, eased closer to him as a couple of older women neared them to place casserole dishes on the dining room table, paying them little mind.

The amount of money he'd displayed, he now realized belatedly as an unwise move, wouldn't allow her wants to be sated.

"I *could* use another fifty to get Lauren a better winter coat," she plied. "You know I have to take her to the medical center once a month, and, man! It's been colder than a mother fucker out there!"

He immediately relented, mind picturing the group of boys up the street outside Mr. Sam's Car Wash offering up his $1000.00 rims and tires for sale.

"Here," he handed her fifty. "I gotta run, Donna. You know, Shantelle's expecting me over her peeps before they cut the turkey and shit."

She had no problem with that, already mentally spending a part of the money on marijuana, which was available no further than in her grandmother's living room.

"You want to slide out the back?" she said, leading him through the kitchen to it's rear entrance.

He followed, delivered a hug to Aunt Betsy, Grandma Short, Miss Lena before leaving.

His SUV was untouched, though a few young men (they were among the same group near the corner store, he realized as he neared them) were leaning on a fence now just yards from his vehicle, eyes apparently appraising the shiny rims and expensive tires.

"Yo," he said by way of greeting, throwing his head back in a common acknowledgement to the youths.

"Wassup?" three gruff voices returned his greeting.

He climbed into the vehicle, motored it and sat for a moment to allow warmth to blow upon him, the compact disc bass to shake the ride to its very foundation. He placed the 9mm on the passenger's seat beside him, removing it from his beltline with a motion which didn't go unnoticed by the three young men leaning on the fence. Then, while still sitting there, he speed-dialed Mumbles on his cellular.

"Y...ye....."

"It's Ellis," he said quickly, out of habit not waiting for his cohort to stammer out a greeting. "I'm gonna stop by your place on my way back to Southeast. Look out for me."

He motored out of the neighborhood, onto the parkway heading south. There was a need to ensure that the remaining bulk of his product was on the streets before celebratory dinners concluded; many crack heads, afforded a meal and, he knew even from his own personal experiences, having access to uncommon monies due to the seasonal charity of kinfolks, would be out upon the streets before sundown looking to additionally feed their addiction.

"Might as well put all this shit out now," he uttered plans to himself, nearing the Suitland Parkway, a road which always reminded him of the vast amounts of money available on streets quite accessible through its many lower-income arteries. "We re-up for Christmas this weekend, get paid big-time."

Chapter Nine

There was no doubt that Darren knew who was responsible for the deaths of QT and Lil' Marshall. Fat Boy was sure of it, and after stuffing himself at his grandmother's Southeast home, he excused himself to meet up with his partner Dru and do a little research around nearby Shelter Road after sunset. After all, QT's father, long-ago crippled and still in mourning, specifically asked that his nephew and QT's cousin, Marquis "Fat Boy" Clease, find out who was responsible for QT's death and level "nonjudicial punishment," as the wheelchair bound man had put it, upon those responsible.

Fat Boy was passing gas in the closed confines of the old Cadillac, and even with the heat blasting against the winter's chill, Dru could no longer stand it.

"Damn, Fats! Fuck you eat over your grandma's: Half a cow or some shit?"

He motored the window down, stuck his head out into the cold air.

Fat Boy shook in jolly laughter, still puffing on the marijuana blunt.

"Some good shit, boy! That's them sweet potatoes got my stomach boiling. And that potato salad. That ham and turkey and fried chicken! Apple pie. Grandma served up some shit, boy! Better bet it!"

He belched, blew marijuana fumes, eased sideways to lift a cheek and farted voluminously.

"God-*damn*!" Dru sputtered, freed the door and climbed out of the car.

Clearing his eyes as if affected by tear gas, he shook his head and smiled, looked across the hood of the car onto the dark surroundings of two apartment buildings, where shadowy figures engaged in what appeared to be secreted drug exchanges. Dru was well aware of the mannerisms, the cautious gazes up and down the street by the young men, for he and Fat Boy were themselves drug dealers, though they'd suffer under penalty of death if they even attempted to pursue their trade in this, a neighborhood firmly in the grips of a local posse. But the dim lights filtering from an apartment hallway momentarily cast an identifiable glow on one particular figure, a lighter-skinned young man fitting the description of the one named Darren they were seeking.

Dru bent down near the open passenger's side car door, crimped his head in the direction of the apartment building.

"That look like that red nigga we looking for," he said, and Fat Boy, a hand over his own mouth and nose against the noxious fumes he'd emitted, eased his window down and peered in the direction of the apartment building.

He pulled a gun from under the seat, struggled to free his 300-plus pound frame from behind the steering wheel.

"We can't just up and bust on his ass like that," Fat Boy puffed, moving to join Dru at the rear of the car. "Bust one in a leg or something, scare away his boys, and grab his ass back here so we can make him snitch on who was behind them killing QT and Lil' Marshall."

"Yeah," Dru, a skinny kid of 17, said. "After that, *then* we bust his ass."

Fat Boy slow-wobbled towards the building, Dru trailing him in his own looping gait. Darren was on the main sidewalk running before a string of three-story apartment buildings, exchanging words with a group of young men who seemed to have little concerns, eyeing cars slowly rolling by and lowly announcing their possession of "that bomb shit." No one paid the approaching duo any mind until someone belatedly noticed the huge figure raising an arm and directing a gun in their direction.

Three rounds caught Darren in his legs as he attempted to join others in dashing away from the scene. The skinniest of the two gunmen did what appeared to be a little dance/skip, arriving above Darren as he grappled at his wounds, and bent to ensure that the bullet he directed tore right into Darren's left foot. He grabbed Darren by an arm, as Fat Boy arrived and assisted in hoisting the wounded figure upright with little effort.

"Come on here, boy. You got some 'splaining to do," Fat Boy said, looking around to ensure no "come-back" was being directed at them from the shadowy corners and now deserted street.

With Dru to one side and Fat Boy to the other, then quickly ushered a moaning Darren to a blackened parking lot between two apartment buildings, pitched him to the ground besides a row of decorative bushes and placed pistols to within inches of his head.

"Now, young'un, all you need to do is tell us who was behind them shooting QT and Lil' Marshall," Fat Boy said.

"Talk, mother fucker, then your peeps can get you to a hospital and the shit be over with…for you that is," Dru said.

"No! Y'all gonna kill me anyway! Fuck that!" Darren said, the fear torturous but a realization quickly setting in that, should he finger Mumbles and Ellis, his death would be assured anyway.

"We ain't gonna kill your punk-ass," Fat Boy said. "We don't want you. We want the mother fuckers killed our boys."

"Yeah," Dru said. "Ain't no need in killing your punk ass."

Darren had second thoughts, looked up to the threatening pair and decided to perhaps extend his life, at least for the moment.

"You know that dude can't hardly talk, dude they call Mumbles?" he whispered in agony. "Him and his boy Ellis. Mumbles did the shooting, but Ellis the one put the word out on them. That's who did it."

Fat Boy and Dru stood upright, presented smiles to one another.

"You know them niggas?" Fat Boy asked Dru.

"Yeah. Ellis the supplier. Mumbles the one be putting the shit out here with this bitch-ass nigga and his boys around here." Dru said.

Then both turned and leveled their guns again at Darren, as he raised his hands before his face as if for protection.

"Come on, y'all! I told you what you wanted! Y'all said y'all wasn't gonna kill me I tell! Come on y'all—"

Four shots tore into Darren's head, three through the upraised hands before they fell in a spastic motion to his side.

"Why you tell the mother fucker you wasn't gonna kill him," Dru asked as the pair quickly moved to the parking lot where they'd left the Cadillac.

"I know," Fat Boy said, wobbling into a gait which for him amounted to a sprint. "Psych!"

Chapter Ten

The shooting of Darren put a serious crimp in the holiday night business along Shelter Road, and Mumbles received word soon enough that he and Ellis didn't dare even approach the neighborhood Thanksgiving's night. The potential financial loss was tremendous, they considered while remaining camped out in Mumble's sparsely furnished apartment. The loss of Darren, a longtime friend and associate, was given only minor consideration.

"The way Otis told me on the phone," Ellis said, giving a mental review of the event, "they shot ol' boy in the legs first, then took him around a building and then shot him all in the head and shit. That mean probably they wanted to get some info from his ass before they killed him."

"Ru...ru....ru....right."

"They say Fat Boy was QT's cousin. Bet you that bitch-ass Darren told him we had something to do with QT and Lil' Marshall getting offed."

"S...sh....sh....sh....sh...."

"Yeah. Shit's fucked up, Mumbles. Fucked the hell up. Now they be looking for our ass..."

"Y...y.....y....yep."

Mumbles blunt response was hardly reassuring to Ellis. He hadn't even attempt words to indicate he was not going to simply lie down and wait for the murderers to make the first move. At least, Ellis reasoned, his main associate could have attempted an utterance indicating that he was ready to seek out the assailants.

"We find where Fats and his boy hang out, we might have to make a move on them first, know what I'm saying?"

"Y...y.....yeah....m....m...man! Bu....bu...bust a...a....cap....in...in...in they...ass...first!"

Ellis had been on the phone periodically throughout the day with Shantelle, had been admonished not to bring his "tired ass" back to *her* apartment that night, and hung up on three occasions when he'd steeled himself to attempt another verbal petition. His "other women" had been soothed with monetary dispensations. But he truly loved Shantelle, considered her home *his home*! And regardless of little Ebony's sassy ways, he truly cared for the little girl and her brother as if they were his own.

"We can't afford to be missing out on no more weekend cash like that between now and Christmas," Ellis said, pondering the situation. "And now you can't resupply them other boys Darren had working Shelter Road, and you know their asses gonna be dry by Saturday."

"I...I....I...know...know...know...Fa...Fa...Fa t...B...B...Boy."

Ellis turned with a glare of partial surprise, part disapproval.

"You *know* that fool? How you know his ass?"

"Fr...fr...from....d...d.....down....fr...d...d...d own..th...th...the....way."

"He be around Shelter Road?"

"S..s...some...s..some...times."

"He must got peoples down there then. We need to holla at some of Darren's boys and find out where his ass be on the regular, and who the other dude was with him when they popped Darren."
"R...r.....r....right."

As happened quite often when the two were together, Ellis wished for a more immediately responsive ear for which to bounce his ideas off. Mumbles was certainly his closest friend, had been since the two were pre-teens. But when business, and particularly potentially deadly prospects were on the horizon, Ellis needed immediate feedback on his ideas.

He phoned T-Rock, a casual associate and long-time resident of the Shelter Road apartment complex, where he'd been a childhood friend of and eventual underling in the late Darren Rogers's drug distribution business.

"T-Rock! Ellis! How's it hangin', bro?"

He listened, a good minute, expression growing remorseful as Mumbles, quite adept at gauging persona through listening and observing, shook his head as if the recipient of some bad news.

"Yeah...sorry about that, bro...We coming back, better bet it....Yeah...Umm huh...Down on Mississippi Avenue, huh?"

Mumbles nodded his head as if the words Ellis spoke rang familiar to him.

"Yeah...We gonna take care of that shit, fo'
real...Yeah...No joke....Yeah, peace out."

Mumbles eyed Ellis for a moment, the two silent
as the phone call was ended. Still without a word,
Mumbles arose and moved to the back bedroom,
returned quickly with a sawed-off shotgun, a box of
cartridges.

"Miss....si...Miss...si...sippi...A....A...Ave...n
ue."

"Yeah. And I got the exact address too."

"W...w....w....we.........bu...bu...bust...they...
they...they ass....fi.....first!"

Chapter Eleven

Ellis really didn't have the heart for the task at hand. But he was unsure exactly what about his business, his home life, his movements, Darren had divulged to his slayers before being permanently silenced, and having finagled his way once again into Shantelle's bedroom, he was leery that weekend of even venturing out again, fearful that Fat Boy and some of his minions lay in wait outside Shantelle's apartment complex with anxious eyes watching for any movement towards his SUV.

Conversely, Mumbles was just itching for Fat Boy or any of his associates to approach him. He went about ensuring that the Shelter Road boys were restocked with their joint product as the Thanksgiving's weekend continued in an explosive fury around the streets of Washington: More than seven deaths had been reported by Saturday evening, three allegedly fueled by alcoholically-driven conflicts, and the other four, though unconfirmed, assumed to be the results of drug-related violence.

As Mumbles went about his business Saturday evening, Ellis would ring him on his cell phone, almost hourly. As was common between them, he'd recognize Ellis's name and number on the caller ID, activate the call and for the most part just listen. He was well aware that Ellis grew impatient quickly, and more often a spastic "R...r....right" was all that was required on his part to confirm that the subject discussed was agreed upon.

Mumbles was standing in the hazy darkness outside Shelter Road's most active drug corner, conversing with T-Rock, who'd immediately assumed the head position along this corridor even before his friend and the mentor he'd replaced, Darren, had been placed in a cold grave. Among the dozens of young men who operated in this area, not three of them had ever even held official employment, and with the economy continuing to move into unprecedented catastrophic disarray, most viewed the sales of drugs to the few employed venturing their way as the only means to paying bills and feeding children more often dependent on quite youthful parents.

Mumbles felt quite safe doing business at the present time on Shelter Road, for all around him were well aware of just who was responsible for the slaying of Darren, and the incursion by Fat Boy and Dru had been viewed as a most egregious intrusion upon the turf of all along this strip, even those who competed with product from competing sources for the same dollars. He, in time, communicated to T-Rock his plan to equal Fat Boy's intrusion, sneak onto *his* Mississippi Avenue turf, and blast him and any others in his circle away with fatal efficiency.

"I'm   not....I...I'm   not...gu...gu...going at...th...th..them with no...no pistol!" Mumbles was explaining, freeing the front of an overcoat to briefly display the sawed-off shotgun.

"I'm....gonna....t...t...t...take.....I....I'm........ gonna...ggg.......t.....take......t...t....take.....'em....a ...a..apart...in....in...p...p...pieces!"

"I got your back, son, you going up at 'em like that," T-Rock said, displaying the handle of a huge pistol tucked in his beltline. "I say we go over there *now* while they out there trying to make this holiday bank! They probably think we doing the same, and won't be expecting shit."

Mumbles, quite comfortable in pursuing the planned assault on his own, was not one to look a gift horse in the mouth though. He surely considered a lone assault on the Mississippi Avenue haunts of Fat Boy at best fraught with potential danger to himself, but prided himself on being one to fear little.

He shook his head, looked T-Rock dead in the eyes and turned towards his pick-up.

"L…l…l…l….let's…..Le….Le….let's….d….d …do…that….sh….sh…sh….shit!"

Chapter Twelve

For years, Marquis "Fat Boy" Clease had been a fixture, literally, on the corner of Mississippi Avenue and Common Drive, deep in a section of Southeast Washington just steps from the Maryland line. His always generous girth had been a regular presence on the corner since he was a little boy (well, he'd never been considered "little, even when coming into the world at 9 and a half pounds!). And within proximity of the Shelter Road apartments, he'd actually attended school with some of the same youths with whom he now feverishly beefed, including the slain Darren Rogers, who'd sat beside him in class at Malcolm X Elementary School.

As the drug trade blossomed in certain sections of the city, Fat Boy was among the league of young men bearing arms, blasting one another, fighting over "turf" which neither they nor any member of their family would every hold title to. A jolly character who was even more buoyant when induced by one of the blunt marijuana joints he so cherished, Fats seemed oblivious to the cold this November night, holding court at Mississippi and Common, laughing joyously and even cutting a few crack heads slack when they came over to his crew with seven, eight dollars for a ten dollar rock.

The pick-up eased down Southern Avenue, the border separating D.C. from Prince George's County, MD. It had taken Mumbles the entirety of the ride to spit a few words telling T-Rock that he was *not* about to commit a "drive-by" on Fats and his cohorts. Mumbles was set on parking a few blocks away from the Mississippi Avenue Boys, walk upon them unexpectedly and, selecting Fats foremost, blast them from a distance close enough to ensure that they were fatally wounded, thus also ensuring there would be no "come-back" from some shattered, even wheelchair-bound victim (it had famously occurred just blocks away from Mississippi Avenue) at some future date.

"I...I....I...see....see his fa...fa....fat ass!" Mumbles whispered, a block away from the gathered crew and quickly, stealthily approaching.

T-Rock removed the .357 Magnum from his beltline, held the powerful weapon just before his crotch with two hands and pulled the knit cap from atop his head into a mask, completely blurring his identity with only eye holes and a mouth opening visible. Mumbles apparently had no such concerns, leveled the shotgun and dashed directly to the crowd before any of the young men realized what was about to occur.

"K...K.....K...K....K.....K...KILL MUMBLES! K.....K.....K....KILL!" he shouted his signature phrase.

The accompanying sound of four shotgun blast shattered the cold air even as the first assailant uttered the apparently reinforcing cry to inspire his mayhem. Instantly two young men crumpled to the sidewalk, fatally wounded. The masked gunman blasted away with the high-powered pistol, but the very weight of it in his considerably frail hands sent errant shots harmlessly tearing into nearby ground and automobiles along the street. The largest, voluminous man among the Mississippi Avenue Boys seemed to have found Olympian dexterity, taking off in a wobble-dash towards the rear of a building. But the man with the shotgun, still sputtering his "K....K...KILL" mantra, stepped over one wounded, wriggling figure while lowering the shotgun to deliver a final, fatal blast to this prostrate form, then dashed in the direction of the fat man.

"M....M....Mumbles....Mu...Mu...Mumbles.. *tired* ...of this....this...shit!" He was speaking softly now, let go a blast at the shadow fighting feverishly through underbrush behind an apartment building. "M...M...Mumbles...t...t....*tired*!"

Some of the scattering pellets from the shotgun blast had apparently found flesh, and as Mumbles neared the underbrush, moaning could be heard as also a flash and the sound or returning gunfire pierced the darkness. The round went errant though, and Mumbles acted as if it were not a threat at all. What it did additionally was send a momentary light from the gun barrel, pinpointing the assailant. Without hesitation, Mumbles directed a more precise blast at the lower portion of the underbrush, stepped closer and pumped three additional blast into the form now clearly visible amidst the weeds.

There was no additional return fire, and Mumbles, reloading the shotgun, moved back upon the avenue, now deserted but for six shattered bodies, and his cohort in the ski mask.

Chapter Thirteen

Christmas was fast approaching, and after heat from what was being termed the Thanksgiving's Weekend Massacre died down, business returned to normal among the Shelter Road Crew, and the Mississippi Avenue Boys. Ellis felt at ease now making appearances at his favorite neighborhood haunts, and the week before Christmas he paid a visit to his "mentor," the wheelchair bound "old school" player, Big Mack, alongside the Shipley Terrace Liquor Store.

Immaculately dressed as he'd always been even when upright, Big Mack sported a fox fur hat and matching jacket, the shine of his alligator shoes visible a block away as they sat on the footholds at the front of his electric wheelchair. His chemically-blackened beard and moustache took at least a decade off his 60 years, and the gold watch and chain which shone from below his sleeve and from around his collar were known to be the "real deal" among the younger men and women who whispered about him on area corners. But only a fool would dare attempt to "raze" Big Mack; many had broached the possibility to neighborhood regulars, but were just a quickly advised that even members of a potential assailant's extended family would be quickly funeralized should such a misguided adventure occur.

"You don't mess with Mr. Mack," was all an authoritative voice needed to say, and any plans to raze him quickly abated.

"So, young buck, you putting any of that long bread you're making to any good use?" Big Mack said, smiling from behind a gold tooth up at Ellis.

"I'm doing aiight," Ellis said, even then tortured by a vision of life prospects growing dim.

"How many kids you got spread around the city? How many women?"

This was a sore point to Ellis, and he wouldn't discuss his social situation with anyone else. But Big Mack seemed to always have some pearls of wisdom for him, even if he didn't often heed them. His current situation with Shantelle was dicey at best, and she'd already let him know that he needed to find a place of his own at the beginning of the New Year.

"I ain't got but..urr...two...just two kids, maybe three that's mine," he said, somewhat embarrassed.

"Same woman?"

"Naw." Embarrassment rankled him now. "Two women. But the one I'm with now, her two, they're not mine."

"You paying for yours?"

"I'm paying. Damn right, Big Mack. I'm paying for 'em."

"Legally?"

It took a moment for Ellis to gauge what Big Mack meant. The elder clarified.

"I mean, they take you to court for child support?"

"Oh! Naw, not like that. I just pay 'em, you know, a little something-something every now and then."

"Young buck, that's not gonna last but for a while. They're still babies, right?"

"Young. One three, the other just over a year old. That other one girl claim is mine, that bitch might need to go on the Maury show or some shit."

"You know they get more expensive as time goes by. And they're mother's mother, grandmother, aunt, girlfriends, they're gonna eventually get all in your baby mama's heads that the only way to get you to pay, and pay rightly, or dearly, whatever the case may be, is to take your ass to court."

"I don't know, Mack. You don't know them girls. I treated 'em right, and, you know," he paused, placing a hand in his crotch and smiling, "I served them like they ain't never been served, know what I'm saying?"

Big Mack allowed a light laugh, displayed the gold tooth and its surrounding glistening white capped ones.

"Young blood, it's all about the money now, times as hard as they is. I don't care if you're a buck-tooth bama from Birmingham. If you got bank, you got some method of negotiations with a broad. That's if you're not married to her. If you're married, that's a whole nother vault in the bank, as it were, young'un. You've gotta be doling out substantial funds to keep a broad from taking you downtown for child support nowadays. And even then, if you slack up, you're *still* going before the judge. Many a young man locked down today behind child support payments. Used to be they didn't press a man and lock him down like they do now. Things have changed, Ellis. You can't just call yourself a hustler and not mind the paperwork, know what I'm saying to you young'un? Find yourself hustling backwards, after all the bank you bought in then you're my age, and ain't got nothing to show for it."

"I hear ya, Big Mack. I hear what you're saying."

Chapter Fourteen

"Mumbles?"

"Yeah. That's what they call him."

Seventh District investigators, along with homicide detectives who covered the entire city, were certainly bent on stopping the carnage brewing between two Southeast Washington drug crews. But they were equally intrigued by reports being received by a number of their "CIs," confidential informants, about one particular gunman who was verifiably involved in at least two of the shootings.

Donte "Biscuit" Millsbury had just provided detectives at the Southeast substation yet another report that a "BM-20 – 24 yo" (black male, 20 – 24 years of age) with the nickname Mumbles had been one of two gunman involved in the Thanksgiving's weekend slayings along Mississippi Avenue. They had been led to "Biscuit" after he turned up at the Greater Southeast Hospital emergency room weeks after the shootings with an infection from what doctors determined was a bullet wound. Required by law to notify police of such trauma, Biscuit was met by Seventh District detectives even as he hobbled towards a bus away from the hospital. It didn't take but a minute in an interrogation room before Biscuit began singing like the proverbial canary.

Detectives ran a computer program to search for any previously arrested persons in their system that had an alias of "Mumbles." To their surprise, there were seven individuals in D.C. who went by the nickname, and further perusal indicated that nearly all of them were black men who suffered from a speech impediment. None, however, fit the description of the suspect described in two particular Southeast shootings. But every one on their list (except one, who'd been shot and killed years earlier) was investigated, interviewed, and considered not the "Mumbles" they were currently seeking.

Additionally, a number of reports had the shooter actually calling out his own name while committing the crimes. This led police to seriously consider that they had a deranged killer roaming the neighborhood, undergirding his commitment to murder by urging himself on with an inspirational call out to "KILL!," a few of the CIs confirmed.

Detective Robinson took a particular interest in the more recent Southeast shootings. A 22-year veteran of the Metropolitan Police force, Robinson came from the same streets he was now charged with protecting. An African-American who'd attended public schools in the District, Matthew Robinson had a son just completing training at the Police Academy, another in his second year at the city's Howard University, and a daughter working the 911 telephone call unit at the city's emergency response center. His wife Gloria was a nurse in the trauma unit at Greater Southeast Hospital, so the family, who for years had maintained a home in a more prestigious section of Southeast boasting half-million dollar houses, had eyes and ears constantly attuned to the city's array of social maladies.

Matt Robinson also headed a church-based community outreach group at his family's Baptist church in a lower-income section of Southeast, not blocks from the Seventh District headquarters. Within the Mt. Horab Community Center, he gained an even deeper awareness of activities among the neighborhood youths, his outreach as a mentor to many fatherless young men from the community endearing him to many who would not otherwise be caught dead (or might face that status thereof) talking to a police official.

At six feet, three inches tall and quite muscular for his age, Matt Robinson was well respected among his peers, held in high esteem among the brass downtown at police headquarters, and was not averse to joining with a team of lower ranking police officers on the company bicycles and cruise Southeast neighborhoods during spring and summer months. His most pressing concern during the current heated holiday season was holding down the city's homicide rate, which had been in decline continuously over seven years before the current economic malaise and acute joblessness was said to have contributed to a major surge in inner city violence nationwide.

This morning he wanted to interview "Biscuit" on his own; unbeknownst to the young man, Detective Robinson was quite familiar with his kin, the Millsbury brothers, their mother, their grandmother, from the old Garfield public housing project. Indeed, Matt had dated one of Biscuit's aunts when the two attended Southeast's Ballou High School. Young Donte, "Biscuit," of course had no way of knowing this.

Dressed in his "combat" gear, blue cargo pants, a matching shirt, black boots, Matt entered the interrogation room bearing a soda and chips, and a clipboard with sheaves of paper affixed to it. He placed the soda and chips on the table before the visibly frightened young man, took a chair on the opposite side of the table.

"Go ahead," he said with a smile, nodding towards the soda and chips. "Know you've gotta be hungry, all that time over in the emergency room, then in here."

Biscuit looked at the officer with cautious eyes, then ripped the bag of chips open and seemingly devoured the entire, measly contents in two mouthfuls. He popped the top on the soda, guzzled thirstily.

"So," the officer began, "they tell me you heard the gunman down there on Mississippi that Saturday shouting something about 'Kill, Mumbles, kill?'"

"That's what that fool said man, no joke."

"You get a good look at him?"

"Shi-i--....I mean, that dude was firing a shotgun! I ain't try to peep at his ass like that man! I was trying to get behind a car, and still some of that firepower got me all in the thigh and leg. Other dude had on a facemask, but the dude..the one talk that 'Mumbles kill' mess, he was just all opened up. Dark-skinned dude. About my height, but maybe a little older. I told your boys that when they asked me earlier."

"You'd never seen him before?"

Biscuit hesitated, quickly considering his own safety.

"I...dude be over on Shelter Road sometimes. I think, like, he one of them be wholesaling crack around that joint. Used to supply that dude called Darren, but his ass got killed there a while back."

"Yeah," the detective glanced down, flipping through the papers on the clipboard. "Darren Rogers. Word around the way was that Marquis Clease, fellow they called 'Fat Boy,' was responsible for Darren's death. And since...'Fat Boy' seemed to be the main target on Mississippi, the shooting there was retribution for the killing of Rogers. You know anything about that?"

"Naw! Hell, that mess ain't none of my business! I don't sling...and most of the dudes got hit, they was slinging."

"Slinging? Selling crack?"

"Right. They was slinging along with Fats. That's all I know, man."

"So, you were just in the wrong place at the wrong time, huh?"

"That's about it, man. Like that. Just like that, know what I'm saying?"

"I hear ya," Detective Robinson said, arose and freed the youth's arm from the cuffs which had him tethered to the conference table. "Go on out to the front desk and get your belongings. You're free to go."

He was escorted to the front of the substation by a lower-ranking officer, but not before another neighborhood youth, in a current drug distribution sting, was being led to a rear holding cell. Biscuit, seemingly awe struck, locked eyes momentarily with the new detainee, tried to shrug his shoulders as if to allay fears he had that the other youth might identify Biscuit, evidently free as being casually escorted from the facility, as a snitch.

He shook his head at the other youth, but his gesture didn't ring true.

"Snitch-ass mother fucker!" the new detainee mouthed the words, and Biscuit knew then that, through communications in the city jail akin to ancient African drums, his neighborhood would be awash with word that he was an informant within a matter of days.

Chapter Fifteen

Shantelle had again become fed up with Ellis's cheating. Again he'd come into their shared bed smelling of some unknown female's fragrance, and for the past few weeks had seemed sexually depleted, parrying away her nightly advances and pleading exhaustion. A couple of attempts by her at arousing him orally, a sexual deliverance which in the past never failed to have him solidly erect within seconds, had only resulted in a flaccid, unresponsive organ lolling about between her experienced lips. She was certain he was being sexually depleted elsewhere, and that, in combination with the foreign fragrances, had finally convinced her that she no longer had as firm a hold on him as she'd believed.

It was just before Christmas, and mostly out of concern for little Ebony and Derrick, she was putting off his eviction until after New Years. Complicating matters, she'd just found out that she was nine weeks into a pregnancy, had been with no other man but Ellis for the past two years, and had grown dependent on his financial largess for the luxuries she and the children experienced. Her financial aid from the D.C.

government, food stamps, a Section 8 housing subsidy, a considerably minor monthly payment for support of the children (their father, drug strapped since his teens, spending more time in jail than out), was considered a pittance for the attractive young lady. She'd generated the attention of "hustlers" since her early teens, and had grown accustomed to benefits which would hardly paint a picture of her as a "welfare mom." Ellis was the latest, and in her views most financially successful, of her live-in boyfriends.

But now, he had to go. The pregnancy assured her that she'd always have ties to the tall, handsome man with the winning smile. But jealousy was one emotion which Shantelle could not bear, and after a period of analysis of their situation, she was by now certain that, eventually, he would have ended their relationship anyway.

She was spending a Saturday afternoon discussing her prospects with best friend Lana, a year older and countless affairs wiser. Little Ebony occupied Derrick with a video game in a rear bedroom, affording Shantelle rare quiet time to discuss her plans with Lana.

"Girl, I'm serious," Shantelle said. "January 2, I'm packing up his shit and telling him for the last time it's over."

"For the last time," Lana smiled. "For the umpteenth time, girl. I hope you mean it this time. I ain't want to tell you, but his ass had the nerve to try and holla at me once out there at Martin's. Even after y'all was hooked-up and he *knew* you was my girl."

"What?!"

"Yeah, girl. I wasn't gonna say nothing, 'cause, you know, he was drinking his Remy and showing off around his boys. But still, I don't care how much he had to drink, girl, he should *know* better than to be trying that shit on one of his girl's friends."

"Tired ass..."

They sipped from a considerably expensive bottle of champagne, a bottle Ellis had stated quite vocally he'd put aside for New Year's celebrations.

"But, dag girl!" Shantelle continued. "I'm gonna miss that...you know..."

"Dick?" Lana was not one to bite her tongue.

"You know!" Shantelle blanched with embarrassment. "Well, yeah! But you ain't gotta go all and say it like that!"

"Well, it is what it is…"

"And his ass *is* fine…"

"Yeah," Lana agreed. "Tall, fine, black-ass. With that Colgate smile of his…"

Shantelle took a generous sip of the champagne, then hesitated before refilling the crystal flute.

"You know," she said, hesitantly. "I maybe shouldn't be drinking. With…with…"

Lana took the bottle and refilled her own champagne flute.

"With *what*, girl?"

Shantelle put her glass on the coffee table, began rubbing her stomach with both hands, leaned forward with a smile, a faraway look in her eyes.

"Oh, *hell naw*!" Lana near shouted. "I *know* your ass ain't pregnant! Girl, no!"

"Yep. About nine weeks."

"How you know...I mean..hell! Well, I *know* you'd know. After Ebony and Derrick! But....daaaa....aaag!"

They sat smiling silently for a moment; Shantelle relented and refilled her flute, took a generous swig.

"You tell him yet?" Lana asked.

"Oh, *hell no*! And you don't say nothing either, he come in here!"

"When you gonna tell him, Shantelle?"

She smiled, somewhat wickedly, eyes cowered, looking towards the back bedroom from where the sounds of her two children playing filtered out.

"Right after he's out. Even if I have to get the police to escort his ass out, he's going out on the second, third of January latest. Then when he calls, like he always do, trying to get back on my good side, I'm gonna tell him. *And* tell him he's gonna support this child even if I have to take his ass to court."

"Go on, girl," Lana smiled, hoisted her glass as if making a toast.

Chapter Sixteen

At the immaculate home in a gated community deep in Southern Maryland, Ellis was engaged on Christmas afternoon with his key supplier, negotiating a deal for the largest volume of cocaine he'd ever scored and trying to convince his supplier that, due to the volume and his willingness to pay straight cash for the volume, he should be given a little leeway on the standard asking price. The next weekend would see business blooming with those who deemed drugs a necessary part of their holiday celebration, and with the New Year fast on the following weekend and weekend business always the best in the drug trade, Ellis was set on ensuring that he had enough coke, and the best quality available in his specific arena, to guarantee profits which would allow him a period of rest as the New Year began.

He'd also been in serious conversation with Big Mack, had been hit with some most acute realizations, and, certain that Shantelle was the most beloved of his current female acquaintances, was convinced that it was time for him to "put away childish things," as Big

Mack had so biblically phrased it, and settle down, in marriage, with Shantelle Bridgefield.

His host Reynaldo listened for a good while to Ellis's ruminations about his personal life, his plans for the future, his troubles with potential "stick-up boys" in Southeast, before bringing the visit to an abrupt conclusion. It was nearing four o'clock; he'd scheduled a major purchase with another dealer from Washington and, as was his long-term practice, neither the two should meet.

Seated in the comfortable living room of his multi-million dollar home, Reynaldo puffed lightly on an expensive cigar, swirled around a fine cognac in a large crystal glass, sipping from it on occasion. Tanned well beyond his normal Mediterranean tone even on this midwinter afternoon, the drug wholesaler with the ever present slight smile studied Ellis from a short distance, perched on the edge of an expensive, brocade sofa. On occasion he'd glance to his constant companion Miguel, a good thirty feet away, seated in a chair at the dining room table.

"You've got that package at the price you're asking, Ellis," Reynaldo turned his attention directly to Ellis, sliding a bound package across the oaken coffee table. "Merry Christmas, my brother."

He arose, and from previous experience Ellis knew that it was time for him to leave. He left the bound stack of money on the table, stood and retrieved the package.

"'Preciate it, Reynaldo," he said, moving to engage his supplier in a customary embrace. "Till next time."

"Next time."

Reynaldo returned to his seat on the sofa as Ellis moved across the living room, Miguel silently easing up behind him. Ellis stopped in the foyer; he knew better than to open the door to the home. He awaited Miguel, who nodded to him and swung open the heavy ornate entrance.

Miguel stood there, watched as Ellis entered his SUV and approached the heavy gate at the foot of the driveway. From the entrance, Miguel hit a switch on the wall beside him, and the gates slowly swung open inward. He waited, watched the SUV ease out the deserted lane leading up to the home, sent a signal which motored the gate closed. Returning to the living room, he followed the motion Reynaldo indicated, sat before his boss.

"I've been hearing from our friend in the Seventh District that Ellis's boy, that...the one who finds it hard to speak, that he's been calling a lot of attention to their business in the Southeast," Reynaldo said, pausing for a puff, a sip. "The reports are not good, Miguel. Do you think Ellis is one who will break under pressure, should he be taken in and questioned by the federales?"

Miguel, a short, barrel-chested man with a handlebar moustache which made him appear as if some Hispanic cartoon character, nodded and looked off into the distance, as if giving the question serious consideration.

"He's a weak one, boss. He talks too much anyway, about his women, his children, his desires. He is not one who would hold up under any pressure from the federales, boss. I don't believe that he has ever gone hungry, and is not one to last long without missing a meal."

"I agree," Reynaldo said, arising.

Habitually, Miguel stood erect also.

"Let him have his Christmas celebration, his New Years," Reynaldo said, moving to the dining room, then on into the elaborate, stainless-steel appointed kitchen. "You know where he stays with the girl Shantelle, and where the guy who has trouble speaking lives?"

"I know," Miguel, feet behind him, said.

"The two should be taken care of before the first weekend of the New Year ends, Miguel. We have plenty of the boys from the city to carry on with putting our products out there. No need to take chances on an operation getting sloppy such as the one Ellis leads."

"Understand, boss. I understand."

Chapter Seventeen

For some, the economy had Christmas resembling a Fourth of July celebration with dud fireworks. For even others, it was as if they had an economy pack of firecrackers but couldn't find nor bum a match or lighter to set them off. Along the streets of D.C. where many depended on their "hustle" to get by, many lacked the fuel for the giddy-up. Others were provided "fuel:" alcohol and drug substances which only served to further extinguish their already dying financial flames.

Ellis was lauding gifts on his grandmother, the only close family member he'd known in recent years and the sole kin who'd raised him after being deposited with her as a boy by a wayward mother and the man he'd known as a stepfather. She still maintained the unit in the historic housing project unit in the Southeast section of the city, the home and neighborhood where he'd grown up among such playmates as Little Man Jones, "Block" Thurman, and the boy whose name had never been established, but was simply referred to as Mumbles.

His SUV stood out in the ramshackle neighborhood, which had a decade earlier experienced a considerable upgrade only to be immediately forgotten and allowed to digress once again when crack cocaine sales took hold there. Now drug sales there were all but nonexistent. But the residual effects, the countless missing young men doing long prison stretches as a result of drug busts, the ruptured families, never well off, had been further depleted financially. Financial destruction was further assured by them having to send scarce funds off to some prisoner's commissary account, or undertaking expensive treks to visit a young man in North Carolina, Western Virginia, even as far away as Walla Walla, Washington. Additional expenses drained the community through the burial of uninsured youths, which virtually sealed the monetary coffins of the three-hundred families still living there.

Grandma Davidson never wanted to leave the community though, even after Ellis offered to purchase her a home in nearby suburban Maryland. But she'd raised him after all, and knew immediately that his offer was merely a way of getting another place where he could lay his head, outside of the array of women he extended funds to, because his means of income, and certainly background lacking any official banking or job-related mentions, wouldn't allow him to acquire anything even resembling a home in his own name.

"You'll never get me out my home and in some place you *say* you're buying, then have some gov'ment peoples come by later on placing me and all my belongs on the street," she'd said by way of declining his offer. "You had any legitimate concerns about yourself and your....*business*...you'd be able to get a place of your own, and not always be depending on them little hot-ass girls you always running behind."

He'd called her earlier, and had bought over the ham she'd requested. Grandma Davidson now saw after two great-grandchildren, and on occasion their father, Melvin. He was Ellis's half-brother, but four years older and in jail more than out. Just like their mother, Melvin was a seasoned heroin addict, and much like their mother also, hadn't any plans on ceasing his particular death march.

Ellis spent a few minutes that afternoon playing with Jordan and Jamal, the four-year-old twins currently in the care of Grandma Davidson for an undetermined period of time. He'd bought them toys, small hand-held video game devices currently the rage among those of their age, and begged off staying for dinner. His grandmother's long-time friend

Winston was there, and the arrival of his adult daughter Dierdra hinted to Ellis that Winston was more than a casual visitor.

His grandmother interrupted his frolicking on the living room floor with Jamal.

"Ellis, I fixed you a plate to take with you, since you can't find the time to have a holiday meal with your kin," she said, holding forth a foil wrapped plate while wiping a hand on her apron. "I'm gonna put this on the side table there. Don't forget it."

The smell of collard greens most overpowering struck him as if he'd just entered the home. His hunger pangs reactivated, his mind began rushing again, and the business he needed to attend to resurfaced.

He arose, exchanged a handshake with the little boy, called out a goodbye to the boy's unresponsive brother.

"Alright, Grandma," he said, moving into the kitchen and giving her a hug. "Merry Christmas, Mr. Winston, Dierdra."

He retrieved the foil wrapped plate, moved out into a biting wind. Quickly, he motored the short distance to Mumbles' apartment, retrieved the plate and a small satchel, rushed to the building and climbed the stairs to Mumbles' unit. He was unaware of the two men behind tinted windows in the nondescript vehicle parked nearby, watching his every motion with professional, dissecting eyes.

"You had something to eat," he greeted Mumbles, handing him the plate of food. He'd already retrieved and devoured only a fried chicken drumstick from the platter, not wanting to return to the home he shared with Shantelle completely full.

"N..n....n...not...nothing....g...g...goo...wo...w o...worth a...a...shit!"

Mumbles unwrapped the foil from the plate, held it in two hands under his nose and smiled broadly.

"Gr...Gr..Grandma's! M.........mmmm........ M....m....uuu...uuu...ump....umpp...umph!"

He sat at the dinette table, delved into the dish while Ellis unwrapped his package, the size a couple of bricks, and began dividing it further down into the "wholesale" quantities underlings would purchase and convert into the most addictive crack cocaine form. As he measured amounts and placed them in individual sandwich bags, a smile gradually surfaced. The amount he'd just purchased would generate his greatest margin of profit ever, and he mentally gave thanks to Reynaldo once again.

"Mumbles," he grinned broadly, holding a bag high giving it a little shake. "We're going into the New Year with big bank, my man!"

Forking collard greens into his mouth, Mumbles just peered up momentarily and nodded.

"I broke down ten packages for the young'uns down Shelter Road. You see they get them tonight, and take a good piece of this shit and keep it in your freezer. Ain't no need to break it down further right now. These ten oughta be enough. And I got a nice package I'm taking home, just in case one of my other boys call and done run out."

He arose, secured his jacket and his own considerable package, peered through the peephole of the door out of habit, looked back to Mumbles and left the unit. The two men behind the tinted glass watched as he walked quickly towards his SUV. They'd already ran the tags on Ellis's vehicle, and a computer in the plain, city-owned vehicle quickly identified the SUV as being registered to one Ellis Davidson. Seeing that Ellis was now empty handed, a summation was made.

"He left the package with...," the man in the passenger's seat paused, looked to a sheaf of paper, "Johnson, Delano, aka 'Mumbles."

"That's the shooter from Mississippi Ave," the driver said, still watching the SUV.

"Right. Well, we know where Davidson is headed, to the place he shacks up with the girl Bridgefield and her two kids. Johnson's probably preparing to resupply the kids on Shelter Road. He'll be armed, naturally."

"Sure. Better call for back-up."

Chapter Eighteen

Out of habit, Mumbles moved into the dark back bedroom, bent the Venetian blinds and scanned up and down the street. The exhaust from the black Mercury Marquis parked across the street, windows tinted beyond what is legal in the District, caught his attention. He moved to the living room, dimmed the lights and peered out the front window there. The view afforded him a glance at the rear tags of the car: The combination of letters and numbers, the "Taxation Without Representation"-slogan on the tag's bottom, assured him that the car was registered in the city, and most definitely one previously confiscated by the police and now being used as a presumably nondescript surveillance vehicle.

Ever since he'd moved into this building, Mumbles had endeared himself to a few of its residents by fronting them modest loans and, some, cocaine on "tic," before they had the means to pay for a dose. Miss Charlene, a woman of 34 who lived in a first floor unit to the building's rear, had been a casual user upon Mumbles' arrival there. After two years, she was now a full-fledged addict, and although words struggled to find their way out of the drug dealer, his mind, quite developed, never ceased scheming and dreaming.

Quickly he gathered all the drugs in the apartment, including stashes remaining from previous scores. He retrieved the sawed-off shotgun, its rounds, two pistols and the cartridges that went with them, placing all the items in two pillow cases. He did a secondary surveillance of the car, now most assuredly detectives, even then being approached by a secondary one of similar make-up, and that one trailed by a marked Metropolitan Police Department vehicle.

Mumbles stepped apace to the front door, peered through the peephole, then rushed out of the unit, to the first floor and to the rear unit belonging to Miss Charlene. The peephole to her unit visibly darkened, and the door was swung open without hesitation.

"What's up, Mumbles?" the reed-thin, ashen women said, stepping back to let an apparently anxious Mumbles into the unit.

"Fi...fi...five....o....o....O!" he said, watching to ensure she secured the door.

A rush of four unkempt children, from toddlers to pre-teens, skittered into the living room.

"Hi, Mr. Mumbles!" a chorus of squeaky voices rang out.

"You got some potato chips?" a child of around five pleaded up to him.

"We hon-grey!" one of about ten said sadly.

Mumbles reached in a pocket, peeled two twenty-dollar bills and gave them to Miss Charlene.

"Y....y....you....go ...s...store....an...a....and I wa...wa....watch...I watch....them....for you."

Seeing the money, apparently in denominations both foreign and exciting to them, the children grew even more animated, two rushing to a rear bedroom and returning with an armload of coats, shoes, baby jeans.

"We go with you, mama! Let's go to the carry-out!" one screamed.

"Get y'all asses back there in the bedroom with all that mother fucking noise around this mother fucking joint!" she blasted them, and the buoyancy evident in the children flushed away immediately. The four, crestfallen, dragged themselves back into the rear of the dirty apartment, suppressed sobs trailing them.

"You think they gonna raid your joint?" Miss Charlene asked, sitting and pulling on a pair of brand-named tennis shoes.

He was peering out the peephole, a view down the hallway to the front entrance discernible even as three of the four hallway light bulbs had been twisted loose by addicts who used the hallway for a quick consumption.

"Th...th...they...pr...pr..probab...bably...w... w...was....s.s.....scoping...m...my..my...man....Ellis. N...n...n...no.....he...gone...they...they...m....m...m m...maybe ....wa...waiting...on...mm.....mm....me!"

Miss Charlene grabbed a tattered overcoat from a hall closet, moved to the exit.

"I'm going to get these kids some food from up Joe's," she said.

Mumbles stepped aside, allowed her to peer through the peephole.

"I'll be back in a few minutes. Scope out them police while I'm out there for you too."

He secured the door behind her.

Just as Miss Charlene was about to push her way out into the night, a phalanx of officers in black, SWAT attire with automatic weapons at the ready rushed into the building, two shoving her aside and adeptly twisting her to the floor, demanding silence. The bulk of the team rushed up the front stairways, the second in this crew bearing what was evidently a heavy metal battering ram. Suddenly, the echoing crash, the thud, of the battering device could be heard echoing from above, quickly followed by the shouts of "Police! Police!"

After a moment of rustling and subsequent bangs, the entire building grew eerily silent. Two officers, now removing the facemask which had blurred their identities, descended from the upper floors.

"He's gone! Where the fuck he get off to?" one asked no one in particular among those still amassed on the ground floor, two still immobilizing Miss Charlene.

"We have personnel to the building's rear. He couldn't have gone out a window," a black-clad figure on the ground floor said.

Miss Charlene, apparently appearing to the law enforcement officials as not one who required any measure of respect, was twisted about by an officer.

"Where your dope-dealing neighbor get off to?" he asked, standing above her with an automatic weapon pointed down directly at her.

"I don't know no mother fucker be dealing no dope around here, mother fucker," she spat, literally, saliva pitching forth from the space where two front teeth should have been.

A female officer stepped into the hallway, apparently summoned, donned rubber gloves and began frisking Miss Charlene as she sat against the wall on the cold hallway floor. Pulling the two twenties from a pants pocket, the female officer held the bills up, looked to her fellow officers, then back down to Miss Charlene.

"Bitch, it's not the first of the month yet. Where the hell your pipe-head ass get this kind of money?" the female officer asked.

"I got it from you daddy, bitch," Miss Charlene spat. "That nigga like to eat some good pussy now and then."

The female officer was visible rankled, looked around to her fellow officers, evidently seeking some unspoken approval. A few nodded, and the female officer whipped a couple of practiced fist upside Miss Charlene's head. She then stepped back, swung a combat-boot clad foot into Miss Charlene's midsection.

"I got your daddy, ho," she said, stepping back and turning to the approving grins of her fellow officers.

"Now see," Miss Charlene folded to the side, attempting to wipe bleeding lips on a jacket sleeve, "that was some fucked up shit right there you did."

Behind her apartment door, Mumbles had a partial view of what was going on to the front of the building. But he couldn't see Miss Charlene, though he knew she'd been taken back in the building when the officers entered. The stairs leading to the upper levels blocked his view of her beating, but he was quite sure that she was not being treated kindly by the officers he could see addressing some figure (most assuredly Miss Charlene) who was apparently on the hallway floor before them.

He moved to a rear bedroom of the unit, where the four children were huddled together on a bare mattress, watching a small television. He peered out onto the grassy expanse behind the building, was reassured something he already knew: Black-clad SWAT team members were gathered there, peering up at windows, scanning the rooftop, cautiously pointing flashlights affixed to the underside of weapons into the dense foliage to the building's rear.

"Sh…sh….sh….sh….shit!"

Chapter Nineteen

Ellis stopped by Shantelle's mother's home after leaving Mumbles'. He'd dropped her and the kids off there before making his run to his supplier, but was told by a steamed Mrs. Bridgefield that her daughter had long gone, taken home with the children be an uncle a few hours earlier.

"Damn!" he uttered, knowing that he'd have to deal with trauma when he arrived at the unit they shared. "I told her ass to wait; I'd be here in a few minutes!"

He headed the short distance to their apartment. But before he'd barely parked the SUV, his cell phone chimed its melodious, rap-based ring tone.

It was Mumbles, the caller ID and a stammering, evidently shaken more than was common voice confirmed.

"What's the problem, man?"

"P...p...po...lice!"

"What? On Shelter Road?"

"N...N...N....Na...na.....Naw!   All....all....all up in....in....my....shit!"

"At your building?"

"Y...y...y...yeah!"

"Damn! Where you at?"

"M....M....Miss...Cha...Charlene's!"

"Cool. You got the shit with you?"

"Y...y..yeah! Th...they bu...bu..bust...in..in..in my...my...joint...I...I...I th..think."

"Man!   Mumbles, just lay low at Miss Charlene's till they finish. Long as they don't find no shit in your joint, you're cool. What about your pieces?"

"G...g....got....I...g....g....got...I.....g...g.....ge .....the.....the....sh...sh...shotgun...and...and....the pistols....o...out."

"Good.   I gotta go in here and deal with Shantelle. I'll holla back once I finish with her ass."

At a fast clip, Ellis walked into the building. He worked his keys, pushed the door, but was stumped by the security chain Shantelle had evidently put in place. He called out to her, visible through the small opening, seated in the living room.

"Hey? *Hey*!! Open the damn door, girl!"

She was unmoved.

"Shantelle!!?? What's wrong with you? Open the damn door!!"

She still didn't move, and he could see through the limited space the tears streaming down her cheeks. He stepped back in the hallway, leaned against the far wall shaking his head.

"Girl tripping! Damn!"

The nosey neighbor across the hall, a lifelong resident of the complex, stuck her grey head out the door.

"You alright, young man?" the old woman said, familiar with Ellis and Shantelle and, not really concerned about his well being, merely starved for news as well as companionship.

"I'm aiight, Miss Mary," he said, stepped back to the cracked apartment door.

"Shantelle? Come on girl, let me in."

She pinned him with eyes so piercing they made his own widen somewhat. Then she arose, padded over to the door, pushed it shut then freed the chains. She didn't reopen the door, but returned to her seat on the sofa. It seemed an interminable period, but eventually she could hear his keys rework the lock, one unnecessarily, then ease the door open and hesitantly step into the warmth of the apartment.

"I don't know why you're tripping," he said, passing by her to place his jacket in the hall closet. "Know I had to take care of my business like that..."

Little Ebony cracked her own bedroom door, stood and looked out at Ellis with eyes near mirroring those of her mother minutes earlier.

"And don't you start," he said, looking to the child with equally callous eyes.

"Ain't nobody thinking about you!" she blurted out, slammed the door.

He returned to the living room, sat in the chair he favored across from the sofa.

"Y'all open them presents?" he asked, looking to a smattering of opened and unopened packages scattered beneath the Christmas tree in the corner.

"Fuck you, Ellis," she said, picked up a Jet magazine from the coffee table and began thumbing through it. "Just fuck you."

He looked at her for a moment, tried formulating some response in his mind then eventually gave up, moved to the bedroom they shared and began making calls on his cellular. First he called Donna, the mother of his three-year-old. She reassured him that his daughter was pleased with the gifts he'd left for her, and that the money he'd given Donna that morning was sufficient at present. He then called Linda, his year-old daughter's mother, received similar reassurances in an equally brief conversation.

He then called Mumbles.

The tumult in his apartment building was growing to a close. Tactical police, SWAT, narcotic task force officers, Seventh District detectives, had come to the conclusion that Delano "Mumbles" Johnson was not on the scene, though a pick-up truck identified as his remained on the street before the building. A second car belonging to him, an expensive, late-model foreign luxury vehicle, could not be located. Investigators assumed he was out in that one carrying on either holiday celebrations, or furthering his illegal trade. His associate, Ellis

Davidson, had apparently used the apartment above to partition the new package of cocaine officers suspected was about to hit the streets around Shelter Road; residual powders were found on Johnson's coffee table, and the surveillance team was being blamed for not arresting, or at least searching, Davidson when he'd been in their sights there earlier.

Miss Charlene was questioned, then allowed to return to her unit after pleading that her children were alone, and that she'd only been headed to the grocery store to get them snacks. The female officer who'd frisked her and debated whether or not to charge *Miss Charlene* with assault on a police officer was half the pair who finally assisted her to her feet, removed the handcuffs and suggested she probably was well aware of her neighbor's crack dealer, and perhaps one of his customers.

"I don't know what that fool be doing, for real," Miss Charlene said, rubbing her wrist where the handcuffs had bitten into them. "The dude sell rocks, he ain't stupid enough to sell them in his own building like that, know what I'm saying?"

The female officer wasn't buying it.

"The way your stank ass smoking it, I don't see how you could avoid not knowing he was selling.

Probably begging for a hit every time you see him," the officer said, looking to her colleagues for agreement.

"Well," Miss Charlene began to step towards her unit, "that's just what you think. And give me back goddamn money, bitch!"

The female officer hesitated, smiled then handed Miss Charlene the two twenties.

"Don't spend it all in one place, ho."

"Fuck you," Miss Charlene retorted, snatching the bills. "And I got your name, mother fucker. I'm 'bout to file police brutality charges against your ass!"

Three officers looked to their female associate, one motioning her towards the door with a supportive arm around her shoulder.

"Police brutality? Officer Williams, I could have sworn that nasty thing there was the one assaulted *you*!" a black-clad officer smiled.

"You want us to take her in on that assault on a police officer charge?" another said, stepping towards Miss Charlene.

Miss Charlene, knees visible weakening, struggled as quick as possible down the hallway to her unit, to the laughter of the gathered officers.

"Fuck all of y'all!" she spat over a shoulder, reached her unit and quickly entered.

The only signs of life in the living room and adjoining dinette and kitchen were the common roaches, lolling about in their regular nonchalant manner in search of scarce crumbs. She called out to "Kanisha!," her ten-year-old, and the four children sprinted from the rear.

"What you get us, Ma?" the skinniest, tallest of the brood said, looking up even then to her mother's bare arms.

"Police got some shit going on out there, girl," the mother said. "I didn't get a chance to get to the store."

"Dag, Ma!" her four-year-old son Michael said. "We ain't had nothing to eat since breakfast! And it's Christmas!"

"I know!" seven-year-old Ricky said, throwing himself on the battered sofa.

"Mumbles?" she shouted, looking to the rear.

The bathroom door opened, and Mumbles eased out, a shotgun at the ready. In his other arm, he struggled to tote the two pillow cases and keep a cell phone to his ear. He entered the living room, placed the pillow cases on the floor, the shotgun on a coffee table, moved to the front door and peered through the peephole.

"T...t...th...the po...po...police...gone?"

"They gone, Mumbles. Gave me some shit though. They busted in your joint. Asked me all these questions about your ass. I ain't say nothing, though. They don't know you're back here."
"Go...goo....good."

He held his cell phone towards Miss Charlene, and the cold glares of the children did not go unnoticed.

"T......talk to..to...to my boy...E...Ellis. About....about....wh...wh...wh..."

She'd known Mumbles long enough to sense when he was struggling for words, and long enough to make out what he was trying to say. She took the phone and addressed his "boy....Ellis."

"Naw man, Five-O busted in his crib....He was down here already. I think he got his shit with him, least   he   got   his   shotgun   and   some bags...Naw...Okay...Later."

"He say he's gonna make sure the Shelter Road Crew is down for tonight, Mumbles," she said, handing him back the phone. "You can stay here long as you want, man. But I got to still try to get up to the store and get these kids a little to eat."

She moved to the door, peered again out the peephole.

"Keep your eyes on them for me, baby. Then when I get back, we can go on back there in my bedroom and get a little busy, you want to."

He eased onto the sofa beside little Michael, put an arm around him playfully.

"And if you got you got your shit, man," she said, turning from the open door with an awry smile, "maybe you can break me off a little something-something, ease my nerves a little, you know? A little Christmas blast, know what I'm saying?"

She secured the door, and he moved to the peephole again, watched her make a solo trek down the now deserted hallway.

"Mr. Mumbles?"

He turned. Kanisha was tugging at the hem of his jacket.

"You ain't got nothing to eat in your bags?" she said plaintively.

He moved to the dinette table, plucked a pair of mating roaches from the surface and took the inventory of one of the pillow cases.

"Ai....ai...ain't got...no...no...food...gu...gu...girl," he said, began busying himself further dividing some packages of cocaine."W...w....wait...fo....for....for......w...w...w ...wa..wait...for...yo...your....m....m...mother."

Chapter Twenty

It was not what he had planned for Christmas night. He'd given a lot of thought to his situation with Shantelle, and had even found time to venture out to the jeweler at the Capital Mall and purchase a pretty decent diamond ring. Satisfied that he'd done a good job of providing Christmas gifts in Kenilworth, Barry Farm, and a few other housing complexes where he'd either planted seeds successfully or was still sowing them, he'd planned on securing the saved bottle of $120.00 champagne and, once little Ebony and Derrick were abed, create a romantic mood in the apartment, incense and candles afire, and ask Shantelle to be his wife.

The near catastrophe at Mumbles' place had put a damper on those plans though. The Shelter Road boys were clamoring for more product; they'd been particularly busy as the neighborhood had benefitted from a string of recently successful armed robberies, and the largess from those heists were making their way through the community, a sort of ghetto trickle-down economics paradigm, where loot from robberies made their way to others through gambling, drug sales, and the necessary endowments to lady friends. After all, in the grand scheme of things, during a time surpassing the Great Depression in certain communities, little was free. Including the sexual "favors" of young ladies some otherwise considered girlfriends.

He just had to make the run.

"Shantelle," he began his practice plea, and she knew immediately what was forthcoming. "I got to make this little run down the way. Shouldn't take but a half hour or so. But when I come back, I got a little surprise for you."

He moved to the faux bar to the far side of the living room, reached behind it to where he stashed his favorite champagnes and, surprised, came up empty handed.

"What the fuck?" he blurted out. "What happened to that bottle of Majique I had behind the bar?"

Shantelle, for days regretting her indulgence with friend Lana but at the moment quite pleased, smiled a wicked smile to him and was glad to assume responsibility.

"Oh, that?" she said, grinning. "Me and Lana killed that bottle some days ago."

He was pissed. But hesitated and took a moment, gave thought to the plans he'd made, the ring secreted in a jacket pocket, relented.

"Well," he moved towards the door. "I'll get another bottle on my way back. And don't you be falling asleep on a brother! I got something serious I want to get with you about."

He moved back across the living room, bent and planted a kiss on her lips.

"Merry Christmas, baby. Be back in a minute."

In truth, Shantelle was glad that he was gone. It gave her the opportunity to engage her friend Lana in an ongoing conversation the two had been having since Thanksgivings: How Shantelle might secure a good portion of Ellis's wealth, which he'd long assumed was hidden, before the break up and even before he'd be held legally responsible for the new life forming within her. She called Lana, schemed on how to get Ellis to make more regular deposits into her checking account, which had been his "safety net" mechanism since the two had become a pair. After all, Ellis couldn't establish legitimate banking, having never actually held a real job. And he'd always been trusting of Shantelle, sure of, and reassuring her, that they were together for life and would one day eventually marry.

"He always be giving me two, three-thousand to put in my checking," Shantelle was telling her best friend over the phone. "One time, eight-thousand. He say if you do any transaction over ten-thousand, the bank has to notify some kinda authority or some shit. That old hustler Big Mack be telling him about how to…how they say? *launder,* his money. Fool got about thirty-thousand in shoe boxes under the bed now."

She went on for a good three minutes, Lana, always trusted, known to possess a mind quite manipulative and scheming.

"Naw, girl!" Shantelle continued. "I haven't hardly spent a dime out of my checking. Transferred a lot over to savings, you know, an interest-bearing account. But he don't never ask nothing except I write checks to pay for little shit, car insurance, that kinda thing. I pay the rent and utilities out of it, but that's nothing compared to what he give me to put in checking."

Again, she listened.

"A Lexus?   Girl, I was thinking about something like a Camry, or an Explorer or some shit. You serious, ain't you?"

A nod, a smile, a response.

"You right, Lana! I might do that! Shit...he can afford a Lexus. But that might take some time, and you know, I was planning on kicking his ass to the curb first thing in January."

Advice was being administered, and for a moment Shantelle only listened and nodded.

"Yeah, well, I'm going to be showing soon, and you know, we *do* get it on now and then. He's gonna be able to tell I'm pregnant by then..."

Cruising onto a particularly active Shelter Road for a holiday night with temperatures in the low 20s, Ellis was merely set on making a quick exchange with crew members who'd been anxiously anticipating an emergency deliverance from Mumbles. Instead, Ellis had raised two of the local dealers on their cell phones, was set to meet them at a prearranged location just off Shelter Road, quickly exchange product for money, and Ellis make his way back to Shantelle before she'd grown further incensed. They recognized his SUV, flashed the lights on their older model Chevy and a Ford which quite resembled a police detective car, left their vehicles and quickly approached Ellis's, climbed into it.

"Merry Christmas, El," the two young men said almost in unison.

"Merry Christmas," Ellis said with little warmth.

He handed each a sandwich bag, both burgeoning with an amount of cocaine both young men found quite attractive.

"This some nice weight," one said, handing over a fold of money to Ellis. "I ain't got but a grand."

"I got a grand too," the second man said, examining the bag handed him. "This looks like a lot more than that."

Ellis smiled, self-satisfactorily.

"Ol' dude out there in Maryland hooked me up decent, you know, for the holiday," he said. "Just passing it on."

The front seat passenger expressed skepticism.

"So, what more we own you on this, Ellis?"

"Nothing. Like I said, I'm just passing it on. We cool."

"No shit, Sherlock!" the back seat passenger said. "That's aiight!"

Ellis glanced over a shoulder.

"Aiight. Now I gotta spend the evening with my lady. I'm out."

The two, visibly elated, hurried out of the SUV, conversing between themselves as they moved back to the blackened shadows where their own vehicles were parked. Ellis eased into reverse, backed out of the parking lot and slowly rolled back towards what for him was considered home.

"He's back," Shantelle whispered into the phone, attempting to end what had been a long, and for her enlightening, conversation with Lana.

The door opened, and it was then that Ellis reached for the ring in his pocket and realized he'd forgotten the champagne. He secured the door, moved to place his jacket in the hall closet, went to the kitchen and retrieved a considerably inexpensive bottle of wine from the refrigerator. He twisted the screw-on cap from the bottle, filled two fine champagne flutes with the cheap liquid and returned to Shantelle, who was wrapped in an oversized robe on the sofa.

He handed her a glass, sat his own on the coffee table, moved to one knee and retrieved the ring box from a rear pants pocket.

"Baby, I know I've been sending you through a lot of changes lately, but you know too that I love you," he said, the practiced spiel fumbled in his mind. "You know I want to marry you, Shantelle."

He removed the ring from the box, took her hand and placed the ring on a finger.

"Baby, marry me."

She was taken aback. Tears welled, blurring her vision somewhat as she put the ring closer to her eyes, examining it as if an expert for size and clarity.

"I don't know what to say," she said demurely, a phoniness evident which she belatedly became aware of, but one which evidently skimmed by Ellis's presently veiled eyes.

"Just say 'yes,' baby," he said, smiling broadly.

"Oh, *yes!*" she screamed, throwing her arms around him and embracing him in a powerful hug.

Still, over his shoulder, she held the left hand out, examining the size and clarity of the diamond.

Chapter Twenty-one

Miss Charlene had spent an antsy twenty-minutes in the nearby Eddie Wong's Carry-out, anxiously awaiting a pizza, French fries, and colas for the children. Although she hadn't eaten herself Christmas Day, Mumbles was in her apartment, surely in possession of generous amounts of crack cocaine. Her anticipation of the drug quelled the hunger in her taught, rumbling stomach. She munched on a few of the fries while rushing back to the apartment, but was more so fingering the fresh butane lighter she'd also purchased, an item worth more than gold to a crack cocaine addict.

Entering the apartment accompanied by a blast of frigid air, she was immediately swamped by the children, hunger not allowing for any measure of parental respect as she fought her way to the despoiled dinette table, flipped back the cover on the pizza box and deposited the French fries and soft drinks. The children tore into the food as if they hadn't eaten for days, which was close to being the case if paltry bowls of dry cereal without benefit of milk and small servings of Ramen noodles were subtracted from the equation.

She let them have at it, peeled a pack of menthol cigarettes she'd also purchased and fired up one. Mumbles was seated in the living room, and she motioned with her head to him towards a back bedroom. He secured his bundles, the guns, and followed her.

Miss Charlene's addiction didn't allow time for formalities. Once in the putrid confines of one of two bedrooms, she moved up to him, undid the zipper to his pants and got on her knees. She guided him to a seat on the bare mattress of a full-sized bed, eased him a bit upwards to move his pants to just above his knees, freed his already stiff organ from a pair of denim boxer shorts and put practiced mouth to work. In less than a minute he exploded, words struggling to surface amidst moans, gripping fists and a body wrenching in ecstatic pleasure.

He lay back, she arose, retrieved a glass crack pipe from a dresser drawer and, without asking, fumbled through his cases until she found the packages of cocaine. Disappointment immediately washed over her ashen face.

"This shit raw? Powdered? Damn man! I thought you always cooked your shit up into rocks?"

Miss Charlene had her acutely anticipating mind set on cocaine in crack form, and the powdered cocaine, in quite a pure and powerful measure, only provided a cruel disappointment to the seasoned addict.

"Y...y...you co...co....cook up....up some," Mumbles said, easing upright.

"Man! I don't have the right shit, no baking powder, one of them glass things, you know, to do it right! Can I snort some of this shit and you go up to your apartment and cook some up?"

"Sh...sh....sh...shit! Po...po...police........... ju...ju...just.........busted....m....m...my joint! Hu...hu...how............how.....hu...how......the....th .....the...the...,the fu...fu...fuck...I...I...I'm going ba...ba...back..........in...in.........there...a...a...after that...sh...sh...shit?"

Miss Charlene eyes suddenly widened, as if she were hit by an acute realization.

"Mumbles? Man, let me take one of these packages down the street to Little Man or Damon or

Geezey or one of them young'uns and trade it for some rocks. I know they'll go for it like that."

She tore off a piece of a matchbook cover, folded it and dipped into a bag of coke, put a mound under her nostrils and whiffed it in like some expensive vacuum.

"Sh...sh...shit's...go...go....good!" She was mumbling now, the cocaine immediately stunting her own limited acuity.

"G...g...g...g....g....go...head," Mumbles said. "J...j...just....just...*one*...and....th...th..then...you... you...you.....come........ba..back...and......l.....l...let m...m...me....w...wax that...that...ass!"

He didn't have to tell her twice. She took another generous whiff of the powder to steel her resolve, left the bed and passed by the now despondent children, picking about the leavings of the paper aligning the pizza box from bits of cheese, crumbs, any visible morsel where there were now scant offerings.

Chapter Twenty-two

She gave in fully to him, one leg pointed skyward, the other planted widely upon the silk sheets, granting him full access. In a room infused with the smell of jasmine incense and the dim glow of a blue light bulb, she emitted her practiced sensual moans, meeting him thrust for thrust, and, occasionally, removing her left hand from upon his ass and stretching it towards the ceiling, peering through slit, moist eyes at the diamond engagement ring.

Of course, he wasn't originally supposed to get any tonight; Shantelle had been convinced by Lana to deny him access, hint at his needs to still shower money and gifts on his "baby mamas," of whom she was well familiar with. The "little skeezer Linda" from the Barry Farm housing project. That "hood rat Donna" from Kenilworth. Yes, she knew at least some, though not all, of his "hos," she'd planned on telling him. But the ring changed all of that, and although she'd said yes to his proposal, she had yet to acquire all that she wanted of Ellis, and was sure that, before they'd even settled on a wedding date, he'd provide her an excuse to call the whole thing off.

But he'd *never* get the ring, the anticipated Lexus, or the considerable amount of funds in her bank account, returned to him.

"Aww, baby!" she moaned, pulling him deeply into her. "Oh, yes! Yes! This all yours, baby! All…yours!"

While at the same time she was reflecting on the shoe boxes just a foot below them, secreted under the bed and, when she last counted their contents, containing over a hundred fifty-thousand dollars in cash.

"All mine!" she moaned, picturing the money, not the long, dark figure who thought he was about to bring her back into the realm he truly believed ensnared all of his female conquests.

He exploded, gritted teeth, head thrown back, hands gripping her shoulders. She faked it, quite convincingly, then as he folded down upon her in exhaustion, stroked his head and whispered nonsensical words into his ear.

"That's alright, baby. You know you always got this. Always."

She tried easing him aside, before he fell asleep on her with all his weight. He was even then headed off to slumberland, his breathing quieting, his previously taut muscles relaxing. With their combined sweat as a lubricant, she slid a bit sideways, until he was partially on the wetter portion of the sheet. Deftly, she twisted free, eased to the edge of the bed, arose and went to the bathroom.

Again, in the bright lights before the bathroom mirror, she studied the diamond.

She had a considerable nest egg in the bank. Ellis had discussed with her the possibilities of them acquiring a home together; she *did* work full-time, and with her mother seeing after Ebony and Derrick when they were not in day care, her monthly expenses were minor when she took into account the monies Ellis gave her whenever she requested any amount.

The only thing which gave her pause about leaving him was that she was quite the jealous type, and even with the benefits she planned on leaving with, it would not sit well with her if Ellis wound up in a more serious relationship with either Linda or Donna: The three were quite familiar with one another and had indeed been in an unspoken competition Shantelle to see who would eventually wind up in a live-in relationship with him before Ellis moved in with her.

"Bitches!" Shantelle whispered into the mirror, reflecting on a future without Ellis. "All up in his grill all the time. Dropping their drawers anytime the fool put a little bank in their pocket."

She took a washcloth to her more intimate parts, donned fresh panties and a silk robe. She looked in on the sleeping children before returning to her own bedroom, where Ellis's rumbling snore gave clear indication that he was out for the night. She moved to the far side of the bed, felt the sheet to ensure she was not on a portion chilly from their sweat, eased under the comforter.

Soon, she was deep in sleep. Her dreams however had a smile creasing her face ever so often. She was cruising the city streets in her new Lexus, body bouncing and heart vibrating to the beat of the heavy bass echoing from custom speakers and sound system she'd had installed. On occasion she'd peer over a shoulder, to the shoe boxes setting on the rear bench seat. She was heading to the bank, but at a stop light, Ellis stepped into the crosswalk before her, and even when the light changed, he would not move out of her way.

"Move!" she shouted, laying on the car's horn.

"Huh?'

He twisted about in the darkness, put an arm around her. She realized that she'd allowed her sleeping visions to filter into the clear and present, recognized that she'd actually shouted out to the Ellis who'd just eased his body tight up against hers.

"Go to sleep, baby," she whispered in his ear, twisting to place a leg astride him, an arm slung over his waist.

"Umm huh," he muttered, then eased back into a dreamscape of his own, one which was quickly growing dim.

In his dream, now a reflection of thoughts behind closed eyes and a mind seeking to reacquire sleep, his supplier Reynaldo was being led away from his immaculate home in handcuffs, a large contingent of black-clad men with yellow "ATF" and "FBI" logos emblazoned on their SWAT uniforms. Ellis stood just outside the complex's gates, staring Reynaldo straight in the eyes.

Reynaldo mouthed the word "snitch," and it was then that Ellis noticed his henchman Miguel on an upper balcony of the home, directed a high powered rifle at Ellis.

He fell back into a fitful sleep, eventually entertained by a more pleasing dream, and one more familiar. He was at his favorite table at Martin's, and was surrounded by women, beautiful and unfamiliar. Just the scenario he so wished for; women, fine and splendidly attired, each and every one at his beck and call. But upon awakening, only the scenarios with Reynaldo kept resurfacing. He recalled the admonitions of his grandmother when he was a child, that every vision "showed unto you by God should be heeded."

His demeanor was unusually calm that morning, and as he awaited a chance to use the shower, even little Ebony noticed his uncommon persona.

"What's wrong with you, man?" Ebony asked as he sat in a dinette chair.

"Aww, nothing, Eb, nothing."

But the little girl, quite astute and like her mother, not one to refrain her thoughts, wouldn't let it go.

"I bet you scared about something have to do with your selling drugs," she said, walking away to the living room before he could form a response. She continued, her voice higher to ensure that he could hear her. "I don't care if they come after you, but you better not have me and my brother and my mother all up in that mess."

Chapter Twenty-three

Detective Robinson was meeting with the Washington Regional Joint Operational Task Force the week between Christmas and New Years. The task force consisted of members from the Metropolitan Police Department, FBI agents from the Washington Regional Office, and members of the Bureau of Alcohol, Tobacco and Firearms. Additionally, a team of officers from other area police forces, Prince George's County, MD, Fairfax, VA and Montgomery County, MD were part of this contingent, and this week they were focused on the drug-related murders in the Southeast section of the District, and how many of theses were tied to drug and gun issues with roots in the surrounding counties.

Leading this meeting, Robinson was called upon particularly to give his take on the various "crews" peddling crack in the Seventh District. It was agreed by all that the poverty pervading the Seventh D/far Southeast section of the city virtually guaranteed that the volumes of drugs and expensive firepower there was coming from outside the area. The Task Force, with arrest and investigative powers which overlapped the region's borders, had already put some of Robinson's most seasoned investigators at the forefront of a surveillance of three specific Southeast crews, and had tailed one particular leader to the home of a naturalized citizen from Bogota, Colombia: Reynaldo Hernandez-Rios.

Meeting in cramped quarters at the Seventh District substation, Robinson used a PowerPoint presentation to give a graphic outlay of drug operations along Shelter Road, with pictures of Ellis Davidson, Delano "Mumbles" Johnson, the recently deceased grouping of Darren Rogers, Marquis "Fat Boy" Clease and Raquan "Dru" Andrews, and, near the top of an organizational chart, Reynaldo Hernandez-Rios and Miguel Pena.

"We've observed Pena most recently sneaking around the places where Ellis Davidson does his business, and even where he camps out with the present lady in his life, one Shantelle Bridgefield," Det. Robinson said, using a laser pointer to put a light on Pena's photograph. "Some of our colleagues from DEA also have observed him in the past three days watching Davidson as he visited with the mothers of his children in the Kenilworth and Barry Farm neighborhoods. All indications are, gentlemen, that Hernandez-Rios is growing uncomfortable with the association he's had with Davidson over the past few years, and is planning perhaps on ending that relationship. And as you all know, the method used in firing an underling in these arenas does not consist of offering one a buy-out and a cash-in of ones 401k."

"They're getting ready to hit him, you're saying," Agent Thurmount from the DEA stated, not as an inquiry.

"Most certainly," Robinson said. "Rarely do either Hernandez-Rios or Pena venture into the city. Especially into the neighborhoods cited. Davidson, I do believe, has run his usefulness. And it's not like they don't have dozens, perhaps hundreds of young men in the same areas, along Shelter Road, Mississippi Avenue, in Barry Farm and Kenilworth, just eager to step up their game, as it were, in the drug distribution game there. Yes, gentlemen, I think if we don't bring him in on some charges within the next week or so, Ellis Davidson's days are numbered."

Sandra Wills, a most attractive agent detailed to the Task Force from the FBI's Washington Field Office, raised a pen before her to gain the floor.

"We don't have enough on Hernandez-Rios and Pena yet to issue warrants, bring them in?"

"Not quite," Robinson said. "Hernandez-Rios is one crafty bastard. We know for a fact that he gets regular deliveries of massive quantities of cocaine, home deliveries. We suspect he has a worker somewhere in the bowels of the ASAP Air Delivery company responsible for the region where his home is located. He gets regular deliveries, but even after our colleagues at DEA put the dogs and scanners on the packages, there's never any justification gained which would allow us to open them up that would stand muster in a court of law."

"You have footage, I understand, of Davidson visiting Hernandez-Rios' home," DelWayne Plant, a grey-haired veteran of the D.C. Police Department asked.

"Plenty," Robinson responded to his old colleague. "Most recently, Christmas Day."

"And the move made into the guy Mumbles' apartment, nothing discovered. Don't you think that move might have put them on notice?" Sandra Wills asked.

"We're hoping exactly that," Robinson said. "You see, these boys, they're a few cans short of a six pack. Not your neighborhood intellectuals. We shake 'em a bit, they tend to trip up, understand? Right now, they're readying business for New Years. We have eyes on them 24/7. It's reasonable to anticipate that some among them are going to make some major errors. But we don't expect the same of Hernandez-Rios or Pena. We have other operations in the works to break those two."

Chapter Twenty-four

With little regard to his personal effects, the Parkdale management followed police directions and placed a fitted piece of plywood in the entranceway to the apartment of "Delano Johnson." Of course, Mumbles had already sneaked back into his unit and retrieved items he deemed necessary: Underwear and outer clothing, seven various pairs of Timberwolves, the hiking boots favored by urban youngsters, and some fresh linen, most of which he knew were stolen but which he'd bought for little or nothing from area drug addicts.

He moved in, quite temporarily he reasoned, with his first-floor neighbor, Miss Charlene.

Surprised by her sexual energy and varietal expertise, Mumbles was, in the most commonly familiar descriptive, "pussy-whipped." The frail but agile woman, often fueled by readily available cocaine, had the muscular drug dealer stuttering for relief on many occasions, and she'd obediently relent, thankful to have laid him to rest for a period while she delved into her favored and necessary pastime: smoking crack cocaine.

With Mumbles' in the home, even her four children were expressing thanks for his presence: They were fed with an unaccustomed regularity and, unlike their diverse fathers and the varietal men who visited their mother's bedroom or joined her in crack consumption in the main quarters, Mumbles merely communicated with them through warm smiles. On occasion, he'd emit struggling but playful words to them, but he generated no fear in their youthful hearts, and was most welcomed. Besides, with "Mr. Mumbles" in the house, the more threatening men, some of whom even cast lecherous glances at 10-year-old Kanisha, were no longer welcomed by their mother. Indeed, many of the men who'd previously been regulars had come calling in recent days and stepped into the unit uninvited, only to see Mumbles seated unconcerned on the living room sofa. The sex-seeking visitors, to a man, then seemed to beg forgiveness of the known dealer and retreated with a measure of fear quite in evidence.

"They scared of him," Kanisha had whispered to younger brother Michael on one occasion. "He bad, but he's not gonna mess with us, so he's okay."

Only four days had passed since the raid on his unit and his forced joining with Miss Charlene and her brood, and they had never been more than passing acquaintances before then. After all, she and most all of the building's residents knew, Mumbles distributed cocaine a measure above street level, and the neighborhood addicts, indeed the vast number of those in the general metropolitan area, favored cocaine in crack form exclusively.

They'd developed a quick means of communicating, Miss Charlene's addiction often allowing little time for formalities. When he wanted to engage her in his favorite position for sexual intercourse, he'd merely grab her around the waist, twist her back to his and move her to a kneeling position on the edge of the bed. When she wanted a coke break, she'd just show him the crack pipe and butane lighter, often going into the bathroom and locking the door for a period of uninterrupted consumption.

His friend and business associate Ellis was none too pleased though at the arrangement. He was repulsed at first to even enter Miss Charlene's unkempt apartment for meetings with Mumbles, and was really taken aback when it appeared that Mumbles seemed to have some visible feelings for the "crack head ho" and her children. New Years Eve, the two *had* to meet, and by cellular phone, Ellis requested that they have a "set-down" at Melody's Bar-b-Que Rib Shack.

The place was bustling just after noon when the two were afforded a booth amidst a throng aligning the wall and waiting in line for phoned-in holiday orders. The two men who abruptly moved from the booth appeared to be undercover police, both Ellis and Mumbles thought, and they were glad the two were leaving as they took to the booth to discuss holiday matters.

Miss Melody, husband David and son Dexter were swamped, two grills sizzling with slabs of ribs, the slathered sauces dripping down on red-hot hickory logs and filling the establishment with steam and a pleasing, savory aroma. With all the tables filled and conversations throughout joyous, neither Ellis nor Mumbles thought much of the pretty young woman and older man in the booth directly to their rear. But DelWayne Plant, the D.C. police veteran, and Sandra Wills, the FBI's Washington Field Office agent, were both sure that the "street dress" they wore, and the savory ribs they were devouring, painted them as among neighborhood regulars. And with the boisterous crowd in celebratory conversation around them, they were sure that the hidden microphone secreted under the table Ellis and *"D. Johnson"* occupied was picking up fully their conversation. They were leaning forward after all, straining to hear one another and making their conversation even more accessible to the omni directional microphone, placed there moments earlier by two colleagues from the Task Force.

"Man," Ellis was continuing his plaintive missive, "I know that bitch is smoking up a bunch of our shit! Don't tell me she ain't. And you gotta be a fool to convert our powder into rocks in her crib! You *know* our business plans was to *never* have rocks in our possession. Just in case some shit go down, we won't be all facing them big-ass sentences they hand out for crack. We get, like, you know, white-boy sentences...like that. Know what I'm saying?"

"I....I.....I hear...hear ya. B..b....but I....I...don't...don't...don't dice...dice..dice up...the coke...l...l...like...like...that. She g....g...g...get one of...d...d...dem..........b...b..b......boys...g...g...give her rocks...f...f...f...for...p...p...powder."

"That's still our fuckin' money, Mumbles. You know all that shit's coming out of your end."

"S...s....so! I.......uuuu...uhhh......I...I...I g..g...got it....l...l...like....that!"

He smiled broadly, but Ellis failed to see the humor in his statement.

"Anyway, after you done gone and blown a gram with that bitch, and I had to put the Shelter Road Crew down with my last, I had to make arrangements to see Reynaldo again sooner than expected. We're meeting up on the Third, two o'clock. You ain't got to baby sit or no shit, do you?"

Mumbles chuckled.

"M…m….man…f…..f…*fuck you!*"

Both glanced deep into the eyes of a lifelong friend, Ellis shaking his head and laughing as Miss Melody's son deposited a large closed bag before them.

They arose, Ellis handed Dexter a twenty-dollar bill and waved away the change.

Before they were out the door good, the man and woman seated to their rear arose, deposited their waste in a large trash bin, then moved together to the picture window, watching as Ellis and *D. Johnson* left the parking lot in separate rides.

"With the photographs your people have of Davidson visiting the home of Hernandez-Rios, and this tape, I think we have enough to get a warrant for the premises of Hernandez-Rios," the huge man said.

"Our offices," the woman whispered, "would probably want to move on his premises on the scheduled day of the next meeting. It's assured he'll have something to deliver to Davidson and Johnson, and we'll have an even firmer case if we get the two known dealers at Hernandez-Rios' place, along with the drugs."

"Yes. I think my chicf would like that scenario even better," the man said, securing his coat and heading out the door. "January third, two o'clock, we got their asses."

Chapter Twenty-five

Economic pressure didn't allow the stick-up boys much leeway for planning. The unemployment rate in the District was hovering around 15 percent. In the far Southeast and Northeast sections of the city, predominated by African Americans, the rate was 24 percent, and studies indicated that, among black males between the ages of 18 – 30, there was an unemployment rate of 34 percent.

Arrest rates were soaring in association with the figures being reported of the effects of the economic malaise on the nation, particularly in most inner city communities. And with hundreds of thousands of primarily young men and women, the majority of African American and Hispanic descent, social organizations were also doing their studies, and one particular report which made the front page of local Washington newspapers, and some televised national news reports, highlighted the great profits being made by a few industrial conglomerates who found the use of prison labor a boon to their bottom lines. In a statement which caused an uproar on Capitol Hill, this particular report noted that the nation's prison/industrial complex was proving to be 29.5 percent more profitable than *slavery*!

The stick-up boys, of course, were little aware of these statistics, and hard pressed for immediate cash, probably wouldn't have cared anyway.

Around the holidays, such robbery crews nearly outnumbered often inebriated celebrants. Whereas money continued to flow in abundance throughout the Northwest communities of Georgetown, Adams Morgan, and gentrifying parts of the historically black Shaw community, monies had slowed to a trickle across the river, in the Anacostia, far Southeast and Northeast communities. Those who still maintained well-paying jobs were being depleted of funds through familial support of those who didn't, feeding some, housing others, and when possible, giving handouts to the league of friends, neighbors, even strangers who loitered about the community streets in search of sustenance.

Three of Mumbles' street-level distributors had been "razed" the week between Christmas and New Years. One had been shot dead when he "bucked," attempting to pull his own gun when the stick-up boys, already leveling guns at him, relieved him of $740.00 cash and an equal amount in crack as yet unsold. Unfortunately, the two who'd committed this particular heist had been recognized by a crack head woman who'd been cowering in fear inside the door of a laundry room near the scene, and when others among the deceased's crew began asking around New Years Eve, the woman came forth, was rewarded with a generous, celebratory, complimentary amount of crack, and quickly escaped the scene in anticipation of additional deadly fireworks.

The robbers were from Congress Park, a community not a mile from Shelter Road consisting of modest, single-family homes flush against a pocket of rental apartments, where many residents were suffering the blunt of the economic downturn. The crack head had identified a couple from the Congress Park apartments, a boy of 17 known as "Two Shoes," and his partner and a boy said to be his cousin who went by the name of El Rod. When told of their identities, Mumbles knew full well who the two were. They'd not a year earlier left Shelter Road, having been fronted a generous amount of crack by Mumbles to get them established in the game, returned to Congress Park to sell *his* drugs with no intention of ever paying Mumbles for his generosity.

He'd let the initial disrespectful malfeasance slide, considering that the two were "kids," and giving consideration of their in depth poverty, both Mumbles and Ellis agreed that the two should only be disciplined through their being banned, for the considerable future, from doing business or even visiting the Shelter Road area. But the present stick-up necessarily called for more critical retribution: If these "young'uns" were allowed to get away with a heist, and indeed the *murder*, of a member of the Shelter Road Crew, then the posse might as well gather their crumpled soda cups of secreted crack rocks and commit to flipping burgers at the local Mickey D's.

"Y'all back up my boy Mumbles," Ellis instructed four Shelter Road Crew members, who were being allowed a "recess" from New Years Eve crack sales to motor to nearby Congress Park and provide support for Mumbles, the only gunman Ellis, or Mumbles for that matter, trusted to make a most public example out of Two Shoes and El Rod. "Y'all don't let nothing happen to my boy."

They'd already secured a plain, frowned-upon minivan, stolen particularly because it was viewed as the type of vehicle only a family man, and one of the demographic common among those who hid alcoholism and/or drug addiction from their upright peers, would even consider spending good money on. Four members of the Shelter Road Crew occupied the vehicle, a most trusted one behind the steering wheel, Mumbles in the passenger's seat. They parked the minivan in a short-term parking space at the nearby Congress Heights Metro station; Lil Tony deposited quarters in the parking meter, the crew vocally agreeing that this possible infraction should be avoided, the planned murders and auto theft paradoxically given lesser consideration.

They cut through an opening in a fence which separated the Congress Park apartments from the subway station, crouching and sprinting and appearing much like some professional assault unit of Army Rangers. Mumbles knew well where the volume of crack was sold in Congress Park, therefore reasoning quite accurately that his targets would be on that secluded corner now, hours before midnight. He held his .357 Magnum pointed to the ground as he sprinted, rounded the rear of a three-story apartment building and immediately spotted Two Shoes and El Rod hoisting 40 ounce malt liquor bottles amidst a clutch of some nine other young men.

"K...K...Kill!"

The uttered voice of the gunman could barely be heard as accompanying "BOOMS!" from the high-powered weapon shattered the night. Repeatedly.

Mumbles' cohorts had come upon the scene from around the opposite end of the apartment building, directly in the direction many of the Congress Park boys took when fleeing the presumed lone assault by the apparently crazed gunman. They leveled weapons and, not sure if the targets were among the fleeing youths, tore into them with automatic weapons fire.

"K.....K...K...Kill Mumbles! K....K...Kill!"

He'd already sent Two Shoes and El Rod to the ground, wrenching around in pain. The .357 was out of rounds, and although he had more in a jacket pocket, he didn't feel the need to reload. He took the "minor" .32 from a pocket, tucked the .357 in an inner jacket pocket, then stood over the two youths, an awry grin visible on his dark features.

"Y...y...you.......boys...sh...sh...shouldn't   of f...f...fucked wi...wi...with us li...li...like that!"

He squeezed off two rounds into each boy's head, spat at the twitching figures and turned casually, pocketed the gun and returned with little rush back down the path on which he'd arrived.

Chapter Twenty-six

"Happy New Year!!!"

Martin's was a spot favored by a leagues of young men and women from the Southeast and Northeast sections of D.C., particularly due to its location and, for young women, because a number of young "hustlers" frequented the nightclub. For young men, the reverse was true: Young women by the boatload favored the club Thursday, Friday, Saturday and Sunday nights, and among the young men, word spread quicker than wildfire, or as fast as the identified legs, about which regulars among the females were exceptional "freaks," or exquisite "head nurses."

Ellis was celebrating New Years there with Shantelle, who was well aware that two of Ellis's "baby mamas" were also in attendance. They cut eyes at one another even as the strains of Auld Lang Syne were being drunkenly belted out, even though Donna and Linda were each in the company of their own current boyfriend.

Mumbles had arrived, immaculately dressed, just a half-hour before midnight. Familiar to many in the club, he made his way through a throng of greetings, high-fives, daps, to join Ellis and Shantelle at the table reserved for them alongside the dance floor. Ellis greeted Mumbles with a common unspoken communications gesture, jutting his chin in the air and receiving a confirming nod from Mumbles.

"D...d....done," Mumbles said, bent and kissed Shantelle on a cheek, took a seat.

Shantelle, quite bubbly with a half-full bottle of expensive champagne before her, held a hand across the table before Mumbles, displaying the engagement ring with a broad grin.

"He tell you we're getting married?" she said, slurring her words.

Mumbles smiled broadly, took her hand and studied the ring, then looked to Ellis.

"C...c...congrat...u...u...lations!"

"Thanks man. You know I'd been planning to make things legal with my baby for a while now." Ellis seemed to be blushing. "We probably tie the knot this coming June, right baby?"

"Yeah," Shantelle gushed, took a generous swig from the glass of champagne.

Ellis poured a glass for Mumbles, placed it before him.

"Bet you must have had to give that ol' girl you be with a rack of our shit to get her to leave you alone and let you hang out for the night," Ellis smiled, his eyes communicating to Mumbles that he was expecting some sort answer or response.

Mumbles rapped on the table with his knuckles three times, nodded. Ellis took that to mean that his assessment was not that far from the truth.

"Your ass hustling backwards now," Ellis said. "Shacking up with a ho smoking up all your profits. Letting your dick make a bum out of you like that."

Mumbles smiled, shook his head and just had to explain away this view Ellis was expressing.

"M….m….man….Su…su..some…t….. t…times a…brother…got……….to…g…g…give……..u……up a…a…little..su…su…something………t….t….t……to knock….d…dem…boots!"

Shantelle was displaying her ring to a friend, oblivious to the conversation being carried on between Ellis and Mumbles. They were both though glancing at her when Mumbles completed his blunted response, and the irony of his statement didn't go unnoticed by either at that particular moment.

Well past midnight, the revelries were mounting and the dance floor bouncing. Some late arrivals, party hoppers, were greeted by familiars, gathered into the ongoing fold of heated celebrations. Among the late arrivals though were some who had not been to earlier celebrations around the city, but who, out of business necessity, had been on area streets, monitoring the sales of massive stores of illegal drugs, occasionally making collections and resupplying their street vendors.

"Block" Thurman was among this contingent.

Noted for a near perfectly flat rear cranium since he was a child, with the rest of his head spreading horizontally to near deformity, Block was also a childhood friend of Ellis's. He had branched out on his own when the two jointly entered the realm of cocaine distribution, was not a competitor of his friends and had virtually cornered the wholesale cocaine market in the city's Kenilworth neighborhood. He still had family and friends in the Shelter Road and Congress Park areas, and had just made his way through the Southeast headed to Martin's for his final New Years celebrations. He saw

Ellis in joyous wonder from across the dance floor, excused himself from a clutch of young woman and made his way over to his old friend.

"Block!!!"

A chorus of greetings rang out from the men and women at Ellis's table.

"Happy New Year, my peeps!"

He exchanged handshakes, kisses to the women, then took Ellis's hand in a grip and wouldn't let it go.

"I need to holler at you for a minute, my brother," he looked down to Ellis. "In private."

Ellis arose, bent and planted a wet kiss on Shantelle's lips.

"Be back in a minute," he said, followed Block as he weaved his way through the crowd towards the men's room.

Inside, a few men were primping in front of the mirrors, a couple drunkenly spilling words at the urinals, the moans of a female filtering from within the locked door of the rearmost toilet cubicle. Block stepped to the rear of the room, just beside the stall where the voice of a woman moaning "Yes!" creased smiles upon the faces of the other men in the room.

"Ellis," Block said quietly. "I went past Shelter Road on my way out here, a little past midnight. Police was all up and down that joint. I had to drop off some cash to my sister down there, and I got to holler at a couple of pipe head bitches in her hallway. They told me that some of your young-young crew down there, think they said a boy named Lil Tony and one named Wade and another boy named 'Quan, girls say them boys was killed by some Congress Park boys after a shooting in Congress Park earlier."

Ellis shook his head, turned and threw his head to the ceiling, tears beginning to form.

"You know something about that?" Block asked.

Ellis hesitated, then turned to face his old friend.

"Them young'uns had to get back at them Congress Park boys about some shit went down on The Road other day. Damn!"

He paused, grabbed Block in a serious embrace.

"Thanks for giving me the 4-1-1 on that mess, Block. Now, this shit done turned into a war."

Chapter Twenty-seven

The Congressional Committee on Homeland Security and the Senate Armed Services Committee had pushed through legislation allowing military surveillance aircraft to be used stateside by local and national law enforcement officials, so long as the aircraft were stripped of their abilities to launch missiles and were used solely for high level surveillance. The *HAD* (High Altitude Detection) drones were authorized to be used starting in the new year, and the Washington Regional Joint Operational Task Force was among the first to use one during an operation slated to occur on January 3rd.

Miles above the palatial estate of Reynaldo Hernandez-Rios, a drone was transmitting a crisp picture of the grounds and surrounding streets. Resolution from the drone was so clear that even the tag numbers of vehicles on the ground could be made out. A block from the Hernandez-Rios estate sat a cable television van ostensibly ready to install service to another of the immaculate homes in the area. But inside the van, Task Force officials were monitoring screens displaying a close view of the Hernandez-Rios estate, and another trailing an SUV leaving the Washington Beltway and moving towards the gated community.

As the SUV grew closer to the gated front of the Hernandez-Rios estate, the screen displaying the estate's grounds grew active with the forms of armed men in camouflage uniforms scaling the rear and side fences and moving in low positions to surround the rear of the home. In the home's living room, Reynaldo was enjoying a fine Cuban cigar and his favorite cognac while his henchman Miguel moved to the front window, checking his watch and nodding his head as Ellis, with customary precision, pulled his SUV up to the front gate. Miguel moved to the front door, electronically activated the gated entrance and pulled the heavy wooden front door open, comfortable that Ellis knew the procedure and would enter and move directly to the living room. He moved over to the dining room, resumed sipping on a bottle of spring water and taking a seat there to allow his boss the privacy he'd requested of this meeting.

Ellis mounted the decorative brick stairs two at a time to the open door, and didn't see the armed men in bulletproof vest until they were nearly upon him. Two grabbed him firmly, wresting him to the ground while a countless number now surfaced from surrounding ornate bushes and plants and rushed into the home. It was only then that the silence was broken, as shouts from the heavily armed contingent demanded that the home's occupants grab the floor.

Someone apparently didn't get the message, for a quick burst of automatic weapons fire could be heard coming from within, followed by a series of crashes from the rear of the home, additional officials evidently gaining entrance from that location.

Inside, Miguel Pena lay dying, chest, skull pierced by unforgiving high powered rounds, a pistol which had apparently only served to extinguish his life lying near a trembling hand. Reynaldo Hernandez-Rios, for some reason presenting a smile to the invading force, remained on the sofa, hands clasped atop his head. He was frisked, handcuffed and led out of the house while another contingent of officials, less armed and dressed in suits covered by bullet proof vests, marched into the house and began tearing it apart. Two officials had Ellis, hands cuffed behind his back, standing to the side of the walkway, asking him questions, as Reynaldo was led by. The Spanish man looked to Ellis with cowered eyes, spat at him.

"Que te den por el culo, Marricon!" Reynaldo growled at Ellis in his native tongue.

May you be fucked up the ass, faggot!

Ellis had no idea what Reynaldo has just said. But what he *did* know that, whatever message had been uttered, more than likely amounted to a death sentence for him.

Chapter Twenty-eight

Mumbles had wanted to make the trip out to Reynaldo's, finally meet him. But Ellis had relayed the request to Reynaldo, and it had been callously dismissed.

"I don't need to meet with that non-talking mierda (shit)," Reynaldo had said, and upon being informed of the widely-aired news reports of the bust, Mumbles finally caught a newscast of what was being touted as the break-up of a major drug distribution network, and was counting his blessings.

Ellis, meanwhile, was counting the number of men of obvious Hispanic descent lolling about the common area in the District's pretrial holding facility. There was a goodly number, all gathered in a group among themselves, away from the overwhelmingly black population. Ellis had seen a few men from the neighborhood, many who'd become drug-strapped at his own hand, and others who'd been busted selling drugs, some of these too for whom he could be partially responsible. And he was sure that Reynaldo's reach, and his immense wealth, reached well into the confines of the District jail, and for the most part, his neighborhood compatriots were powerless.

He saw a small group of black men at one metal table, all wearing the kufi caps fitted tightly to the skulls of those who worshiped in the Islamic faith. Ellis had never been particularly religious, even during the brief period as a child when he was taken to a Baptist church Sundays by his grandmother. But right now he felt he really needed help from a Higher Power, decided to throw his chips in with Allah.

"As Salaam Alaikum," he hesitantly greeted the men, inching over to their table.

"Walaikum salaam," a chorus of voices responded.

A tall man who was apparently an avid body builder, stepped over to him.

"What can we do you for, brother?" Mr. Atlas said, standing before Ellis and flexing.

"I just...you know...thought maybe y'all was the knowledgeable fellas up in this joint. Just wanted to holler, that's all."

"And what brings you into these pristine confines?" another man, seated, asked.

Ellis was lost momentarily, struggled to grasp what the question meant.

"What's your charge," another put forth for clarity.

"Oh. They got me on a drug distribution charge," Ellis said, releasing a light laugh. "Some phony shit I'm 'bout to crush, know what I'm saying?"

Muscle bound took a step to within inches of Ellis's face.

"You're in the wrong area, my brother." He nodded towards a group gathered across the room, pants sagging, tennis shoes unstrung. "You go over there, get with your...*homies*...know what *I'm* saying?"

Ellis got the message immediately, stepped off.

"Alright. Alright. A Salaam Aliakum, mother fuckers."

"Walaikum Salaam," a chorus responded.

"See you at evening prayers," Brother Atlas said, pinning him with a cold, telling gaze. "Walaikum Salaam."

Ellis moved back over to a group of men whom he'd known casually from the Southeast neighborhoods who were also among the group the Muslims had pointed out, with sagging pants and untied tennis shoes. As he approached them, he took notice of three Hispanic men who seemed to depart in response to his arrival.

"Wassup, fellas?" Ellis said, but the greeting went with only cold glares in return.

"You're wanted, fool," one young man said in a low voice. "You need to go find you another camp to pitch your tent in."

Ellis scanned the entirety of the social hall, and as his eyes reached individual gatherings, the members of each group cut eye contact with him. Death loomed, he felt seriously, moved to the door and glass cubicle which separated the overseeing correctional officers from this segment of the population.

Upon arriving there, four uniformed officers also abruptly turned their backs to him.

Chapter Twenty-nine

"He called you collect?"

"Yeah girl. From D.C. Jail. And I said I couldn't accept the charges, that I was on my way out to take my children to their grandmothers."

Lana shook her head, grinning. Shantelle had Ebony seated between her legs, braiding the girl's hair.

"Then that old black-ass Mumbles come by here, talking some mess about some money. Now, that mug take so long to get his point across, I just told him to write it down on one of Ebony's notebook pages. And even *that* took the fool damn near half an hour. And he write down some mess about Ellis's lawyer got in touch with him and said Ellis wants me to give him, like, five thousand dollars from his stash to pay for bail."

"What?!"

"I ain't lying, girl! So look: He left a nice piece of change here. And you *know* I've been banking off his ass big-time. So the way I see it, and he been blowing up my cell phone but by now I know the ID so I don't *even* answer that mug. And like, you know I was about to raise up on his ass anyway about that girl in Kenilworth he *swear* he don't do nothing with but look after their daughter, and that one down Barry Farm I *know* his ass still fucking 'cause I seen the bitch and we almost bumped heads and she was all up in my grill like that and I smelled that nasty, ho-ass perfume she be wearing and his ass coming in here some nights smelling like that ho."

"For real?"

"Yeah, and, I know Ellis gonna do some time, so like, what I'm thinking is, like, I was about to kick his ass to the curb anyway. So like, girl, I'm looking at a place out in Laurel, and about to move even though we still under a lease."

"You moving to Maryland?"

"That's what I said, girl: Laurel."

"You gonna need a ride out there, girl."

"Shit! I got enough to get that Lexus I was trying to get him to buy for me."

"He left that kinda bank here?"

"Sure did. And anyway, much time as he's facing, he ain't gonna have no use for it, not where he's going."

"Damn..."

Little Ebony, always one, as her mother said often, "into grown folk's business," just couldn't resist putting in her two-cents worth.

"I don't know what you saw in him anyway, Ma," Ebony said. "You could just *tell* he was gonna wind up in trouble. Running around thinking he was all that..."

Shantelle jerked on a plait, silencing the child.

"You just hush!" she demanded. "Regardless, Ellis was good to you and Derrick."

"Sure was," Lana allowed. "He *did* take care of home, girl. You got to give him that."

"He took care of *homes*!" Shantelle corrected. "Spent as much time over Kenilworth and down Barry Farm as he did here."

"I know that's right," Lana said.

"Well, Mumbles and his lawyer just gonna have to look for us," Shantelle said. "'Cause I got this man I work with got a truck and a crew, and soon as we get the lease on the place in Laurel and I get my ride, we're out of here."

Lana looked at the diamond ring as Shantelle's hand worked expertly on her daughter's hair.

"You gonna give him back the ring? Leave it over his grandmother's house? At least to let him know the plans for the marriage is over?"

Shantelle paused, looked at Lana with a look of incredulity, then stretched her hand out again and stared at the ring.

"Nigga please!" she said, and both of them, and Ebony, broke into uncontrolled laughter.

Chapter Thirty

He was sure that he was being watched. The pick-up was registered to him, as was the fine luxury vehicle which usually sat in the parking lot of the apartment complex unused. Since moving in with Miss Charlene, he'd only used the pick-up to do his business, and he even parked that over a block away when finished doing his little business. Now Ellis was jailed, as was their key supplier, and his drug stores were quickly running short.

He'd done what he could to attempt a coordinated freeing of his friend through stumbling submissions between Ellis's grandmother, the lawyer she'd acquired, and a few conversations with Ellis. Attempts to involved Shantelle had proven futile, and all the while Mumbles was forced to take leadership of an organization in tatters: Five of their underlings along Shelter Road had been killed, as many jailed, and even though he had secreted away a considerable amount of cash, his new contacts for buying additional "weight" of cocaine proved much more costly than the deals they'd had with Reynaldo.

The jailed wholesaler was an additional concern to Mumbles. Ellis had told him in no uncertain terms that Reynaldo had issued what amounted to a deadly threat when the two were busted, and Ellis said quite convincingly, and sorrowfully, that he believed he'd be "shanked" with fatal finality within the confines of the supposedly secure confines of the D.C. Jail.

Mumbles, Ellis had warned, should consider himself a target of the Hispanic drug lord also.

A mid-January blizzard further put a damper on his operations. Whereas a crack addict would ford a crocodile-infested river or try a desert storm in pursuit of crack cocaine, the blizzard, historic for the Washington region, had even dealers unable or unwilling to shovel their ways out onto their customary corners. And many an addict, "fiending" for the drugs after a secondary front dumped an additional foot of snow on the region, were rapping the door knockers on dealers homes who lived in their community, a serious breach of narco-protocol and an action which would normally lead to a beat-down at best, with a shooting of the miscreant a distinct possibility.

Mumbles, still in contact with Ellis and his people by cell phone, was content to wait out the January blizzard in the home he'd made with Miss

Charlene and her children. Indeed, he was enjoying antics with the four youngsters almost as much as he pleasured in the varietal sex engaged in nightly with their mother. By now he'd acquired the necessary tools and ingredients for converting powdered cocaine into crack, right there in the small apartment's kitchen. And even though Miss Charlene's consumptions saw a good portion of his profits go up in smoke, she could hardly continuously consume the volume of coke he converted, as even a seasoned addict such as she had to take time off every now and again.

As the second blizzard continued to rage outside, Mumbles spent a Saturday morning tumbling about on the living room floor wrestling with four-year-old Michael and seven-year-old Ricky. Kanisha, 10 and eldest of the siblings, attempted to participate, but Mumbles, in a few motions and fewer words, convinced her that the madcaps were not something a little girl should be engaged in.

Miss Charlene, as was more common of late with her smoking cocaine well past the midnight hour, remained in bed, and would probably do so for the better part of the day. With driving all but impossible, Mumbles had trekked on foot on two occasions to the corner grocer and carry-out since the first storm came: The grocery store, owned by immigrant South Korean who lived a distance away in Virginia, nevertheless was open the day the first blizzard hit the region, and even though an hour or so later than their regular opening time, had been ready for business each day since. Their most popular items, the 40-ounce bottles and six-packs of malt liquor, fortified wines, Newbreeze menthol cigarettes, were still being snapped up with gusto, and those items were in short supply by the time the second blizzard hit. But the resilient Koreans, their private four-wheel drives stuffed with resupply items, managed to make their way to the Southeast each and every day, and did land office business.

The Chinese immigrants who operated Eddie Wong's Carry-out weren't letting a couple of feet of snow hamper their business either. The steamy front Plexiglas of their establishment summoned those suffering from cabin fever from noon till well past midnight throughout the storm, and it appeared that many of the eight Oriental figures secured behind bulletproof glass were camping out in the facility's rear through the blizzard.

Besides an extensive menu of Chinese dishes, the carry-out tended to do most of its business serving the dishes favored by their almost exclusively African American population: Fried chicken wings, pizzas, steak-and-cheese subs and, of course, super-sugary soft drinks and, certainly among the non-food items prominently displayed flush up against the Plexiglas partition, Newbreeze menthol cigarettes and butane cigarette lighters. Mumbles was thankful that the Chinese were working full tilt during the blizzard, for the children favored the pizzas and subs. He rarely cooked anything other than pot pies for himself, and Miss Charlene had proven that her culinary skills were limited to opening boxes of heavily sweetened cereals, cartons of milk and, when really flexing her muscles in the kitchen, filling a pot of water and boiling a handful of hot dogs.

He'd purchased a PlayStation for the kids, but they quite often seemed to prefer playing with *him* instead. He was an uncommon joy to them, and even as the sounds of their favorite Saturday morning cartoons filter in from the television, and Kanisha and the toddler Patrania were enjoying them while the boys were content to wrestle with Mumbles. But he was growing tired, having "waxed that ass" of the mother well into the previous night.

"Y…y…y'all…g…g…..watch….s…s…some…t …v…f…f…for a…w…while," he said to the boys, breathing heavily. "Mu….Mu....M…….M……… "M….M…Mumbles….t…t..t…tired!"

"Okay," Ricky said, climbing to his feet and helping his little brother to his.

Little Michael paused before following his brother to the back bedroom, stood smiling down at Mumbles and said in a somewhat pleading, childish tone: "Mr. Mumbles? Is it okay if we call you 'daddy?' See, we ain't never had a daddy, and since you living in our mother's bedroom, maybe you could be our daddy too?"

For all his bravado, his willingness to kill at the bat of an eye, his muscle-bound appearance and ever present stoic persona, the four-year-old had struck an uncommon nerve in the man. If one were to look closely, what might have appeared to be tears were forming in the corners of his eyes.

He took Michael by the hand, gently pulled him to him in a warm embrace.

"I....I...I...b...b...be your...d....d....daddy, Lil Mike," he said, and a true tear crept down his face. "I b...b...be....your....d....d....daddy."

Chapter Thirty-one

They lay in wait for Ellis. A crew returning from an early morning task requested of the city removing snow from the sidewalks around public schools. This had allowed Jose Martinez and his crew uncommon access to the tool shop, where they'd been assigned inventoried gear for the mission into the blizzard, and a small space in time upon their return to acquire a few unconventional items long secreted in the shop by compatriots who worked there as their general daily assignments. Now, Jose, Juan and Brian took their time idling inside the entrance to the recreation hall, awaiting the entrance of the small contingent of men from Cellblock C to enter. Ellis Davidson was among the new arrivals.

During the two weeks he'd been incarcerated, Ellis had made few friends. Indeed, most in the overcrowded facility avoided him, many secretly expressing a certainty that Ellis would been slain before the heavy snows even melted, and no one wished to be anywhere in proximity to the doomed man when the execution took place. He sauntered into the recreation hall with a good measure of space around him, whereby others from Cellblock C, all black, strolled in amidst small groupings.

As they completed entry into the spacious hall, the group of Hispanics began easing their way towards a lonely Ellis, seated on the edge of a metal table near the cubicle housing corrections officers. They hastened their pace towards him, Jose and Juan easing "shanks," razor-sharp pieces of metal, from their rear waistline. But just as suddenly, five men from the group of Muslims, *Brother Atlas* at the lead, rushed over to Ellis and stood between him and the Hispanics.

"It's not happening like that, my Spanish brothers," Atlas said, flexing muscles with two equally muscular men in kufi caps bookending him.

"This not your fight, hermano," Jose said, easing back.

"There *is* no fight, *hermano*," Brother Atlas said. "Just be on about your business. If anything happens to this brother, we're going to hold you personally responsible. Comprende?"

Jose eased the shank back into its hiding place.

"Yeah. I understand, hermano. I understand."

The Hispanics, in unison, threw their heads back, each wrapped in a red bandana, chins to the ceiling. The gesture was more common among the young blacks, and the Muslims took it as a sign indicating that a truce, however brief, was in place. Jose and his boys stepped off, not wanting a battle with "The Muhammads," as they privately referred to all the Muslims as, while the Muslims turned to face down Ellis directly.

"You didn't notice, my brother, but the men back there in the booth, the correctional officers, all turned away from you when the Spanish boys were descending on you," Brother Atlas said.

"Nobody's got your back in this place," another of the Muslim brotherhood said. "We've had a discussion, and decided to accept you into our group, on a probationary basis."

Ellis just nodded, the sweat trickling from under his arms in the considerably icy recreation hall serving as a reminder to him of just how close he'd come to certain death.

"I appreciate it," he said, looking from face to stern face surrounding him.

"We're allowed noon prayers in the back of the chapel, sundown prayers at the same location,"

Brother Atlas said. "Fajr, our prayer which starts off the day, is performed at sunrise. You'll need to perform that in your cell. We have the wherewithal to get you a prayer rug. And a Holy Qur'an. But we'll fill you in on all that after the noon prayer and meeting in the chapel."

"Okay," Ellis said, and for the first time since his incarceration, he actually felt that he might live to see the light of day again.

Chapter Thirty-two

The Parkside Manor Apartment complex in Laurel, Maryland was considered a comfortable enough distance away from the District by many of its residents who'd previously lived in the city. Shantelle Bridgefield, Ebony and Derrick were well ensconced in their three-bedroom with balcony unit by spring, and the family additionally benefitted from the three-year-old Lexus Shantelle had purchased with a hefty down payment; she didn't want the monthly car notes, and could have paid cash out of the considerable largess afforded her by Ellis's sudden demise, but knew well that expenditures of cash in the amount the car cost would generate undesired attention from authorities.

Ellis remained in pretrial confinement, and with all the money he believed he had stashed with Shantelle, he couldn't make bail. After a continuous string of calls from him, Mumbles and his grandmother, which she never answered, she decided to completely discard the phone she had and get a new one with a new number. She could have merely converted the one she possessed to a new number,

Lana had told her, but hell, that one held bad memories and, certainly, she could well afford a completely new, Internet-capable one, with all the bells and whistles.

She'd counted $157,440 cash from the shoe boxes under their bed when told that Ellis had been jailed. That was back in January, and now, mid-April, she had $90,500 cash remaining. Still, the amounts he'd doled out to her in smaller amounts to fill her checking and savings account gave her additional reassurance: She'd managed to save close to $15,000 in her checking account, $27,000 in savings, drawing interest. Her job at the D.C. Department of Public Works office, in the heart of the Columbia Heights section of the city, paid her a generous $24,500 pre-tax salary, so Shantelle, having grown up poor along the same Shelter Road from which Ellis had stripped away thousands in precious dollars, considered her present financial situation as bordering on being rich.

Ellis certainly would never again see a dime of the narco-dollars he'd amassed. Still sporting the diamond engagement ring (more so now to dissuade potential suitors), Shantelle was living high on the hog. Literally. She'd replaced cheap, store-brand bacon for "thick sliced, smoked" brands costing three times as much, and now frowned upon pork chops in favor of smoked ham and a periodic indulgence in pre-cleaned chitterlings. The occasional steak rounded out the menu that she perceived served as an indication that she had arrived, and she just couldn't wait for the Chesapeake Bay blue crabs to come into season, that she might indulge an appetite for seafood previously priced well out of her reach.

She fitted the already immaculate Lexus with chrome rims more common on the urban wheels of young men riding high in GMCs, Chevy Suburbans, and other SUVs on which such wheels were more appropriate. Her friend Lana, behind her back with mutual girlfriends, lambasted her for "Ghettoizing" the luxury car.

"You can take a nigga out of the country, but-," Lana had joked once when Shantelle pulled up in the reconfigured ride, singing a tune passed down through generations of blacks but without adding the concluding stanza *("-you can't take the country out of a nigga.")*.

Ellis was still feverishly seeking her, as best he could from behind bars. He'd adapted to the practices of the Muslim group and "Brother Atlas" (and finally been made aware of the fact that the Muslim brotherhoods leader's legal name, though not his birth name, was now Abdul-Rahman

Muhammad). Efforts by his grandmother, other kin and Mumbles to get in touch with Shantelle continued to prove fruitless, and after being told by Mumbles that he'd visited their previous apartment and found out that Shantelle had moved, he was finally convinced that she had no intentions of assisting in freeing him. After a prideful young lifetime of philandering and having women at his beck and call, Ellis realized that the one he loved most had kicked him to the curb. He was utterly heartbroken. Had he known that, by now, Shantelle was now in the second trimester of a pregnancy with their child, he'd have been totally devastated.

Her pregnancy was in protruding evidence by April, and still sporting the engagement ring, her colleagues were whispering rumors about the possibilities that the wedding was currently on shaky grounds. Her female friends on the job, sworn to secrecy, had released a flood of half-truths and summations placing the baby's father, her fiancé, incarcerated on some most serious charges. He'd already had a preliminary hearing, and with a court-appointed lawyer, was being advised that he might be offered a plea deal, lest he face the more serious charge of maintaining a continuing criminal enterprise.

The U.S. Attorney was attempting to tie Ellis to Reynaldo and his South American connections under the RICO Act (Racketeer Influenced and Corrupt Organizations Act). Enacted in 1970, RICO was intended to be used to prosecute members of the Mafia, but in recent years has been applied more often to those engaged in a "continuing criminal enterprise," mostly drug dealers.

After detailing the circumstances of his arrest to "Brother Muhammad" and the members of the Muslim brotherhood, jailhouse legal minds convinced him that, with suitable representation (read, a PAID attorney, as opposed to a public defender), he could easily beat the charges. He'd not been caught with any drugs on his person, they reasoned, and his "visit" to Hernandez-Rios had been misread by law enforcement officials for more than it was: Simply a casual visit to a casual acquaintance.

Those concerns were given considerable weight by Ellis. But equally vexing in the mix was that he *could* actually afford a good attorney, and at the same time the very thoughts gave rise to the fact that Shantelle, who he'd loved and trusted, had apparently absconded with his monies.

Meanwhile, Shantelle was just having a good old time.

With her souped-up Lexus, she'd deposit the children with her mother as summer approached, done a top which emphasized her always attractive breast but hide her near seven month pregnancy, and arrived at Martin's nightclub surrounded by perfumed air and friends well aware of her financial windfall. Sensibly, she now avoided all alcohol, but was not averse to buying top-shelf drinks for her friends, Lana always the one riding shotgun in the Lexus and in a leadership role in the club. They were spending yet another Saturday night at the favored venue, being hit on by a league of young men with lecherous hearts who were attracted to their group.

"No thanks," Shantelle was saying in her singsong voice to the third young man who'd asked her to dance.

She was still ordering drinks all around, basking in the glow of her newfound popularity, when she glanced towards the entrance and saw two familiar faces from the old neighborhood. Her buoyant persona abruptly faded into a mask of fear and shadow of despondency, as Mumbles and Block spotted her, pinned her with cold gazes and weaved their way through the crowd towards her perch at the end of the extensive bar.

"Hi, baby!" she sang in a voice which put the *false* in falsetto, extending her hand sporting the diamond and realizing belatedly that that was not a good move.

Mumbles just looked down at the outstretched hand, began fighting for words.

"B....b....b....bitch! W...wh.....wh.....w...why you...you....di...di....diss my b....b... boy...l...l...like th...th...that?"

"Ellis say you got a lot of something belong to him too," Block added, clutching his massive hands before him. "What's up with that?"

Shantelle didn't have an answer, or couldn't form one. She smiled, but the two men were actually scaring the piss out of her. For the past few weeks, she had been having to use the bathroom with irregular frequency, and at the moment, she could actually feel a small measure of warm liquid moistening her seat on the barstool. With a lean, tilt and wobble often seen in a woman close to giving birth, she made her way off the bar stool. Mumbles, short on words but keen on observations, peered at her with eyes as if a major discovery were unmasked.

"Sh...sh...Shantelle! Y...y.....yu....y...y...you pr...pr...pregnant?!"

Everyone within twenty-feet paused and turned in their direction, and Shantelle merely presented a plastic smile, looked to Lana for support. Lana took the cue, swiveled off her own bar stool and moved swiftly up beside her friend.

"She gotta go to the bathroom," Lana stammered, took Shantelle by an arm. "Come on girl. These fools don't know what they're talking about."

The other women in their grouping cast eyes at one another, saying nothing.

"That bitch!" Block said, looking to Mumbles, then to the other women who'd evidently been with Shantelle. "All y'all ain't nothing but a bunch of scheming hos. Y'all know what's up with her man, and y'all probably all up in her grill like that telling her shit against him. Bitches!"

"B….b….b…..bitches!"

Chapter Thirty-three

They figured their presence in the club would make her uneasy, and with the large crowd dancing and socializing in two massive, ballroom-sized areas, it wouldn't be at all odd if they didn't run into one another the rest of the night. So Mumbles and Block sat in the Mercedes on the large parking lot across from Martin's with a clear view of the front entrance. They were waiting for Shantelle and her crew to leave, discover what car she, in particular, left in, and shadow them from a distance in hopes of finding out where she had moved to.

Just weeks after the arrests of Ellis and Reynaldo, the Task Force began corralling a number of Reynaldo's associates. In conjunction with law enforcement officials from as far away as Miami and as close in as Baltimore and New York City, a good portion of what was determined to be a major drug distribution web was interrupted. Block, however, was scoring his cocaine from a completely different web, and Mumbles, quickly depleted of drugs after the New Year's holiday had found his childhood friend and arranged to score through his channels.

The two were scarcely in competition, were even friends since childhood, and Block found in Mumbles a well-financed partner to allow the two to cop greater weight at a substantial discount.

By the dawn of summer, the two were even greater suppliers in the Southeast and Northeast sections of the city. Everything was smooth; even the police, for some unknown reason, failed to follow up on Mumbles' presence in the apartment building they'd raided the past winter, though he maintained a base there with Miss Charlene and the kids. The only bothersome aspect of Mumble's business dealings now was the inability to aid his best friend Ellis in fighting the drug charges against him. He certainly had the monies to put forth for his bond, but even in conversations with Ellis, his pal wouldn't hear of it: Ellis *had* money! With Shantelle! He was vehement that the absconding young woman be found, and his substantial nest egg retrieved.

If she had had any wits about her that night, she might have noticed the shiny, late model Mercedes trailing her as she left the club, dropped of one, then another friend, then headed to her Laurel home. But she failed to notice them, and Mumbles and Block were finally able to find out just where Shantelle had acquired new digs. They even watched through the ornate glass of the front of her unit and were able to see exactly which apartment she'd gone into.

It was late, well past midnight, but Mumbles and Block were committed to completing the task without having to leave and return to this location, a distance away from the city, and from their individual digs.

"I'm gonna slip over there and take out the tires on her ride, man," Block said, retrieving a sheathed, near foot-long hunting knife from under his seat. "We get a little shut-eye; her ass can't go no where. Then she come out, we, like, pull up on her ass and act like we offering to help, like that. Won't be all suspicious, people be looking out their windows or some shit."

"Y…y…yeah."

"We show her our shit like that. I got a piece for you under the seat. A .32." He displayed a Mac-10 automatic. "I put this shit up in her ribs, we go back in her crib and get our boy's money. Know the way she spending cash clubbing she got the boxes like ol' boy say up in her crib. She can't have banked all that, or spent it. Anyway, she don't have the money, we know where her mother live, where she leave them kids. We let her know she don't come up with ol'

boy's money, well, her mother and them kids might
be in for a world of hurt."

"Y…y…yeah.　　W…w…we….m…m….make
her…gi…gi..give…give…..up..El…El…El…Ellis…sh
…sh…shit!"

Chapter Thirty-four

Sunday morning Shantelle decided to sleep in. She called her mother, was assured it was okay for Ebony and Derrick to stay until afternoon, and promised she'd pick them up around one. Yes, she also promised mom, she had the hundred dollars her mother had requested last night.

She was suffering morning sickness, she told her mother, though in actuality the confrontation with Mumbles and Block had almost given her a case of diarrhea. She reset her alarm for noon, fell into a fitful sleep teeming with images of Mumbles and Block, ensconced in her new, immaculate living room bagging cocaine while she, in a servile apron and Aunt Jemima head rag, prepared food and drinks and delivered it to them.

When she awakened, a cold sweat had soaked the sheets, and the dreams seemed almost as if premonitions. Her left eye wouldn't stop throbbing, and old lore she'd heard from a grandmother as a child said such was a warning that some bad event was on the immediate horizon. She showered, took in her profile in the full-length mirror affixed to the bathroom door, running a hand over her bulging stomach. There was a baby boy forming within, she'd been told by her obstetrician after asking about the baby's gender. She was looking forward to yet another child, but torturous words continued to play through her mind. No, the father would never be told of the boy's existence. And she was almost sure that he'd have no way of finding her, or finding out about the boy's existence.

Unless her encounter with Mumbles and Block the previous evening evolved into something she was praying that it would not.

Unlike the previous evening, she made no attempt to hide the pregnancy and dressed quite maternally. She took her cellular phone off the charger, scanned the living room to ensure she was forgetting nothing, left the apartment. Entering the car, the flat tires didn't generate any attention until she'd started the car and begun backing out of the parking space. The rough, hobbling motion of the car confused her at first, until it hit her that she probably had a flat. She eased the car back into the parking space, climbed out and inspected the wheels.

"You gonna need some help changing them tires, pregnant lady."

She began to present a smile to the voice, then looked into the cold eyes of Block, turned in fear back towards the walkway to her apartment building and almost stepped directly into the arms of Mumbles.

"D....d....d....don't," he whispered, eased he jacket aside to show the gun tucked in his beltline.

Block moved up beside her, and just in time. Her knees weakened, then buckled, and he had to support her to keep her from crumpling to the ground.

"Let's go back in you crib, Shantelle," he whispered, guiding her back up the walkway behind Mumbles.

Both men had to assist her up the stairs; her legs just weren't working. She handed a ring of keys to Mumbles, who knew which door to use them in. In seconds, they were in the apartment, and Block eased Shantelle down onto the nearest segment of a plush, wrap-around sofa. She adjusted herself, as if for comfort, the plastic furniture cover appearing to deter her from sliding back for needed support.

"You got my boy's money, Shantelle, and that was some cold shit you moving and not answering his calls and his grandmother's calls to try and get together his bail money," Block said, taking a seat across from her. "You don't know, but them Spanish mother fuckers had put out a hit on his ass in the joint. Wasn't for some brothers he hooked up with, they would have been shanked his ass."

"N...n....no...sh...sh....s....sh...shit," Mumbles submitted, still standing by the entryway.

"So," Block leaned forward, dramatically removing the Mac-10 from under his jacket and setting it on the ornate coffee table. "Where you got my boy's stash?"

She didn't utter a word, eyes fixed on the machine pistol.

"Don't have me tear this fine-ass joint of yours apart looking," Block warned. "We'll tear this mother fucker to threads, bitch. You better holla."

"K....k.....k...," Mumbles stepped forward, struggling to make known his view. "E...E...Ellis aw....aw....always......ke....k...k....ke.... k...k...kept a....sh...sh...shoebox...u..u..under the...the....bed. I...I'll....t.t...take...a.....look."

He went to the rear of the apartment, while Shantelle, wordless and visibly shaken, looked to Block with pleading eyes.

In moments, Mumbles returned with two shoe boxes and a broad smile. True to form, Shantelle had followed precisely Ellis's pattern: All the cash she had of his remaining had been secreted under her bed, in the same shoe boxes in which they'd been at the apartment she'd shared with Ellis.

Mumbles took a seat near Shantelle, placed the boxes on the coffee table and proceeded to separate and count the bundles of bills. Her tears began to flow again, and increased seemingly in tandem with the uttered increase in the amount of dollars being counted.

"T....t...two-thousand,,,"

Sniff sniff sniff!

"T...t....ten-thousand..."

"Whimper whimper whimper!"

"F....f....forty-thousand..."

"Boo hoo hoo..."

"N...n...ninety....t...thousand...f...f...five...h ...hundred!"

"BWAAAAAAAAAAAAAHHH!!!!"

"B....b...bitch!   Sh....sh.....sh.....shut....the......f...f...fuck up!"

"Yeah, stop all that fucking crying," Block growled, looking at the mounds of money. "You should have though about this shit when you left your boy to rot in jail."

Mumbles began neatly stacking the money back into the shoe boxes, pointed to the back and looked to Block.

"L....l...look   at...a..all   the....sh...shit....she got...b...b...back there."

Block arose, went to the back and surveyed the bedrooms, returned.

"Bitch got big-screen televisions in every bedroom *and* here in the living room! We oughta take them mother fuckers and sell them too, know what I'm saying, Mumbles?"

"Y...y...yeah."

"Please," Shantelle had her most piteous face on now. "Those for my kids mostly. Please don't do that."

Mumbles put the tops on the boxes, arose. Block stepped to the front windows, peered out then turned back to Shantelle, retrieved the Mac-10 and secreted it under his jacket.

"Wasn't for my boy's baby you carrying," he said, stepping towards the door, "I'd bust a cap in your ass."

"N...n...no...sh...sh...shit!"

She looked to them with pleading eyes.

"Y'all could at least leave me with a couple grand," she sniffled. "You know since I moved in here, I got more bills to pay. And y'all done fucked up the tires on my ride and shit. Mumbles? Come on, man..."

"F....f...fuck you."

Then in apparent afterthought, Mumbles counted out five hundred dollars and pitch the amount, in twenties, onto the living room floor.

They left the unit in no particular hurry, motored back to the city and agreed to meet Monday morning at the law offices of Bernard Macke.

Chapter Thirty-five

For anyone who could afford him, retaining the services of Attorney Bernard Macke was somewhat equivalent to being tried by a jury of first cousins, childhood playmates, and favorite teachers. Macke was renown for his defense in a number of high-profile cases, particularly in gaining an acquittal for Devon "Shep" Shepherd, notorious head of the Capitol Heights Posse. He'd also successfully represented a D.C. City Councilman in his battle against corruption charges, and had even parried away an investigation by a grand jury of a six-term congressman. Macke was "all that," in the words of those seeking his counsel, and the hefty fee he demanded was a pittance when one considered the prison time many would face without his acute manipulative mind and flair for the dramatic while representing them in the courtroom.

A towering black man with a booming voice who favored finely tailored suits and bowties, Macke kept offices on U Street in the District, a stretch of gentrifying Washington once referred to as the Black Broadway. He also had more austere digs on K

Street, NW, home of hundreds of more traditional law offices and the offices of most of the city's lobbyists. For Block and Mumbles to wander into his U Street office with two shoeboxes full of money didn't raise any eyebrows at the Shaw location, and as Macke maintained accounts at the nearby Industrial Savings Bank of Washington, a historic black financial institution, his staff was handing a receipt for $50,000.00 for Macke's services in the name of Ellis Davidson to the two shadowy figures even before the morning rush hour had ended.

With such a deposit, Macke personally assigned two of his most seasoned attorneys to study Ellis's case and meet personally with him that same day. There was certainly enough money in that $50,000.00 to provide for the ten percent needed for the bond which had long ago been set for Ellis, and with practiced efficiency, he was freed through Macke's efforts the following day.

For their part, and because, after all, this was business, both Mumbles and Block kept $10,000 apiece for themselves, a "service fee," if you will. Ellis would certainly understand, and approve, though they felt little need in telling him this. The "change," $20,000.00, would be given to Ellis to assist in getting him back on his feet.

Bernard Macke personally reviewed the evidence against Ellis that week and determined that he could easily convince a jury, if not a judge before trial, that the government lacked enough evidence to pursue their RICO charges against him. He'd surely have the recorded conversations gained at the rib shack thrown out, and that, he believed, formed the bulk of the government's case against Davidson.

"It's a crock of bullshit!" he'd told the two attorneys he assigned to lead in the case, and they were then sure that Davidson's acquittal was assured: When Macke uttered his "crock of bullshit" analysis, everyone knew that his assessment was most assuredly accurate, and that any charges given this determination would not stand up to judicial scrutiny.

Meanwhile, Ellis had been released under the conditions that he maintain his presence in the city at a residence that could be verified. With Shantelle out of the picture, he was forced to return to his grandmother's home, though Block had offered his residence as a place for his friend to stay. Macke's team assigned to him had insisted though that he stay at his grandmother's, a considerably pristine and certainly drug-free abode where his standing could be further cleansed should the U.S. Attorney's investigators do a pretrial surveillance of him, which Macke assured him that they most certainly would.

He'd be under a law enforcement microscope, Macke had told him in a personal meeting, specifically because he had retained Macke as a defense attorney, and this was further proof that the government knew that their case against him was weak.

"You stay your ass away from Shelter Road, Kenilworth, Congress Park, even your friends who paid for our services," Macke told him. "Until trial, you're grandmother's little boy. Get you a suit. Go to church. Believe me, they're watching your every move from here to trial. Bank on it."

Ellis did want to confront Shantelle, however. His SUV had long since succumbed to storage fees and been sold at auction. And if not for the money Mumbles and Block secreted to him through an elaborate scheme involving neighborhood youths, he'd not even have "ends" to assist his ever struggling grandmother with a food bill now doubled. He knew about Shantelle's pregnancy, knew that her Laurel location was easily accessible. But he took the advice of counsel, wouldn't even chance a ride with Mumbles out to confront her.

So for the first few weeks of the summer, Ellis merely lollygagged around his old neighborhood, spending hours in conversation with Big Mack by the old Shipley Terrace Liquor Store. He appreciated the wise counsel of Big Mack, and at least he had the mind of someone not drugged out, liquor soaked, or merely uneducated to bounce his thoughts off of.

"Hope your attorney moved to detach your trial from that of the Mexican, the Colombian, whatever the fuck his ass is," Big Mack said softly, staring from the wheelchair confines across at activity occurring outside the liquor store.

Ellis hovered over him, just to his left, taking in the same view.

"Yeah, he said that was his first action. Reynaldo got a lot of...what they call it? *Notoriety* about him. Tied to some big boys out of Florida. What I heard in the joint, they got him under protective custody. They say a price on his head."

"And what about yours, young buck?"

"Oh, I think they finally realized I was just small fish. I had a little trouble at first over in lock-down, but that was squelched. I don't think they're worried about me. Besides, beyond Reynaldo and Miguel, I ain't really know nothing. And they killed Miguel when they raised up on us out there. If anything, Reynaldo probably would have sent Miguel after my ass."

"Cool. Cool."

The summer was warming quickly, and the heat among a population suffering under increasingly tenuous financial prospects contributed to a further raising of temperatures in the city. Gun violence which had for years been decreasing surged dramatically. In certain parts of the city, and the nation, thousands of citizens growing ever hungrier seemed to be fighting over the same crumbs. The streets surrounding Ellis and Big Mack were a microcosm of the greater Southeast and Northeast communities: Unemployment among black men between the ages of 16 and 30 was near fifty percent. And with little else to do, the most enjoyable thing available was sexual activity, further contributing to the need for cash as the out-of-wedlock population of children soared.

"My old girl should be dropping that baby any day now," Ellis said, watching a crowd of children being chased from the Mom and Pop store by "Mamasan" and "Papasan."

"This is, what? Your third?" Big Mack asked, smiling at the children tearing by.

"Yeah. Little Lauren still out Kenilworth with her mama. Little Michelle down Barry Farm with hers."

"And here you stand with your dick in your hand," Big Mack smiled. "Can't even spell pussy."

Ellis laughed. "Why you gotta be so cold, Mack Man?"

"'Cause all along, I ain't never told you nothing but the truth." He wore dark glasses, a Hawaiian shirt, gold gabardine slacks and shined Neleton loafers perched on the chair's footrests. His gold front tooth was equally polished. "You were in love with the last one, the one that's pregnant now."

It was a statement, not a question. Ellis was slow to answer.

"Kinda…yeah…I guess. How you know?"

"Young blood, you can't fool the fooler. I could see it in your eyes whenever you talked about her. See, you ran around trying to be a player, and as always is the case, in the end, it's the player who winds up getting played."

Ellis had to let this sink in for a moment, couldn't think of a response, stood by silently, watching life pass him by.

"Naw young buck," Big Mack said after a while. "You can't fool the fooler, and you can't out play the player."

Chapter Thirty-six

"Yeah baby! That's it! Go ahead! Go ahead, with your nasty ass! Tear it up! Tear it up!"

Miss Charlene's legs were seeking heaven, her hands clutching Mumbles behind the neck, her torso arching to meet his every thrust. She was on her back, on the edge of the bed since fitted with nice sheets and a comforter, and at the moment, completely sober. Sex when not benumbed by the cocaine was nearly an aphrodisiac to her, especially when being served quite effectively by Mumbles. And he didn't need any stimulus. He was naturally driven, and God had blessed him with a considerably enormous driver.

"Ohhh, *shit*!" she cried, reaching with one hand behind a thigh to further pull open the gateway into which he plunged like some Olympic swimmer. "Hit that shit man, *god-damn* your ass!"

He smacked down into her ravenously, growing intense as even her words served to usher him further towards the precipice. Explosively, he spewed voluminous warmth into her, convulsed, cried out

"Shit! Oh, SHIT!" without so much as a stutter. Then he folded, weak and spent, upon her sweat soaked body at first, then easing himself out of her, rolled to the side.

She'd done much to make herself more attractive to him in recent months, even struggling to cut back on her cocaine consumption, eating some fruits and vegetables, which was rare for her, cleaning the apartment, paying more attention to the kids. She cooked, and for a few days, usually after an extended period of crack consumption, she'd struggle to stay sober, even once advising Mumbles to not keep any drugs in the home. She'd even gone as long as a week at one point without smoking crack. But once she started back, it was full steam ahead until the next attempt at sobriety, surely to be a failed one, when she swear off crack and played as if she were a stay-at-home mother. She'd even put on a few pounds during the spring, then as quickly shed them as summer heated up.

Business was moderate, even seasoned addicts seemed either not able to bum their way to a nickel-and-dime amassment for a $10.00 rock, were jailed, were seeking relief in one of many AA/NA programs throughout the city, or were dying off. Mumbles was still scoring with Block, had managed a midnight rendezvous with Ellis to further invest his now meager funds, and had rebuilt the youthful distribution network along Shelter Road after a good portion of the previous crew was either jailed or buried.

But kids were continuing to emerge into adolescence after all, and even amidst the greatest economic downturn since the Great Depression, the youths still just had to have the latest pair of $120.00 Air Junket tennis shoes, or the $90.00 Timberwolf boots. These were the very same youths who stood around in their costly attire each and every first of the month to watch U.S. Marshals, accompanied by often homeless day laborers, oversee the eviction of the family of one or another of their number.

On most Fridays, Mumbles had already put out enough product to take it easy Saturday and Sunday. As he moved to stretch out lengthwise on the bed, Miss Charlene eased up beside him, planted her naked body next to his and fixed his arms to embrace her.

"I'm gonna chill today, Mumbles," she whispered, committing for the umpteenth time to stay sober for a day. "No smoking. No beer. None of that shit. Just you. You and the kids."

"C....c....cool."

Few knew where to contact Mumbles other than by cell phone. Most of his associates wouldn't dare bother him unless there was some critically pressing matter. Block Thurman was increasingly among his closest associates since Ellis had come under the eye of the police, even though the two, as teens, had "bumped heads" on more than a few occasions. But those fisticuffs were long forgotten, both having attributed the battles to childhood, neighborhood beefs. At present, they were of benefit to one another, and those past conflicts mattered little with the money the two were bringing in with their combined wholesale purchases.

As was common, Mumbles had turned off his cell phone when he'd first determined that he and Miss Charlene were about to engage in a period of sexual acrobatics. After trying his number a few times, Block, visiting relatives along Shelter Road, decided to drive the few blocks and rap on Miss Charlene's door. Little Kanisha answered it.

"Yes, can I help you?" she said, cracking the door open with the flimsy chain still securing it.

"Yeah, baby girl. Mumbles in this joint?"

"Mr. Mumbles back there with my mama."

"Good. Tell him Block needs to holler at him."

She closed the door tight, looked to her siblings before a television displaying Saturday morning cartoons, stepped to the back of the apartment. She tapped lightly on her mother's closed bedroom door, cast her eyes aside as her mother eased the door slightly open, fully naked.

"Ma, it's this big-head man at the door want to talk to Mr. Mumbles."

He heard her words, twisted around on the bed and grabbed his cell phone off the table, having forgotten it was idled. He looked at a few "missed calls," pulled on a pair of boxers, jeans, a t-shirt.

"T...t...that's....m....m....m.....mu..m..…m… my..bb..boy....B…B…Block," he said, recognizing Kanisha's most accurate description. He moved past Miss Charlene. "B…b…be b…b..back…in a …m…m…minute."

Kanisha returned to the living room, joining her siblings. They all cast suspicious eyes at the man whom Mr. Mumbles granted access to what they considered the cherished, private space belonging solely to them, their mother and, of late, Mr. Mumbles.

"Hu..hu…..h…….h…hey….B…B…B…Block. Wh…wha…what…u..u..up?"

They moved to the dinette, Mumbles taking a chair precariously remaining upright on wobbly legs, motioned for Block to sit in a more stable one.

"Some of them boys down Shelter Road hollered at me when I went by there to take my sister some ends this morning," Block said, leaning on the table and giving his spiel as if at some formal conference. "They say Five-O been asking about you again down that joint; something about them killings on Mississippi back there last winter. And one of them boys say that young'un they call Biscuit was in a detective car last night, thinking ain't nobody see his ass. Say they think he a snitch, then that boy Ray Ray say he saw Biscuit up at Seven D right after Fat Boy and his partners got shot on Mississippi. Man, his ass probably been snitching since then."

Block arose, was joined by Mumbles in a quick handshake, a shoulder bump.

"Just thought you needed to know that shit, man. That boy Biscuit know where you be hanging here, know what I'm saying?"

"I...I...I....know." Mumbles escorted Block to the door. "I...I...t..t..take care...of it. H...h...hollar a..a...at you...l...l...later."

Chapter Thirty-seven

In the seedy and dangerous world of police "snitches," Donte "Biscuit" Millsbury was a minor snare. At 20, he barely had any chips in the sordid game of drug dealing, a third- and fourth-string player who'd at best earn a few dollars by getting money from a crack purchaser, delivering the dollars to a true dealer, and be directed to a crumpled paper cup, usually, tossed curbside and containing at best a $10.00 "sack" of crack. The methodology was near universal in the crack cocaine street sales realm, a way of doing business whereby only a stooge such as Biscuit, at best, would ever be caught with any real drugs on their person.

And he was hardly a valued snitch, from the perspective of police. At best he'd often be frightened into divulging sometimes important but for the most part useless information about dealings on the streets around Shelter Road. Always wanting to be the big man, he'd most recently been traipsing around the neighborhood displaying to anyone willing to listen his bullet wound received the previous winter; apparently, being shot, and surviving, was among the highest honors among his peers, while, conversely, being seen in conversation with "Five-O" was almost a guarantee that the next bullets directed his way would be fatal ones.

Mumbles waited until the Saturday night activities were fully active before walking the short distance from Miss Charlene's to Shelter Road. A few young men selling crack at the head of the street saw him approach, ceased their babblings about "I got that good shit!" to potential customers and melted into nearby hallways and dark parking lots. They all knew Mumbles, and even in casual jeans and a loose khaki shirt, they were sure that somewhere on his person was firepower no one wanted to see the business end of.

He marched casually down the street, and summer night revelers abandoned 40-ounce bottles and allowed burning blunts to simmer untouched as the residents and visitors scattered. At the end of the street, a group selling crack mostly acquired through Mumbles watched as he neared, and a few among them knew they were safe, and exactly who their benefactor was in search of. Biscuit, never one to stand well under the influence of a few tokes off a blunt and the full contents of a 40 ounce malt, was basking in imagined glory, his back to the approaching figure who would end his life, and was completely taken by surprised when the others he'd been bragging to suddenly backed away from him.

"What's wrong with y'all fools, man?" Biscuit slurred, a blunt in one hand, 40-ounce in the other.

He turned, was mere feet from the barrel of a gun, and focused with a final gaze to recognized the feared man known as Mumbles behind the pistol.

"M...M....Mumbles....d....d..... d.d....d...don't like....s...snitch...mm......m...mother ....fuckers!" the gunman said, then squeezed of a most powerful round directly between the open lips of Biscuit. "K...K...Kill....M...M..Mumbles! K...K...Kill!"

He released an additional three rounds into the young man even as the spray of blood from his exploding head still speckled the surrounding air. He even had to lower his aim, quickly, as the power of the .357 Magnum sent the frail body pitching backwards, downward, fragments of bone and blood exploding out onto the sideway, despoiling the nearby grass, despoiling the window of a car parked nearby.

The echoing of the gunfire seemed to hang in the air as much as did the last blood of Donte "Biscuit" Millsbury. By the time residents felt it safe to get off the floor of nearby apartment buildings, ease from the confines of hallways, inch their way up from the floors of nearby cars, Mumbles was retreating back up the street, in no particular hurry, testing the warmth of the gun barrel and, finding it too hot to be secreted into the small of his back, holding it by his side, raising it to blow cooling air on the barrel at one point, disappearing over the horizon.

Chapter Thirty-eight

On an extremely hot day in late July of that summer, Ellis Davidson went before a jury of his peers. At least that was the legal term for the twelve men and women who'd sit in judgment of the now 26 year-old, charged with maintaining a continuing criminal enterprise, though the presiding judge had already advised the prosecutor and defense attorneys that the stated charges were highly dependent on evidence the prosecutors assured him would be presented in detail at the trial.

Already the charges had been considerably lessened through legal maneuvers by the esteemed attorney Bernard Macke. Strutting before the court like a black peacock in tailored regalia, Macke assured the jury that they would be presented with clear evidence that his client, solemnly seated at the defense table in a cheap suit which made him appear not unlike a boy accompanying a crew of Saturday morning Jehovah's Witnesses, was guilty of nothing more than visiting an associate whom he knew had possible employment in the subcontracting construction business he owned. And certainly, "Mr.

Davidson" had no knowledge that one Mr. Reynaldo Hernandez-Rios was also involved in the drug trade. Macke had already petitioned mightily to have Hernandez-Rios present to support this fact, but unfortunately, Hernandez-Rios, "in federal custody, mind you!" Macke emphasized, had been mortally wounded within the confines of a federal institution.

"My client is merely among those unfortunate enough to have even known, barely known, mind you, Mr. Hernandez-Rios!" Macke proclaimed, prancing before the jury and crowded courtroom. "And now, with their main target killed, under their watchful eyes even, they want to do whatever they can to bring some...some *meat* before the altar of justice! They want you to feed *my client*, to the wolves in the sordid, mean wells of the federal penal system, where as you already have heard, they could not even guarantee the safety of the one they really wanted, Mr. Hernandez-Rios!"

To Ellis's surprise, an astute Macke, occasionally generating laughter from the courtroom and the judge, effectively debunked measure after measure of the prosecution's case against him, moving the judge to disallow the admittance of key pieces of evidence, ruling that the taped conversation from the rib shack again was inadmissible, and even questioning whether the new High Altitude Detection drone, with its images seen here for the first time in a court on the homeland, had yet been proven valid.

When the court reconvened after an hour's lunch that afternoon, the judge, with concurrence from the prosecution, agreed that there was no case against Ellis Davidson. He walked out of the courtroom surrounded by his legal team, his grandmother, and before a bank of local television news cameras.

At exactly the moment he was presenting smiles to the media, some seven miles northwest of his location, Shantelle Bridgefield was giving birth to their son.

Chapter Thirty-nine

Mumbles of course couldn't attend Ellis's trial. He'd expressed an interest initially, but Attorney Macke had near hit the ceiling when Ellis had informed him that a few of his childhood friends from the old neighborhood had planned to be in court to show their support.

"They want to show their support," Macke had blasted, "tell them to keep as far away from the courtroom as possible! And your friend, Mumbles? Hell, you tell that man I'll pay for a Jamaican vacation for him until the trial is over! Last thing you want is a bunch of hoods in the courtroom cheering you on!"

It was the weekend, moving into the most blistering month of August, before Ellis was even comfortable in mounting a celebration, or even securing the funds Mumbles had been amassing for him to attempt to reestablish his previously high-flying lifestyle. He needed a car, and was back in more regular contact with his Kenilworth "baby mama," Donna, to set her up in a comfortable apartment, from which he could begin anew his own quest for the golden ring. He'd certainly not forgotten about Shantelle, and had his mind set on searching her out as soon as he'd moved out of his grandmother's, obtained a "fine ride," and was again flush with cash. He'd of course been told by Mumbles and Block about her pregnancy, but had no idea if the child had been born. He reasoned it was about time, but had no confirmation. Not until his celebratory night out at Martin's, when he saw her friend Lana along with other female associates, joyous and flitting around the dance floor apparently in a celebration all their own.

Lana caught a glimpse of him approaching as a song ended and she left the dance floor. Well into a session which she reasoned had called for more than the customary champagne, Lana had consumed a few cognacs and cola, which served more than the champagne to loosen an already notoriously free tongue. She waddled over to an approaching Ellis, threw her arms around him.

"Hi baby!" she slurred in a drunken voice which only served to highlight her renowned cosmetic persona. "I heard you got off from that beef they had you on! Congratulations!"

Ellis presented a restrained smile, eased her back to arms length.

"Hey, Lana. See you ain't let up off the drinks none. Your girl Shantelle ain't here?" He glanced over her shoulder at a couple of familiar females apparently awaiting her, then around the club, scanning for his ex.

"Naw, man!" Lana sang. "She gotta spend quality time with y'all's new baby. You ain't heard?"

He guided her to the side of the dance floor, to a table where Mumbles and Block and a few other friends sat sipping drinks.

"I didn't hear nothing," he said, guiding her to a seat. "So, she had the baby? What she have? A boy?"

"Yeah, man!" she said, bobbling in her seat and taking a drink that was certainly not hers. "Y'all got a pretty little black baby, man! She named him Marquis! Man, you don't know?"

"Naw, Lana. Ol' girl ain't try to call a brother or nothing like that. And since her ass moved, and changed her number, I ain't have no way to get in touch with her."

Mumbles and Block glanced at one another. They had a while ago volunteered to direct Ellis to Shantelle's Laurel apartment. But on advice of counsel, he said, he had to avoid many past contacts, including those which might have prompted him to commit some act out of haste. And surely, he'd reasoned then, he might have done something quite hasty had he come upon Shantelle fresh out of confinement, and still facing the possibility of a prolonged stint in jail.

Mumbles and another associate of theirs arose, moved towards the bar. Block stood and pinned two of the girls who'd apparently been awaiting Lana with a cold stare; they and Block moved off, affording Lana and Ellis as much privacy as possible in the packed club with a table to themselves. Ellis sat across from Lana.

"Hey, I know where she took off to," Ellis said.

"I know you know!" Lana said, now belligerent. "And I don't know *why* you had to send your boys out after her, taking all her money and shit! You *know* she got Ebony and Derrick, and now Marquis, to feed. And then that was some cold shit, them fucking up her car tires like that. Man, y'all ain't shit, you know that?"

"Girl, stop talking so loud, drunken-ass bitch," he spat, noticing eyes upon them from surrounding tables.

"Fuck you, Ellis!" she said, stumbling to her feet, upsetting a table full of drinks. "I wish you'd send them mother fuckers out with some shit fucking with me, I'm telling you the truth! You ain't the only one can play gangster around this joint! Like they say, when the man made one gun, he made two. And Shantelle got a man now, so you might as well just step on off to your bitch in Kenilworth, or that skeezer down Barry Farm! Bitch-ass nigga!"

She stumbled off into the waiting arms of two girlfriends, who'd drawn closer to her as she'd lashed into her tirade against Ellis, even as others nearby in the club were inching their ways away from the two.

"Naw," she said, throwing away the arm of a friend. "Somebody need to tell that sorry-ass mother fucker that he ain't all that! Punk-ass mother fucker…"

She was at last silent, moved with her girlfriends to their previous table where addition drinks awaited them. While from across the room, at the bar, Mumbles sipped a Remy, glanced at her with cold eyes, and whispered a chilling word or two to Block.

"T…th…that's…….wu…..wu… one…one…one b…b….bitch…a…a…asking….fu.. f…f..for…trouble.

I...I...don...do...don't   hi...hi...hit....w..w..womens. B...b..bu....bu......but I...gu...gu...gu...I gu...got.... got   a...a...l..l...lady   friend...wh...who...w....will f...fu...fuck a b...b...bitch up!"

Chapter Forty

"Here we go again with that mumbling son of a bitch!" Detective Robinson blasted to the men and women gathered in the conference room. "That boy Millsbury wasn't a bad kid at all. I know his peoples. He wasn't among the worse ones out there on Shelter Road. And here we get word once again that that mumbling son of a bitch is responsible for yet another killing in Seven D!"

He was meeting not only with detectives from his District, but with a few officials who were also part of the Joint Task Force of which he was also a participant. They were setting in after a miserable attempt at trying to interrupt another drug operation which had regional implications: After the effective disruption of the local network supplied by Reynaldo Hernandez-Rios, and his subsequent slaying in a tightly-controlled federal prison (everyone knew that the assassin, quickly identified and caught, had been dispatched by Hernandez-Rios' Miami connections), the Joint Task Force members were focused locally on yet another cocaine network, this one apparently having in record time taken over the market left vacant by Hernandez-Rios' sudden demise.

"You ever put some officers back outside the place he used to stay, the one that was raided?" Sandra Wills, the Task Force member from the FBI's Washington Field Office asked. "You know, the way it's reported he always announces his killings by calling out his own name, he's no rocket scientist. Most certainly feels comfortable in the neighborhood where he previously lived. Probably frequents the area still, wouldn't you think?"

"Although he's not in the system, never arrested before, we do have a police sketch artist image of him, and stats on his car or truck; I think it's a pick-up he has registered, and a Mercedes?" Detective Plant, the 17-year veteran D.C. officer asked.

"We've had someone setting on his pick-up for the past 24-hours," Robinson said. "It's over there by his old apartment unit. Nothing so far. And evidently he keeps the Mercedes elsewhere. But we have a BOLO out on it."

Of course the "BOLO" was not limited to the Seventh District. A "be on the lookout" request was city-wide, and also on the radar of Prince George's

County police in particular, and most other regional law enforcement agencies in general.

"From what I hear from some of our street sources, this guy, Delano Johnson, aka Mumbles, does a lot of his business walking, especially when he's armed and about to take someone out," Detective Plant added. "He's a crafty bastard."

"I got word that he's supposedly seeing a woman on the first floor of the building where he used to maintain a base," Robinson said, rising to indicate that the briefing was about to conclude. "He's also known to do a little partying, at the place, Martin's. Perhaps he'll be coming in from a night out in the early morning hours. Plant, we need to put a good team of the overnight boys outside that unit where he's supposed be shacking up with the lady, see what turns up. We need to get this man off the streets, and quickly. He's a madman, gentlemen, Agent Wills. Let's take this mumbling son of a bitch down, either in shackles, or in the back of the Medical Examiner's wagon."

Chapter Forty-one

Block dropped him off just after 3 a.m. in front of the building where he'd previously had his own unit, and where he'd been staying with Miss Charlene since last winter. Not waiting for him to enter the building, Block took off, tired and anxious to get to his own home. Mumbles caught a glimpse of the two men climbing out of a car in the parking lot to his rear, just barely. But he knew the stick-up boys were well known to await late-night revelers returning half-toasted to their homes and raze them with little effort.

He stepped into the hallway, quickly retrieved a key ring from a pocket, unlocked the metal slot to a mailbox, the one to the unit he'd previously lived in. He never received any mail when he lived in the unit and, still retaining the key, reasoned that the secured mailbox, deep-set in the wall and dark, would be a perfect place to hide an "emergency" weapon, a small .25 revolver which, even if the mailman were to open that particular box for some unknown reason, would probably not notice the gun shoved to the back of the orifice. And even if so, he believed, the mailmen who worked this route, of necessity a rough-and-tumble breed capable of parrying away miscreants set on relieving them of possible first-of-the-month checks, might see the gun and decide smartly that such was none of their business.

The plain-clothed, black, young officers, appearing not much unlike the denizens of this neighborhood, dashed over to the building mere seconds after Mumbles had entered, wanting to corral him, assure themselves that he was indeed their target, before he could enter the rear unit he reportedly occupied and then having access to his alleged arsenal and also requiring a warrant they did not possess to enter the unit.

The first young officer swung the entry door open with force, gun drawn. He was utterly shocked to peer down, for the mere seconds he had remaining, and see their target, crouched, a gun pointed up at him. Mumbles quickly squeezed off two rounds, one striking the officer in the neck, the other plowing harmlessly into the bulletproof vest the officer wore under a floral shirt. The officer threw one hand to the neck wound, the other bearing the gun wrapped around his abdomen.

In the early-morning silence, the gun blasts shattered the previous calm. The second officer put on his brakes, almost skidding in his black utility boots into the rear of his partner. Mumbles, still crouching, squeezed off two rounds into the upper legs of the second officer, then directed another shot to the man's head. That one missed, but two shots, one puncturing a thigh, the other shattered a kneecap, folded the second officer into an agonizing, whimpering figure. He tried to direct rounds of his own at the gunman, dressed as if he'd just come from some wedding reception. But the gunman dashed out of the doorway, over the first plainclothes officer, down the street and into the darkness.

Sirens could be heard wailing in the distance. Mumbles couldn't figure out just where to go, headed towards Shelter Road, where even at this early-morning hour a number of his underlings were sure to be out doing crack business. He was reassured when he saw Lil' Melvin, one of his "new crew young'uns," his posse occupying their regular corner. All among them reached for hidden weapons when Mumbles dashed down the street towards them, only releasing their grips when it became clear that the approaching form was that of their benefactor.

"Mums! Man, what's up?" Lil' Melvin said, sensing fear in the man who'd just recently moved him into the higher echelon of the Shelter Road Crew.

"M..M....mother...f...f...fuckers....s...s...shoot ...a..a...at...m..m...my...ass!"

"Who?" Lil' Melvin pulled his own gun, looking in the direction from which Mumbles had come.

Like a precision army, five other boys were suddenly surrounding Mumbles and Lil' Melvin, guns of various calibers and diverse deadliness at the ready.

"M...m....m....mi....mi......mmm...might...of be...be.......been...F...F...Five....O."

The guns were as quickly put away, as the distant police sirens grew closer.

"Here man!" Lil' Melvin said, handing Mumbles a ring of keys and cautiously stepping towards the darkened shadows of an apartment building with his crew. "You go hide out in my crib, Mumbles. One-o-two in that building across the street. You ain't shoot none of them cops, did you?"

"Y...y...yeah!"

"Shit! Go on, Mumbles! They be all over here in a few minutes, a cop got shot. We shutting down business for the night! I'm up in my girl's place man. You need to holla, hit me up on my cell!"

The sirens neared, and grew in number, in intensity. But Shelter Road was now so silent, so deserted, that the glistening street lights only cast the shadow of a lone, humongous rat on the asphalt, crossing a street even the rats normally avoided.

Chapter Forty-two

Everyone in Miss Charlene's building and for at least a mile around, knew exactly who was behind the shootings of two undercover police officers in the neighborhood, an incident which was leading the local news and had law enforcement officials of every hew and cry descending on the Southeast neighborhood where the shootings occurred, and in an equal presence from there to Shelter Road and Congress Park. The officers suffered serious injuries, but they would survive. And investigators were pulling over cars in the targeted communities, sweeping the streets, asking every breathing soul to name, and point out the whereabouts, of the gunman. But even though most all those questioned were quite familiar with the man police were seeking, investigators nary heard even a mumbling word leading to identifying and locating the gunman.

Miss Charlene and her children were particularly upset. It was certain that Mr. Mumbles could not return to their home in the near future, if ever. The children were near tears, but their mother was reduced to near hysterics. She'd cut back her drug use dramatically as Mumbles engaged her more and more in activities that sated her need for blood-curdling activities, and was even growing to have true feelings for the man. Convinced that she could, she had determined to herself to step the death march that is crack cocaine addiction. But on the Sunday afternoon following the shootings, she was again "fiending," pressed for a hit of crack.

Ellis was preparing to look at new apartments the coming week with Donna, but was at Linda's home in Barry Farm Sunday when he got the call from Block. Throughout his business area in Kenilworth, a good distance from the Southeast location of the earlier shootings, even Block's underlings were preparing for the police crackdown they knew would follow the shooting of two police officers. And even in this corner of the city flush up against the northeastern border with Maryland, word was already spreading that "that crazy-ass nigga Mumbles" was behind the assaults.

"We ought to kill that mother fucker ourselves," one Kenilworth drug dealer complained seriously. "Got Five-O all hot out this joint behind some simple shit!"

Block called Ellis immediately, agreed that, even though they knew within hours where Mumbles was hiding out, that he should be avoided at all costs.

"Shit! I just beat a goddamn beef!" Ellis said. "Now all I need is to be caught up with my boy, even just hollering at his ass, and they'll be sure to pop me for some shit that'll stick this time. Man! Mumbles one crazy mother fucker!"

"No shit, Sherlock," Block replied. "We was doing good copping together wholesale from them Spanish mother fuckers out in Hyattsville. But I know they'll cut me off now if they know I'm dealing with Mums. That's his fault, Ellis. I can't do nothing but cut him back. Know what I'm saying?"

"I hear ya."

Meanwhile, Mumbles was short on cash. He'd secreted a stash in Miss Charlene's, hidden so well, he believed, that unless he gave her specific instructions, even she would never be able to find the money. He figured he had well over a hundred thousand dollars amassed, but at the moment, he had but eighty dollars in his pocket. And the people with whom he was hiding, drug dealing young'uns and a mother addict, were only going to abide him but for so long without him at least putting up a good portion of the money needed for food.

He called Block, who immediately recognized the number in his caller ID and refused to answer.

Similar results were met when he tried calling Ellis. He tried both for a good while, before being convinced that the two would not take his call. And he couldn't blame either of them.

Lil' Melvin, whose apartment Mumbles was hiding out in, was putting his quite limited mental acumen to work. He knew Mumbles was a major player, was indeed the present source of most of the crack being peddled by the Shelter Road Crew. But Mumbles was in no position to leverage his considerable weight now. Lil' Melvin, pretty much Mumbles' key player on The Road since the slayings of his main boys the past New Years' Eve, figured he'd provide the needed legs for Mumbles in these trying times for his benefactor. And at a hefty cost. He would cater to Mumbles' every wish while the wanted man was ensconced in the second bedroom Lil' Melvin shared with a younger brother, in the apartment his mother had been renting for over a decade.

Lil' Melvin walked with a pronounced limp, the results of a shooting in the leg two years earlier, when he was only 20. Frail almost to the point of appearing anorexic, he was six-feet three-inches tall, and weighed just over 150 pounds. His dietary fare consisted mostly of potato chips, sodas, the occasional piece of fried chicken, and French fries smothered in ketchup. His mother, only 35, moved about the Shelter Road neighborhood much like the teenaged and twenty-something mothers she spent her days and evenings with; she'd been guided into the city's social support network by her own mother when giving birth to Melvin Jacks Jr. at 15, maneuvered her way into the system so astutely that, by the age of 24, she had attained doctor's analysis that she was disabled, garnering Supplement Security Income checks monthly, along with a continuous allotment of food stamps, child support payments, and, of course, undeclared regular income when her boys were old enough to work the streets.

She was also quite familiar with Mumbles, his drug dealing, and was more than willing to put him up for a while in her small, two-bedroom apartment. Initially she'd thought about "giving him some," reeling him in sexually and thus, she believed, gaining access to the extensive monies he was said to have stashed away. She even tried moving on him the first full night that he was in residence, but he was evidently distracted, only willing to sit with Lil' Melvin and plot a way to get his money, and a stash of drugs, left a few blocks away at Miss Charlene's.

After mulling over the situation for a day, Mumbles seemed to have finally come up with a plan. He wanted Lil' Melvin to be a key player, and feeling that he might not get his point across accurately through words, asked that the young man get him a notebook, that he might write out his instructions in more detailed. He wrote a most precise plan out, supplementing it with a few detailing words.

"M…Miss Ch…Charlene…y….y..you gi…give her…th…this…f…f…fifty..of..c..crack..a…after…y …you….. t..tell…… her…I….s….sent….you….t…to g…get…some…… of…m….m…my stuff…f…f.from h…h….her….b…bedroom," he instructed, while also writing out with precision where he'd stashed a bulk of money and cocaine, in the tiled ceiling of Miss Charlene's bedroom. "J…ju…..ju…just gi…give her…t…this…ru…rock…and……she…go…ri…right in…bathroom…and…..h…..…hit. You…g…get…in bedroom…c…close….d…door…s…so…kids…don't …s….see…you. Ge……ge…..get…..……….. G…Get up…on….b…bed….m….move…ceiling…r…right…o …over…top……….of…b…bed. Ba…..ba….bag of…m…m…money…coke….r….r…right…th…th….. there."

Lil' Melvin followed the instructions precisely, gaining entrance to Miss Charlene's after announcing he was on a mission for Mumbles. He was even more warmly received when he presented her with the hefty crack rock. The children, suspicious at first, were cursed into immediate submission by their mother, who admonished them with a string of expletives to leave her and her guest alone while she moved to the bathroom, and allowed him to retrieve "Mr. Mumbles' stuff" from the bedroom.

Even as Miss Charlene remained in the bathroom with the door secured, Lil' Melvin quickly found the backpack hidden in the ceiling exactly where Mumbles had told him it would be. Before leaving the bedroom, he opened the backpack, rummaged through the contents. There had to be thousands of dollars there, *and* at least a few thousand dollars worth of powdered cocaine!

Lil' Melvin gave serious thought to absconding with the entirety of the package. Hell, he thought, he wasn't living too good with his mother anyway, and with the package he now possessed, which Mumbles had entrusted him with, he could leave Miss Charlene's and go directly over to his girlfriend Cheyenne's house, miles away and in a part of the city in which he was little known and where even his mother knew not that he had acquaintances. Leaving the bedroom and the apartment, he seriously considered going up the street in the other direction from Shelter Road, board a Metrobus and leave the Southeast area for a long time, flush with cash and coke.

But even as he tried to make his way up the street, a warning voice in his head shouted out for him to do as he had been instructed. He was being foolish, he realized; Mumbles, suffering a loss of what had to be near a hundred thousand dollars, would do whatever it took to find Lil' Melvin, and the results would not be pretty. He realized that eventually he would be found, by a man whom it was rumored once blew a young man's brains all over a city street for making fun of his speech problem.

He made a U-turn, headed back towards his mother's house, back to give Mumbles his package.

"I ain't messing around with that fool," he said to himself, pulling the backpack tightly under his arm. "Man, fuck that shit!"

Chapter Forty-three

Donna Short was "fine," most young men in her Kenilworth neighborhood would agree. Compact at five-feet five-inches tall, the bulk of her small frame seemed equally distributed between a pair of generous breast which seemed to bulge skyward and a globular rear so perfectly rounded that a fortunate child could seek shelter under it during a summer thunderstorm. At 23 now she had but one child, one-year-old Lauren, fathered without question by Ellis Davidson. The girl was a female mirror of her tall, lanky father, with eyes much like his off grey ones, sculpted high cheekbones, and that white, glowing smile which, in her father's case, had virtually melted the panties off of targeted female conquests.

A most heated summer was drawing to a close in the District, and parents couldn't wait for the children, in particular the thousands of teenagers, to return to school. Some unfortunates no longer had this concern: Seventeen young men, and one young lady of middle school and high school age, had been killed during the summer, and under a president who'd taken office with a treasury depleted of all funds, the chronically underemployed and unemployed continued to scrapple, mostly against one another, for available crumbs. Donna, still in residence at the childhood home of her grandmother, was fortunate in that she was afforded luxuries others around her could only dream of, primarily by young men who sought her pleasures with monies gained for the most part through the selling of crack cocaine.

Damon Cantrell was her present suitor. At 30, he was a bit older than many of the young men who loitered about the Kenilworth community, selling crack and "hollering" at the many fresh young ladies who were seeking champagne lifestyles on coca cola budgets. Damon was born and raised in Kenilworth, but now lived in Palmer Park, Maryland in a comfortable home, courtesy the crack he supplied young men in Kenilworth which, a step into the District and along a main parkway, drew customers from far and wide. He was into Donna both emotionally and physically, having watched her mature as a teen and projecting correctly that she would be a head turner as a young adult. Ellis Davidson, a stranger to the neighborhood at the time, had beat him to the punch though, coming into the community with his cat eyes, basketball player height and well-appointed SUV to woo a 19-year-old Donna

Short, impregnate her, then as quickly move on to even more fertile grounds.

Although Ellis had "done right" by seeing after the baby girl Lauren, it was well known that he was a wholesale crack supplier in Southeast, miles away from the seamy streets of Northeast's Kenilworth. And because he had known and serious "backup" in the personage of the feared madman known as Mumbles, he was given a pass, as it were, when he occasionally visited Kenilworth. Many young men who'd met a "Kenilworth girl," perhaps at some city nightclub, had found swiftly, and sometimes violently, that it was quite perilous for a young man to visit the neighborhood and not be there to spend money on the community product. And though Ellis was perceived as a "bitch-type nigga," he was always evidently armed, and in addition was a close friend of "that crazy nigga" from Shelter Road, simply known as Mumbles.

No one, in the hardest regions of Northwest, Northeast, Southeast, Maryland or Virginia, wanted to chance a conflicting meet with the mumbling man.

Ellis was hard back on the scene as the summer ended, still desirous of a voluptuous young lady on his arm and, of more concern to him, in need of someone with a clear record and considerably decent credit score to secure the apartment he now so desperately needed and provide other "on paper" needs. He'd just secured another ride, and his grandmother had bucked at him putting the insurance in name at her address. In truth, he had no official address of his own.

His previous SUV, corralled by law enforcement officials outside the home of the late Reynaldo Hernandez-Rios, had sat in an impoundment lot for so long that the cost of retrieving it now surpassed the potential cost of getting a newer, fresher ride at a local auction. Indeed, the previous one was for sale at a Maryland police auction, but had been snapped up by a used car dealer long before Ellis could even locate it among the many area auto auction sites.

With the particularly well-conditioned Ford Explorer, Ellis was back in Kenilworth, ingratiating himself upon the extended Short clan by handing out ten and twenty-dollar bills to adults and children alike. He was especially generous to Sandra Short, the grandmother who "made a way out of no way," as she was heard to say often, to see that her grandchildren, and their children, had food and shelter.

A stooped, fragile woman, "Miss Sandra" to many, "Grandma" to a few, appeared weathered, as if the combined weight of seven children and five surviving grandchildren sat upon her weak shoulders every wakening hour. She was particularly fond of Ellis; he'd appeared regularly with monies for little Lauren, unlike the fathers of some of her other great-grandchildren, most of whom were either jailed, dead or addicted to some or another drug. She reached high to give him a hug when he arrived, fresh from his bout in the downtown court which everyone was well aware of.

"How you doing, son?" Miss Sandra said, taking him by the hand and leading him into a living room crowded with children, young men lounging, two young women. She looked to Donna, who was seated with Lauren between her legs, braiding the daughter's hair.

Across from her, silent and in an overstuffed chair most all within knew Miss Sandra reserved for herself, sat an older man Ellis did not recognize, but instinctively knew was someone he'd heard of vaguely: Damon Cantrell, Donna's current suitor. He greeted the familiar faces, went to Donna, bent and kissed her, then embraced his daughter.

"How my little baby girl?" he said, taking her aloft, turning towards Miss Sandra but speaking to the girl in his arms. "You know, I'm going to get us a place, then you and me and your mother can live together. You like that?"

"Yeah, daddy!" Lauren squealed. "And I hope before I have to go to school too. So I won't have to go to that ol' raggedy Shad Elementary down the street. Daddy, that school got *rats*!"

"Soon, baby girl. Soon."

"You serious?" Donna said, smiling broadly, then looking to Damon.

"I'm serious, baby," Ellis said, redeposited the girl before her mother.

Damon, all the time, had been "gritting" on Ellis, pinning him with a cold glare which communicated dislike, and disrespect. Ellis caught this, presented a slight smile accompanied by a glare which also sent a message of challenge to the older man.

"So," Damon said, returning the slight smile now, "I hear your boy Mumbles on the run from the Feds?"

This statement furthered the rift between the two, strangers until now, and was meant more so by Damon to indicate that he *knew* that Ellis's street power was gained more through Mumbles than through any "rep" Ellis had for himself and that, with Mumbles in hiding, Ellis had been virtually neutered among competing drug posses.

"He aiight," Ellis said, trying to make light of the comment. "He can handle and direct his crew from where he is."

It was like a boxing match, with words taking the place of fists. The others looked on in silent wonder as the two men sparred.

"Shooting police. Where he *is* 'fore long gonna be in the grave, my brother."

Hard left!

"He can take care of himself, dude. And anybody else come up against him."

Oooh! Shattering uppercut!

"That's in y'all old raggedy Southeast camp, fella. Y'all ain't up for the big stage."

Right hook to the jaw!

"It's all good, *old man*! Anyway, I'm just out here to pick up my girl and my daughter." He looked to Donna. "You ready?"

KNOCK OUT!

Damon nearly tore himself out of his seat, and this time really gritted, teeth gnashing, jaws tight. He looked to Donna as she gathered a purse and Lauren.

"So, it's like that, huh Donna? This fake-ass player come up in the joint and just gonna step with him like that?"

"Sorry Day-Day," Donna smiled, sashaying behind Ellis to the front door. "It was like that before you came out here. And he *is* my baby daddy. *See ya!*"

She waved a hand back to him as he floated back into the overstuffed chair. A few of the children covering leaked guffaws with palms, and Miss Sandra, grandma, moved to secure the door behind them. She then turned, moved over to her favorite chair and stood before Damon.

"You might as well unleash your ass outta my chair now," the old woman said. "And I really don't see no need for you to be around here no longer either."

He arose, moved slowly to the door, gritting now down on the children whose own grins up at him amounted to refrained debasement.

"Fuck it!" he blasted, wrenching the door open with force. "Y'all poverty-stricken mother fuckers ain't worth shit anyway!"

Chapter Forty-four

Mumbles was tired. Tired of hiding out in yet another decrepit apartment with streams of unkempt children, the begging addicts, the loose mother always coming on to him in exchange for some of the massive amount of money all knew he now had. He was particularly saddened that he could no longer engage Miss Charlene with regularity or, as he put it in a mind where the words flowed freely, "jump up and down in them guts."

He went into his stash, recounted it for at least the seventh time since Lil' Melvin had brought it to him, decided to send Lil' Melvin on another mission, to retrieve Miss Charlene. He penciled his wishes on a child's notebook, then doled out a small fortune, in the eyes of the recipients, to Lil' Melvin's kin, suggesting that they spend the day at the zoo, or even the Six Flags Amusement Park in Maryland. Mumbles also gave Lil' Melvin enough cocaine and addition dollars to hire a driver for the family. But certainly Lil' Melvin was *not* to give Miss Charlene any cocaine before delivering her to the Shelter Road apartment. If she were even to engage a single hit of the drug before leaving her own apartment, he well knew, she'd not leave her locked bathroom until every morsel of the drug was consumed.

He decided in the meantime that he had at least a half an hour, and that it would be safe to take a stroll to the supermarket a few blocks away from his Shelter Road hideout. But not ten minutes into his walk, "Five-O," in a marked cruiser, pulled up beside him. He saw them approaching out the corner of his eyes.

"Delano Johnson!" an officer called out a cruiser window, as the car inched along beside him.

Mumbles didn't even look in their direction, didn't flinch.

"Mumbles!" the officer tried again. Still, no response.

The driver parked the cruiser, and both officers got out and moved upon him just as he was about to enter the parking lot of a string of storefront establishments leading to the supermarket.

"Hold up there, buddy."

Still, no response. The closest officer to him reached out, took him by an arm and twisted him around.

"You hear us talking to you, fella?"

Mumbles, quite astutely, presented them with a smile, then put two fingers before his mouth, cupped an ear, smiled and shook his head. It appeared as if he were doing sign language, though none that would have stood muster at the city's Gallaudet University for the deaf and blind.

"What? You deef and dumb?" the second officer said, faking what he perceived as an old Southern drawl and grinning broadly.

Mumbles simply smiled, nodded, and again placed two fingers to his lips and cupped a hand over an ear.

The officers looked to one another, made some silent remarks to one another and then retreated back to their cruiser.

"He's not the one," the driving officer said, easing back behind the wheel. "The guy we're looking for has a speech problem, but he *can* talk and hear."

Mumbles stepped on towards the supermarket, chuckling to himself.

"D ……….d………..ddd…….dd…..….d…dumb-ass….m…m…m…mother…f….f…f…fuckers."

Chapter Forty-five

With Block as his new partner and partial financial benefactor, Ellis was quickly back in the game, resupplying the crew along Shelter Road, expanding to the boys along Mississippi Avenue, where Mumble's incursion the previous winter had effectively eliminated Fat Boy's leadership, his life as well, and created a vacuum among a cadre of street-level crack dealers lacking a true head. The products Block had access to, from a number of sources, were considered among the best quality available in the city, and the Block/Ellis confederation quickly dominated along Shelter Road, Mississippi Avenue as well as in Barry Farm and Northeast's Kenilworth community.

He put Donna and Lauren up in a quality suite at a downtown hotel, quite an expensive one at that, while he shuttled her around weekdays looking at apartments, in more stable sections of the District, and in nearby Maryland and Virginia. By the end of that summer he'd finally decided that the time was right for him to go in search of his newest offspring, and convinced Block to go with him to the Laurel apartment he and Mumbles had invaded to secure Ellis's bankroll from Shantelle. When she looked through the peephole and saw Ellis and Block standing in the hallway, rivulets of urine rolled uncontrollably down her legs.

"Can I help you?" she shouted out, trying to mask her voice.

"Come on, Shantelle. We know that's you. I just want to holler, baby. Don't leave me hanging, girl. Come on."

She put a shoulder to the door, again glanced out the peephole, paying particular attention to the men's beltlines, looking for some trace of a concealed weapon. But she knew both men well, particularly Ellis, and knew that if armed, the weapons would be secreted in the rear beltline. Suddenly aware of the warmth dribbling down her legs, she moved quickly back to the bathroom, took a washcloth and cleaned herself even as the echo of another knock came from the living room. She stumbled back to the front door, took a deep breath, eased it open.

"Hey, baby girl," Ellis smiled, bending to place an informal kiss on her cheek. "How you be, lady?"

"I'm...I'm okay," she said, backing away. "Hey Block."

"Wassup?"

Ellis looked around the place. It remained immaculate, though it was apparent the fine furnishings now suffered from a lack of regular dusting, polishing. Suddenly from a rear bedroom, little Ebony, a bit taller since Ellis had last seen her, strolled into the living room, cradling a fresh bundle, its chocolate head protruding from the blanket. She handed the baby up to her mother, looked with callous eyes to Ellis.

"Hi, Ellis," Ebony said, still glaring. "I saw on TV where they didn't get to keep you locked up. Maybe they'll have better luck next time."

Before he could respond, she poked lips out at him, swirled around and disappeared to the back.

Ellis laughed.

"Girl, that child of yours gonna give a man the blues some day, better bet it."

"She's just like her mother," Block said, taking a seat on an end of the massive sofa.

Shantelle rocked the baby lightly, moved to a seat across from Block. Ellis moved over to her, eased past her, sat close to her and peered at the baby.

"This my boy?" he asked, smiling at the child who looked directly at him with eyes which seemed as if inquiring as to whom he was looking at.

"This is Marquis," Shantelle said, "and, yes, he's yours."

Ellis slumped into himself somewhat, as if weakened, as if not knowing what to say, what to do. He hesitantly reached towards the blanketed infant.

"Can I...can I...hold him?"

Equally hesitant, she looked into his eyes first, then handed over the baby to him.

"Keep his head up," she instructed, then arose and moved towards the kitchen. "Block, you want a soda, a beer, some wine or a shot of Henny or something?"

"Yeah. Give me a shot of Henny with two rocks in the glass."

"You, E?"

"Naw," Ellis said. "I'm cool."

He was making faces at the baby, whose little laughter seemed to indicate he was enjoying the play of his father. It was as if Marquis knew the man holding him, something of a spiritual or blood connectivity. The eyes were somewhat like Ellis's also, though not grey, but a light, almost gold and silver mix.

She returned with drinks, put one before Block and sat with a wine glass of her own.

"E, that was cold the way you sent him and Mumbles out here, taking all the money like that," she complained, but couldn't help but smile at the father/son interplay taking place. "And that crazy ass Mums, I know it was his idea. Flattened two of my tires that cost me a hundred twenty dollar each."

Ellis looked up from the baby, between Block and Shantelle.

"You gotta be kidding me," he said. "Your ass moves, with all my money, and I spend 114 days, seven hours, twenty-two minutes locked the fuck down! The way you did it, no phone and shit, tells me you ain't have no intention of seeing me again. And look: Still wearing the mother fucking ring I spent four-thousand dollars on! You *must* be lunching, Shantelle! Lucky they ain't take more than that!"

She arose, moved over to him.

"Give me my baby. It's time for his nap anyway."

Reluctantly, he handed her the child. She moved to the rear, while Ellis leaned forward, looked to Block and shook his head.

"You believe that bitch? Got the nerve to complain about y'all getting *my* goddamn money from her, and for real, y'all hadn't seen her at the club and found out where her ass moved to, I'd probably still be in the joint. And you know if I hadn't got Mr. Macke on the case, my ass be down Petersburg or in Lewisburg or some shit, locked down till I'm an old ass nigga. That bitch is trippin'..."

Little Ebony pranced in from the rear, went into the kitchen after casting cold eyes at the two. She returned with a soda, popped the top and stood in the foyer leading to the living room.

"I know you ain't come back here trying to live with nobody," she said, looking directly to Ellis.

"Girl, don't nobody need to live with y'all. Especially not with you," Ellis said, smiling. "What you need is to have your dope fiend ass father here with you. Your mother tell me he used to whip that ass when you got smart with him. That's what you need."

"He ain't whipped nothing!" she said with a volume of sass. "And if he *is* a dope fiend, at least he don't be selling that mess to his own people. You just a dog, Ellis! A low-down dog! I hate you!"

Before he could even form an answer, she strutted back to the rear, and a bedroom door could be heard slamming.

"You see what I had to put up with," Ellis looked to Block, shaking his head.

"Girl too big for her britches," Block allowed. "But she sure 'nuff her mother's daughter, you can bet that."

"No shit."

Chapter Forty-six

In a mental description of what he was doing at the moment, Mumbles slapped with full force against the upturned rear of Miss Charlene as she knelt on the edge of the bed and the words "waxing that ass" played repeatedly through a mind overcome with excitement and a body intense with pleasure.

"W..w..wax.....th....th....that...a...a...ass!" he muttered, spurring himself on. "W..wu...wu...wax that ass!"

Miss Charlene leaned forward full on her elbows, looked back under herself to a vision of testicles and upper thighs slamming into her, as much a vision as she could gain between her own spread legs, the sagging breast leaping about, her toes curled just off the edge of the bed.

"M...M...Mumbles...w...w...waxin..t...t...that .....*ass*!" he sputtered vocally, then sputtered physically in a wrenching, forceful ejaculation into the upturned orifice which clasped then tighter upon him in a spasmodic climax all its own.

She cried out, a half whisper, a partial moan. Then he fell upon her, remaining inside her, resting partially on his own outstretched arms, partially on her back.

"D....d...d...*damn!*" he muttered, then rolled off her onto his back.

The evening was growing late, and Lil' Melvin, his mother and his siblings would probably be returning from their gifted outing soon. He was at a loss for words, more so than usual, took a hand, shook Miss Charlene's eyes open, pointed towards her clothes. She got the message, arose and grabbed them, pulled the bedroom door open and went into the nearby bathroom.

Dressed himself, he retrieved a shopping bag of snacks and foods favored by her children, particularly little Kanisha; he certainly missed the kids, who'd shown him rare love and provided a needed sweet spot in a life gone sour. Miss Charlene begged for coke and money, and, having sated himself now sexually, he gave her a generous piece of crack rock and fifty dollars. Now anxious to get home and put flame to the gifted drug, she slobbered a messy kiss on his mouth, tongue just lapping away, and quickly left the unit, tearing up the street in what for her was a speed walk, stick legs doing their darn best to hasten her arrival home.

Outside her own apartment building, plain clothed detectives had been "setting on" the neighborhood, secreted away in a nearby building's parking lot periodically, watching for Delano "Mumbles" Johnson while also observing the movements of the crack addict, Charlene Wright, whom a neighborhood informant had identified as having given shelter to Johnson prior to the police shootings. She'd been tailed for over a week, but for the past few days it was reasoned, almost correctly, that she only ventured out to secure fast food morsels for the children, and with regularity, to proceed on knees to earn a dose of crack cocaine. This very method of attaining her rock lately proved to the officers that she was no longer being provided the drug by her benefactor Mumbles. So the assigned detectives, in pairs of two working eight hour shifts, had almost given up on her leading them to their most wanted quarry.

Detective Nadine Perry, the female who'd put a "smack-down" on Miss Charlene in her hallway the previous winter, shook her partner, Detective Lucretia Ortiz, and nodded towards a weak-kneed Miss Charlene speed walking up the street.

"You see the way she's moving," Perry said, adjusting her gun and killing the plain car's engine and air conditioning. "That bitch looks like she really got paid. Let's tag her ass."

Before she was a step into her building, the two women were upon her like white on rice. She was taken aback, completely shocked and at first thought she was being robbed.

"What the fuck?" she blurted out, strong-armed up against the hallway wall. "I ain't got no goddamn money, bitches? Fuck y'all trying to raze a poor mother fucker for? Damn? Get off me!"

A badge was shoved before her eyes as she was quickly handcuffed.

"You don't remember me, huh bitch?" Perry asked, turning her around.

"Oh," Miss Charlene said, recognition setting in. "You the Five-O mother fucker kicked me in my ribs and shit. Now you all up in my face again. What the fuck you want?"

"Your boy Mumbles," the Hispanic officer said.

Mu…Mumbles? His ass ain't in my crib!"

Need to put flame to the crack was as pressing as it gets, possession nine-tenths of the need.

"Ain't nobody in there but my kids! You can come on back there with me and check if you want to. Ain't no goddamn Mumbles in my joint!"

"And ain't no mother in 'that joint' either," Ortiz said, frisking her and immediately finding the crack rock. From experience, both officers knew that a crack addict, if not keeping the rock palmed, would have it in a place, a secure pocket, where it would surely not be loss.

"We oughta run her ass in," Perry said, "and have them little crumb snatchers of yours put in foster care. You doing this rock, leaving them alone, judge surely will see that as child neglect."

Miss Charlene was mentally tortured, her crack rock now in the hands of law enforcement, and the threat of losing her children, though secondary to the crack concern, immediately pressing down upon her.

"You know where that guy Mumbles is," Ortiz smiled, holding a crack rock nearly the size of a quarter close before Miss Charlene's eyes. "You tell us where that nigga is, we give you back your rock, let you go on in there and blast away. No harm, no foul. We just want his ass."

Miss Charlene weighed concerns for Mumbles, but only for a few seconds. She desperately needed that blast.

"He down there off Shelter Road, 2940 Wade, Apartment 102, with that boy Lil' Melvin and his peeps. Been there since he shot them two cops here."

The cops looked at each other, smiled then communicated with their eyes and a nod. The Hispanic officer gave Miss Charlene back her crack rock, and the small measure of color she did have in her ashen face returned.

"Get your ass on home," Perry said. "And if that mother fucker ain't at the address you gave, we'll be back. For you and them raggedy-ass children of yours."

Miss Charlene stepped apace to her rear unit, turning quickly to issue a reassurance to the officers.

"He's there. Better bet it. Right now. And I laid something on his ass, so he's probably wore out, trying to get some sleep or some shit."

At the same time, Mumbles was greeting the returning occupants of the unit, and engaged in a previously arranged meeting with Lil' Melvin. There was a vacant unit just across the street, in the basement, which his street-level distributors had secured long ago for a base of operations. Management had attempted to shoo them away from the unit, B-1, with little success. Their maintenance crews had placed padlocks on the unit's door, and they were quickly battered off. After a second attempt, the maintenance men had been warned at the barrel of some most serious weapons to cease their efforts, and after reporting the threats back to management, company officials relented. After all, they reasoned, only a fool would have rented the basement unit anyway. So they turned the other cheek, in essence, giving over B-1 to the drug posse.

Mumbles had grown tired of the constant traffic in and out of Lil' Melvin's family unit, and the continuous begging of the mother, siblings, drunken uncle, dope fiend cousin, crack head aunt, children of every age and diverse states of health and most always complaining of hunger. He'd already gathered every item dear to him, pistols, the sawed-off shotgun, the backpack of money and coke, and readied to move out of the two-bedroom hurricane center, assured that the B-1 unit would be more private, more comfortable. He was entering the new location just as Detectives Perry and Ortiz, backed by what appeared to be the entirety of Seventh District uniformed and plain clothed officers, descended on 2940 Wade Place.

Depositing his goods in the basement unit, now fitted with a new lock by Lil' Melvin with one key given over to Mumbles, he watched from the hallway directly across from the police activity. Initially a squad of SWAT officers, automatic rifles preceding them, moved on the unit. The loud crash of a battering ram taking down the target apartment door, all around knew well, was followed by the "FLASH/BANG" of an incendiary device, familiar methodology to those in a community where such raids had occurred throughout the lifetimes of many.

Lil' Melvin's mother, a cousin, two of the cousin's crack head cohorts, and a stream of children were soon ushered out of the building. Numerous officers, both in uniform and plain clothes, moved into the apartment after SWAT team members came out shaking their heads, and the secondary teams moved from door-to-door, floor-to-floor, rousting residents and searching their individual units.

"That crack head bitch you had me go get for you must have snitched," Lil' Melvin said to Mumbles, both gathered behind the glass slot in the building's door, opposite the raided one.

"T..t…t..they…h…h…had….t…t…to….press …..h….her…..ass," Mumbles said, already forgiving

Miss Charlene for the evident betrayal. "G...g...girl was...p...p..pressed i...i....if she....sn...snitch."

They moved back to B-1, Mumbles using Lil' Melvin as an assistant in cutting up a fresh batch of cocaine. They discussed the new methodology in Mumbles' acquisition, through Block and by way of an intricate delivery system of both the money and the drugs. And he found the new location quite suitable, right off Shelter Road and, surprisingly, fitted by the boys of the posse to be quite comfortable.

"M....m...my...r....rides....they...gone." Mumbles said, knowing from Miss Charlene and others that his pick-up and Mercedes had long been towed by law enforcement officials. "N...n...now...I just...st...st...stay....he.....here...t...till...sh...sh..shit cool...d....down...and...j...j...just...b....b...bank."

Chapter Forty-seven

Ellis still hadn't forgiven Shantelle, blaming her exclusively for the torturous time he'd spent in jail. But now she had his baby, his only son, and even though he was now in residence and seriously involved again with Donna, he truly loved all of his children, and was especially committed to being a part of Marquis's life. He and Block were expanding their drug territories extensively, and were now making trips viewed as quite economical and with little risk to New York City, where they were acquiring volumes of cocaine at nearly half the price they'd been paying locally.

Without fail, he'd pull off the Baltimore-Washington Parkway at the Laurel exit when returning from New York, having already phoned Shantelle on the way home and telling her that he'd be stopping by to see little Marquis, perhaps bearing gifts for the baby and some minor funds for Shantelle. And again, Shantelle was falling for the man, the man whose engagement ring she refused to relinquish and wore now with renewed hopes. He was again "rolling," in her materialistic eye view, and having been used to his largess in the past, it was weighing on her quite heavily now, dependent only on her modest salary from the Department of Public Works.

As was common of her, she bounced ideas off of Lana, who was herself now seriously involved with a government contractor, twelve years her senior, but a man who could well afford the extensive "bling" of gold and platinum Lana so cherished. As a most torturous summer in the region drew to a close, they were spending a Saturday evening at Shantelle's, Lana having brought her own five-year-old Sherri over to play with her fast friend Ebony.

"Girl, just 'cause you still wearing his ring don't mean he's gonna come back all up in here with them wedding plans," Lana said, the Moet tickling her nose and her visionary fancy. "He asked your ass once then you kicked him to the curb, moved and shit! Didn't even leave a forwarding number! And, girl, you took all his ends and stuff, and right when he needed 'em? You know he still blames you for him having to spend them few months in jail. And now you all back into him and shit. Girl, you're tripping!"

Shantelle, savoring champagne from the second opened bottle, was well into mental revelry herself, plans for her and Ellis part emotional, but mostly a continuation of her misguided attempt at a method she perceived towards social climbing. Again she was in love with the man who had moved her off Shelter Road as a teen and showered her with things previously unimagined. But when his fortunes had fallen suddenly with the arrest, so too had her love for the man. And it didn't help that she was well aware of at least two of his other female relationships, with at least two children surely involved in those.

"But, you know," Shantelle said, leaning off the sofa to refill both their glasses, "he got his shit together now. And he just *so* fine! You gotta admit it. With them pretty-ass cat eyes! And...you know...the nigga *can* serve a sister, in more ways then one! Know what I'm saying?"

Laughter, and they leaned forth and exchanged a high-five.

"Yeah, I hear ya! I ain't gonna lie to you girl: That habit he got of licking his lips after his take a sip of something? Girl! He have me and a whole lot of other girls getting all hot and bothered behind that shit! I ain't lying!"

Ebony, Sherri and Derrick dashed through the living room, circled around the dinette, apparently engaged in a game of chase.

"Y'all stop running through this house!" both Shantelle and Lana shouted in unison, and the kids disappeared just as fast into the back.

"Yeah, his tall, fine ass used to be all that," Shantelle continued. "But I still got a beef with him about the way he sent Mumbles and Block out here, and Block talking about if I wasn't pregnant then, he would have bust a cap in my ass! And I don't know how he found out I was seeing Jay-Rock."

"Girl, I know," Lana admitted, the Moet loosening her tongue yet again. "You know how I gets sometimes, out there clubbing and shit. I told him, at Martin's right after he beat them charges. I'm sorry, but the nigga was going on about some shit, then I told him about Marquis and said he didn't have to worry, you had you another man, or something like that."

Shantelle glowered at her, the cozy warmth of friendship dimmed.

"You just don't know what to say out your mouth when you be drinking, Lana. Girl, sometimes I can't stand your hoing ass!"

Lana did a little head move, pirouetting head on her neck in a perceived sassy way of making a point. "Look at the pot calling the kettle black. 'Hoing ass?'

I ain't the one sitting here with one man's ring on her finger and another man's nasty-ass ring still around the bathtub."

"Oh, I *know* you didn't, girl! Only reason you ain't *got* no ring on your crusty finger is 'cause all them fools know they can get in them nasty drawers of yours and ain't gotta give up nothing but a 40-ounce at best! Girl, please…"

Lana merely laughed.

"That's cold, girl. You ain't gotta be all like that."

Shantelle feigned sorrow, lips cursed downwards and eyes dimmed. She hoisted her glass towards Lana as if in a toast.

"I'm sorry, girlfriend," Shantelle said, wiping an eye with the back of a hand as if swiping away a tear.

"Apology accepted," Lana said, clicking glasses with Shantelle.

Shantelle took a large swig, refilled her glass and the emptied one being held forth by Lana.

"But you still a stank ho!" Shantelle said, and the two both fell into a fit of laughter.

Chapter Forty-eight

Ellis was "feeling" the lifestyle exhibited in the immaculate brownstone on Adam Clayton Powell Boulevard in the heart of Harlem. On his third trip to New York City with Block on matters related to their business in D.C., he was given a tour of the four-story home by Rachelle, a statuesque young woman with jet black hair which cascaded down her back and shimmered like the nightlights at Time Square. She was either Dominique's wife or girlfriend; no one sought clarity on her specific distinction, and both Ellis and Block expressed to one another privately that it would not be cool to even inquire. She was definitely the woman of the house, both agreed, and so attractive and forthcoming that both of the Washington visitors were more anxious on visits to spend time with her than to negotiate bargain deals with Dominique.

They'd never been above the second floor on previous visits, and were there late August to conclude a deal which should have set them up in Washington well into the winter. Dominique, a swarthy, thin man of 30 whose racial identity baffled even those who'd known him for a while, placed the visitors in the hands of Rachelle while he left the immaculate home to do business elsewhere related to their pending transaction. He was gone for well over an hour, and Rachelle, ever the New York hostess, offered to show Ellis and Block around the upper reaches of the brownstone.

Four bedrooms abounded with four-poster beds, beds with canopies, lush Queen Anne chairs and embroidered settees which made them appear, to the D.C. natives, as if some custom fitted bordellos on movie sets. From the fourth-floor, Rachelle pulled back heavy drapes to display a view downtown across Central Park.

"This is our bedroom," Rachelle explained, squelching the wishes of both Ellis and Block that she was a sister, or at best a casual acquaintance, of Dominique's.

Upon his return, it only took another fifteen minutes before the deal was cut, the money given Dominique, the "package" handed over to Block and Ellis, tested for quality and secured. As was common on these trips, one of the men would have to take the bus back to D.C., a method they used to ensure that, should their car be pulled over on the New Jersey Turnpike (a common occurrence for a late model

Mercedes occupied by two black men, they believed) there would be no illegal "product" in the vehicle.

It was Block's turn to catch the bus with the package. He was dropped off at the Port Authority bus terminal, and Ellis quickly maneuvered familiar streets and made his way into and through the Holland Tunnel.

In three hours, he was rocking to a heavy rap beat, the car vibrating with its enhanced speaker system, as he cruised through Baltimore Harbor Tunnel. Less than twenty minutes later, and well before sundown, he reached the exit for Laurel, Maryland, slowed and moved onto the highway leading to Shantelle's apartment.

This time he'd failed to call, and apparently she was not expecting him. Surprised, she opened the door and stood partially barring his entrance. But he glanced over her shoulder as she stood silent, saw Lana joyously engaged with a young man setting beside her on the sofa, a young man who was a stranger to Ellis. But the bundle on his lap was no stranger: the young man, in pleasant play, was cuddling baby Marquis in his arms.

"E! Man, why you ain't call?" Shantelle said, stepping aside and admitting him.

The young man on the sofa smiled up to Ellis, who gritted in return.

"My cell wasn't charged," he said, looking between the young man and Lana, whose smile was just shouting out to him that there was something awkward about the present situation.

"Hey, Ellis!" Lana sang, and between the empty bottles on the coffee table and Shantelle and Lana's personae, he could tell the two were quite unstable, if not totally drunk.

But it was the man, holding *his son*, who particularly upset him.

Hesitantly, Shantelle introduced the two.

"Ellis, this is a friend of mine, Jay-Rock. Jay, Ellis."

They exchanged a common acknowledgement, pointing chins at one another and issuing a small shake of the head. Ellis stepped over to the sofa, sat and threw both arms back along the back length of the sofa, posturing as if he owned the place.

"I was just stopping by to see my baby boy there," he said, looking to the child in Jay-Rock's arm.

"He…he's….fine," Shantelle said, blanching visible and seeming at a loss for words.

Jay Rock looked into the baby's eyes, then directly into Ellis's.

"Yeah. Right," Jay Rock said. "I can see the resemblance."

He arose, glared at Shantelle and handed her the child.

"Yeah, I'm out," he continued, moving to the door. "Child support. Skank-ass ho."

He left in a huff that could be felt throughout the living room. Ebony, Sherri and Derrick came into the hallway from the rear bedrooms, but held ground there just close enough to see what was going on. With keen, childhood senses, all three knew that there was trouble brewing. Shantelle, appearing embarrassed, took a seat beside Lana and opposite Ellis, cradling the baby closely.

"Child support?" Ellis said, elbows on knees, leaning into the space between him, his son and Shantelle. "You had the nerve to tell that fool my son was *his*?"

Abruptly, Lana arose, moved to where the children were gathered.

"I'll be in the back with the children, y'all. Peace out!"

They sat for a moment, an embarrassing face presented by Shantelle, unspoken venom being spewed forth by Ellis.

"And the nigga was probably paying you too, huh?" he said finally. "Talk about double dipping. Damn! Girl, I ain't know you was so cold hearted! See, if I got with the brother...what's his name? Jay-Rock. See, if I got with him and gave him a little of his bank back, got my lawyer Mr. Macke on the case, I bet I could take your ass to court and get full custody of Marquis. I should do that shit too. Trifling-ass bitch ain't got no business with no more children. Especially my boy!"

"Ellis," she struggled for words. "E, don't talk like that. See, when me and Jay-Rock was together, it was like, it was over between us. And I didn't even know I was pregnant with Marquis then."

"Sh----it!"

"Naw! I'm serious! But, you know, with Ebony and Derrick, and now him," she looked down into the bundle in her arms, "and after I moved out here, the rent was way more than in Southeast, I needed to get a little more bank, know what I'm saying?"

"So, you tell that fool my baby's his, and then you hit him up for child support."

"It wasn't...well, yeah, like that, something like that."

"You ain't shit, Shantelle. I remember you used to have a little class about yourself."

"Baby, it's just...you know...shit just got so expensive over the last few years. I mean, damn! You know how much baby formula costs?"

"I shoot you money for Marquis! Now, that fast ass little Ebony, and Derrick, well, I know their father locked down, but shit, that ain't my problem."

Shantelle was reflective, and even as she directed warmth down unto her new baby, Ellis, out of experience with her, could see the wheels turning in her mind, scheming. He sat forward, awaiting the proposal he knew was forthcoming.

"Ellis? See, now you done blown my thing with Jay-Rock, and he was going to be kicking me a little something-something for the baby. Without that, man, it's gonna be hard on us out here. You know what the rent is on this joint? And gas for my ride?"

"Ain't nobody tell you to move out to this expensive ass joint anyway." Ellis was showing little

love. "And then you used *my* money to buy a fuckin'
Lexus? I'm gonna kick you some ends for Marquis,
but outside of that babe, you on your own."

He arose, moved to her and bent as if to deliver
a kiss. She smiled, turned a cheek towards his
approaching lips. But he planted a kiss on the
forehead of his baby boy, stood and cast glaring eyes
at her, turned and left the place.

Chapter Forty-nine

They were bringing in a rack of money to Mumbles. He'd been resupplied through an intricate web by Ellis and Block, and was now the sole provider of crack on Shelter Road, Mississippi Avenue, in the community of Valley Green a mile south of his headquarters, and even into a few regions of Prince George's County, Maryland. His minions, Lil' Melvin and seven others from the Shelter Road Crew, ensured that deliveries were made and monies returned with corporate precision, and Mumbles had little reason to leave B-1, now befitted with cable television, two large screen televisions, and varietal women whenever he so summoned one. Or two. Or three. Mumbles was growing extravagant, in both material and sexual tastes.

A few drug posses had tried to move in on the blossoming Shelter Road market, some from as nearby as Congress Park. The Road was drawing traffic from far and wide, from other parts of D.C., Maryland and Virginia. Any crack posse worth its salt just had to attempt the occupation of a corner along Shelter Road, or nearby thoroughfares leading there: Mississippi Avenue, Southern Avenue, The Savannahs (St., Pl., Terr.). But word of any attempted incursion reached the ears of Mumbles almost immediately, and in what was a rarity for him now, he'd secret out onto the dark streets, more often just after midnight, and always well armed, violently extinguish any potential competition. "Kill, Mumbles, Kill!" was so popular a phrase among youths in the Southeast region that one entrepreneurial spirit had put the slogan on hundreds of XXX tee-shirts, along with the image of a man in black, bearing two submachine guns, creeping down a dark city street.

The maker of the initial batch of shirts made a killing. For just over a month. Then his silkscreen machine, original shirt images, and a massive supply of XX, XXX, and XXXX shirts were taken from his storefront shop in a Southern Avenue center adjoining Melody's Bar-b-Que Rib Shack, and soon thereafter both crack and the popular tee-shirts were being sold along Shelter Road.

Detectives Nadine Perry and Lucretia Ortiz were still on the hunt for Delano Johnson, aka Mumbles. They were sure he remained somewhere in the far Southeast community. But trying to wrangle any information about him from even their most tested informants proved futile: no one was willing to even discuss Mumbles, and to even be seen speaking to the by-now well known undercover officers was most certainly asking to be marked for death.

It was a not too well kept secret in the Seventh D that Perry and Ortiz were lovers. With the recent legalization of same-sex marriage in the District, the two were planning on an elaborate "coming out," although they'd never hidden their sexual orientation. The planned event though would be a wedding and reception where all their friends and colleagues were invited. Then they were planning to take a well-deserved period off from the job which was weighing so heavily on their private lives that they feared that recent, testy exchanges between them was putting a crimp in a relationship that had blossomed over 12 years. Ridding the Southeast landscape of Delano "Mumbles" Johnson and his murderous organization would go a long way in allowing the two to settle into a more reasonably sane existence. They were determined to close the book on him and at least his Shelter Road posse before winter set in.

They just *knew* he was being protected in someone's apartment either in the Shelter Road area or along nearby Mississippi Avenue. His fingerprints were on at least three shootings that had occurred as summer drew to a close, and the kids running around in "Kill Mumbles Kill" tee-shirts was as if the drug boys were rubbing it in the faces of law enforcement officials that Mumbles was so elusive even trained detectives were falling on their faces in pursuit of him.

Both Perry and Ortiz were particularly attractive women, both 35, and although none would have voiced such a concern, many of their male colleagues were none too pleased that the two preferred one another and brushed off the many come-ons from male officers which skirted the realm of sexual harassment. Ranking officers had even worked behind the scenes to separate the two in the workplace, but in a city teeming with women activists and, to be sure, the recent legalization of same-sex unions, these attempts might have jeopardized the hard-earned rankings of the disgruntled officials. So not only were the two abided, but were treated with particular respect by other officials in the Metropolitan Police Department.

They pulled down Shelter Road all of a sudden early Tuesday evening, the last week of the summer before schools restarted and a week preceding the Labor Day holiday and the first of the month, considered by some a holiday in and of itself with the influx of public assistance monies, food stamps, and general revelry in some communities.

"Coming down!" a series of shout-outs alerted drug dealers, drinkers and general ne'er do wells of the approach of known police officials.

"Five-O," was hollered by a few in a similar vein.

Ortiz and Perry smiled as they watched a few known dealers lower their heads and stroll of slowly towards the back of apartment buildings.

"I'm not about chasing any of these fools," Ortiz said, seated in the passenger's seat of the unmarked vehicle.

"Naw," Perry responded, scanning the faces of a league of preteens aligning the curbs, peering at them and many sporting "Kill, Mumbles, Kill" tee-shirts. "But we see that kid Lil' Melvin, get on his ass."

"Agreed."

Lil' Melvin, even as the officers were rounding the corner, had already disappeared into the apartment building where Mumbles was locked away in his B-1 hideout, a local "head nurse" on her knees serving him for a minor dose of crack rock. Mumbles didn't flinch, nor did the head nurse, when Lil' Melvin worked a series of recently installed deadbolt locks, for which only he and Mumbles had keys. Lil' Melvin stepped across the spacious front room to where Mumbles was leaned back on a sofa, stood above the pair and delivered his message.

"Five-O out that joint, Mums," he said. "Them two dyke bitches always be up in a nigga's grill like that. They put the word out they gonna mess up our sells out on Shelter and Mississippi until somebody snitch about where you is."

"F...f....fuck......aw....aw...all...uh...of..'em. .....ai....ai...ain't...n....n....nobody...'b...'...'bout.... to...t.....t.....tell...uh....uh....about.....about........... about...th...th...th...this....p...p...place....l...l...'less they wanna...g....g...get a cap...b...b...b...bust in....t...t..they...a...a...ass."

He threw his head back, clenched eyes and teeth and cupped the woman's head, thrusting to meet her bobbing deliverance. Lil' Melvin smiled, sensing that Mumbles was about to reach the penultimate of enjoyment. He recognized Tondra even from the back of her head, had experienced her himself on a number of occasions, and stepped back to allow his mentor to enjoy the explosive outcome. He placed a hand down the front of his sagging jeans, fondling himself, not having planned on this but now most surely aroused.

He was next.

Outside, Perry and Ortiz were just before the building, outside the car now and making small talk with the children playfully gathered around them.

"Hi, baby," Perry said, kneeling before a seven-year-old. "What's your name?"

"LaShonda," the tot said, twisting about from side to side.

"You live in that building?" Perry asked, pointing to the three-story unit behind them.

"Yep. Me and my mother and my brother and sister and my brother's boyfriend sometimes."

She nodded to a group of other children beginning to gather around them.

"What's up with those tee-shirts?" Perry said, pointing to three teenaged girls wearing the "Kill, Mumbles, Kill" XXX tees.

"You know what's up with them," a fresh faced girl of about 14 said, grabbing LaShonda by the hand and stepping away. "People trying to get paid around this joint. Ain't no jobs out this bitch! At least Mumbles got some work for the young'uns around here."

"Yeah," a series of low-keyed voices agreed.

Perry stood, preparing for the debasement she knew from experience was forthcoming.

"By selling your mother, your cousin, your brother, crack?" she shouted.

"Lady, fuck you!" the 14-year-old shot back. "And that Mexican bitch of yours, standing over there looking like a fool! I bet both of y'all dykes."

Laughter rang out, as some kids wandered over as a tumult seemed to be developing, while older teens, leery and apparently upset that their business was being put on hold, loitered around the hoods of cars and the deserted, curbside brown-bagged 40-ounces.

Ortiz moved up to Perry, who appeared as if she were about to step after the mouthy teenaged girl.

"It's not worth it, baby," Ortiz whispered into Perry's ear, motioned her back towards their vehicle.

"Anybody know where Mumbles is hiding out here," Perry shouted over a shoulder, "you'd better holla! Or we're gonna come around here every five, ten minutes and just fuck up all your tacky business out here! Hear me? Y'all hear me? And you can count on that!"

They got into the cruiser, slowly rolled out of the area and towards Mississippi Avenue, where they'd further disrupt business in a search for the evasive Mumbles.

Meanwhile, Mumbles was trying to catch his breath, having denied Tondra the promised crack rock until she completed a similar deliverance upon Lil' Melvin.

"Y'all some cold mother fuckers," Tondra complained, anticipation of the crack rock most acute after finishing with Mumbles. "You said after I did you Mums, I could get me a nice rock and roll out."

Mumbles stood, handed a small rock sack to Lil' Melvin, went into a rear room and closed the door. Lil' Melvin, all smiles, freed himself from his pants, sat with them around his ankles on the edge of the sofa where Mumbles had just been.

"Y'all some cold mother fuckers," Tondra repeated her complaint, wiped her mouth on a tattered sleeve for the second time, eased to her knees between Lil' Melvin's legs and went to work once again.

Chapter Fifty

He was at the supermarket, a trip he'd promised Donna he'd make after ensuring a few deliveries were made and before coming home for the holiday weekend. He'd also promised to stop by Discount Wholesalers and secure school uniforms for their daughter Lauren, had already made that trip, and with a list in hand, entered the supermarket a few blocks from his old Shelter Road haunts. The bedraggled man who approached him was visibly a crack addict, probably a customer down his own extended delivery system, and Ellis immediately knew what the man wanted upon his approach.

"You paying cash for your food, main man?" the addict asked, and Ellis, quite familiar with the forming ploy, made up his mind then to assist the struggling crack fiend.

"Yeah, my man," Ellis said. "What you want: Fifty on a hundred?"

"Whatever you get, main man," the addict responded. "I'll pay the whole bill for half in cash."

Usually Ellis would reject such an offer; he'd been approached numerous times before by an addict proffering their Electronic Benefits Transfer Card, or EBT, which was each month loaded electronically with funds to buy foods and foods only, in exchange for half his food's cost in cash. He reasoned that many of the addicts, mostly female, were stealing food from the mouths of children, though he'd vehemently deny that his very business, the selling of crack cocaine, was the prime contributing factor to this ruse. But this time it was a disheveled man, a seasoned crack addict he believed, and hell, if he didn't save fifty percent on his own purchase, then someone else surely would. And the man assured him that he had at least two-hundred dollars on his card, having just received his first-of-the-month allotment.

Ellis agreed to meet the man at the cash register, got a shopping cart and began to do more shopping than he'd intended to. He had no way of knowing that Detectives Perry and Ortiz had formulated this particular ruse, had been tailing him since he'd made a few assumed surreptitious deliveries of powdered cocaine to some mid-level minions and, actually wanting to corral Mumbles more so, set up the EBT-armed "addict" and pointed Ellis out in particular. They were a distance across the supermarket parking lot, watching the transaction through binoculars. Once they received assurance through the hidden microphone on the EBT bearer, they moved separately into the supermarket, shopping themselves and situating themselves to visually observe Ellis and the "addict" conduct the EBT transaction at the cash register.

Once that act was completed, the detectives were outside the store to witness Ellis pass seventy-dollars (for his $140.00 grocery bill) to the addict. They then descend on him with guns drawn.

"Alright! Grab the wall!" Ortiz instructed a shocked Ellis, who immediately complied as Perry instructed the addict in a hushed voice to move on.

"This is entrapment like a mother fucker," Ellis complained as he was frisked and handcuffed. "My lawyer gonna have a field day with y'all asses. And you better bet we gonna sue the fuck out of you, too."

"Shut the fuck up!" Perry said, twisting him around and grabbing him by one elbow as Ortiz grabbed the other.

A crowd was gathering, and Perry, with a broad grin, looked to the crowd and nodded to the large cart of food Ellis was leaving.

"This boy won't be needing that food where he's going," she shouted, looking with a broad grin to the crowd. "Y'all split that shit up!"

Like black ants on a spilled splotch of the sweetest ice cream, the standers-by were upon the food cart in a fevered frenzy. Steaks were being twisted between the competing hands of shoppers who'd left small bags of their own meager victuals aside for the abundant take, and before Perry and Ortiz could even get Ellis into their car, the ever present uniformed officers from inside the store were out upon the crowd in attempts to prevent a riot.

Chapter Fifty-one

Mumbles knew that his friend Ellis had been arrested even before he was booked into the Seventh District police substation. And he was worried that Ellis had weakened; he'd noticed a particular weakening of his never strong personae upon his beating of the Hernandez-Rios associated drug charges, and felt that, even though their ties went back to childhood, he was not going to chance his own incarceration, on murder charges at that, to the whims of Ellis's refusal to "snitch."

"M….m….my……b……… boy….he….he….he gotta…g…g…g…go," Mumbles told Lil' Melvin and four young drug associates. "H…h….h…he g…g…get……….o………o……o…………. over…the j….j..jail…w…w…we…get….a….a….couple….o… of our…..f…f…friends…in….there…put……….. him away….l….l…like…t…t…that."

The young men gathered were all in agreement.

"You know he gonna snitch," Sho Breeze, a 17-year-old dealer, said. "Sorry Mums, but I always said your boy was a bitch-ass nigga. You know, business is business, man. His ass gotta be silenced."

"No joke," Lil' Melvin said.

"And just in case," Donnie, a 15-year-old added, "we need to move you and the operations out of here. Like, maybe across Southern Avenue into Maryland or some shit."

"R...r...r..right."

"I say we don't wait till he in the joint," Lil' Melvin said. "It might take a week or two to get somebody to shank his ass. And anyway, he probably already snitching up there at Seven D, with his bitch ass."

"We get that lawyer Mr. Alphonse to bail him out right now," Sho Breeze said. "We all throw in a little bank, get his ass out with the quickness, blow his ass away soon as he come home."

"Y...y...yeah. Thats...even....b...b...better."

There was a general agreement, and Lil' Melvin and Sho Breeze were dispatched the following day to the Southern Maryland office of Attorney Alphonse Riley.

"Mr. Alphonse," as he was known to his extensive string of criminal defense patrons, was a powdered cocaine addict. Had been for over fifteen years. At 55, he maintained a considerably prosperous legal practice by catering to the family and friends of drug miscreants throughout the Maryland and D.C. region. He still maintained a pretty astute legal mind, but most all of his clients, and a few prosecutors and judges, knew that Alphonse Riley was fighting a drug problem all his own. Or not fighting it, depending on who you asked.

When he arrived at court Tuesday morning (arraignments having been delayed Monday due to the Labor Day holiday), he stepped forth when the judge called for any legal representation for Ellis Davidson. Surprised, Ellis looked to Donna, who shook her head to indicate she'd not put any money out for an attorney. Then the attorney identified himself, and Ellis immediately recognized the name: Mr. Alphonse, he realized, had been dispatched to represent him. And that could only mean one thing: He was going to certainly be freed, and just as assuredly silenced.

"I don't want him!" Ellis shouted to the judge when a smiling Mr. Alphonse stepped to his side. "I refuse release! I want to wait for my trial!"

A brief bench exchange between the judge, Mr. Alphonse and the district attorney took place, while Ellis scanned the courtroom, comforted by Donna's presence, but almost floored when he saw the back of a young man, he could have sworn it was Lil' Melvin from Shelter Road, leave the courtroom just after his outburst.

"Mr. Davidson will be remanded to pretrial confinement, as requested," the judge said when the bench conference ended. But before the marshals could usher him away, Mr. Alphonse whispered into his ear.

"You're not going to be any safer over in the jail," Mr. Alphonse whispered, and handed him a business card. "You keep your trap shut, you hear? And then give me a call when you want to squelch this mess."

Chapter Fifty-two

He was late on his child support payments, and Shantelle was seeking legal advice to have him forced to pay, and to have payments for little Marquis increased. She had no way of knowing that Ellis was already in jail, and was completely taken by surprise when, returning from work and from picking up little Marquis, Ebony and Derrick from her mother's, a team of masked men accosted her as she climbed out of her Lexus in the Laurel parking lot. She screamed, but was quickly silenced by the gloved hand of one of the gunmen. Ebony let out a yell, little Derrick began sobbing uncontrollably, and the men smacked Shantelle's hand away when she offered up her purse in perceived acquiescence.

But that was not what they wanted.

One man undid the child safety seat Marquis was belted into, grabbed the baby and tore off to a waiting car with him, speeding off into the night even as potential rescuers were descending on the distraught mother and her remaining children.

"They got my baby!" she cried, stumbling up the parking lot in the direction the marauders had taken. "They got my baby!"

* * *

Mumbles loved children. He even chanced arrest to ensure that Kanisha, Michael, Ricky and Patrania, Miss Charlene's children, had food and, for Kanisha, a uniform for the new school year. But he also knew that Ellis also loved his offspring, in particular his first boy, little Marquis. And activities by law enforcement officials, an unsuccessful raid on B-I (they'd already relocated to Maryland) gave indication that Ellis, now in protective custody, was, in the analysis of his minions, "snitching like a big dog."

So the taking of Marquis was considered to be a most effective way of silencing him. Mumbles had even come to an agreement with Block, and had received an almost threatening message from NYC's Dominique, that the silencing of Ellis by the D.C. boys was paramount, or it was hinted, in no uncertain terms, that the entirety of the D.C. connection would be permanently silenced. Even Mumbles, in his most heightened state of bravado, didn't want to chance a violent confrontation with Dominique and his army.

It didn't take law enforcement officials but a brief interview with the distraught mother to get the name of the baby's father and link him to the Southeast drug cartel. And although officials sought to keep word of the abduction from Ellis, Shantelle called Lana who called a friend who knew Ellis's current girlfriend, Donna, who immediately made arrangements to visit Ellis and inform him of the abduction. Ellis, who'd been giving bits and pieces of the drug operation to investigators, suddenly shut up tight as a clam.

They threatened to remove him from close confinement and place him with the general population at the D.C. Central Detention Facility, to no avail. He was apparently willing to give his own life, if it would save that of his only son. Detectives Perry and Ortiz, who had taken the lead on the case and were anxiously seeking the whereabouts of Mumbles, sat with Ellis in a close conference room at the jail in a final attempt to get some critical information.

"If you have any idea where they moved off to from down Shelter Road," Perry was pressing into him, "it might be where they're keeping your baby. Can't you think of anywhere they'd move off to, some place familiar, and nearby, perhaps in Valley Green or Congress Park or somewhere?"

Ellis, still completely distraught over Marquis, merely shook his head.

"They wouldn't move to Congress Park," he said. "They got a beef with them boys go way back, though they do supply some of the young'uns down that way. I don't know..."

"What about over the line, in Hillcrest Heights, Eastover, that region?" Ortiz asked. "We heard that Lil Milton has a cousin out there near Iverson, or over off Branch Avenue. Any places out there they might have moved their camp to?"

"Shit!" he blurted, eyes welling with tears. "I told you I don't know! Damn!"

The officers leaned back, relaxed, allowed him a chance to revisit his thoughts, to perhaps lead the conversation.

"But I know y'all can do something to find my boy," he said finally. "Hell. Y'all find him, I swear, I'll open up about a whole lot of shit y'all don't know."

"Like you and Block Thurman's New York connection?" Ortiz said. "We know all about that. Our federal friends are not too far away from having enough to get your friends Dominique and Rachelle. And you *know* they're going to blame the D.C.

connection, Ellis. Anyway you look at it, your ass is grass."

Ellis pondered this for a moment, reflecting on the beautiful Rachelle, and the pleasant Dominique. He'd always sensed that they were not to be toyed with, and never had any plans to. As long as he and Block kept their business on the up-and-up, he thought, the NYC connection was quite lucrative and posed little danger.

"I don't know what y'all talking about," he said finally. "I think y'all oughta be concentrating on finding out where them fools got my son. And, like I say, y'all get him back, then I swear I have a whole lot of stuff y'all might be interested in."

Chapter Fifty-three

Just to look at Rachelle, one would think she was a former super model, a bit beyond her runway years at perhaps 30, but an even more striking and desirable woman and progressively more appealing as she graciously matured. But among her few associates in America, only Dominique knew that she was truly one of the most deadly persons engaged in the sordid international drug trade. She was a professionally trained killer, an assassin only available to the highest level drug merchants, and only called upon, at a quite exorbitant price, to eradicate those deemed a most serious threat to some measure of one of many billion dollar drug cartels.

Trained in a number of martial arts since a child, Rachelle had studied mysticism in the Far East, deadly combat techniques in South Korea and Japan, studied alchemy in the halls of some private institutions, received weapons training from a family friend who'd retired from a number of international spy agencies. Her parents were themselves operatives of two CIA-type organizations, world travelers, and had given their tacit approval when, at quite a young age, Rachelle had found her way into the services of South American drug merchants for monies rivaling the incomes of many of America's corporate leaders.

She was deadly, to say the least. But only Dominique, and a few foreign associates who could call on her, knew that the exceptional beauty could strike with the deadliness of a cobra.

The problem in D.C. was one she considered well below her pay grade: She had received $300,000 cash to complete her most recent "elimination," a quick, deadly silencing of a former high-level operative in the Maldivian Consortium who'd left the organization after it was discovered that he'd, over 10 years, secreted away nearly a billion dollars in joint Consortium funds in a host of Swiss and Cayman Islands accounts.

The way in which she'd eliminated this "problem" was now spoken of with high admiration by some in the Gulf, Tijuana, Sinaloa, and Miami cartels. Rachelle had patiently ensured that she had a first-class seat opposite the target on a London-Washington Dulles flight, engaged him in pleasant conversation and, minutes before landing and without the slightest hint to the twelve other first-class passengers, planted a most sensuous kiss on the target, delivering at the same time three deadly but unobtrusive blows to vital organs of the man, then returned to her seat, secured her seatbelt and prepared for landing.

When the target didn't arise to leave the plane, the flight crew called medics, who thought the man appeared to have suffered some major medical trauma. It was days before a medical examiner discovered that he had been efficiently slain, midflight, and every first-class passenger but one was tracked down and questioned.

The beautiful woman who had befriended the decedent, as reported by all other first-class passengers, would never be found. Even the passport she'd used was later discovered to have been so professionally faked that it hadn't even raised any concerns either in Great Britain or America.

Now she was being asked to carry out an erasure on the homeland, and Rachelle had to be carefully convinced that the operation was in the best interest of both she and Dominique's business, and further the pipeline to South America which guaranteed with efficient regularity that the two continued amassing wealth beyond imagination. She protested for only a few minutes with their Medellin associate, who was in NYC on a rare visit specifically to address the "D.C. problem."

"The Mumbles fellow must go," Mr. Medellin said, seated in the Harlem brownstone on a crisp, fall afternoon. "He has taken the business as some sort of self-aggrandizing operation. The tee-shirts, the self-proclamations upon killings. He must go, and by extension his associate with the block head, and the fellow Ellis who is even now speaking to the police in an effort to save his son."

Rachelle finally relented.

"I see," she said, standing and looking out the floor-to-ceiling window upon an active Adam Clayton Powell Boulevard. She turned to Dominique. "I'll leave for Washington first thing in the morning. Two days of surveillance, four hours to complete the task. You can still get the theatre tickets for next Friday."

She smiled at Mr. Medellin, escorted him to the door.

"Don't worry, my friend," she said, kissing him lightly on a cheek. "We'll have a new operation up and running in D.C. before the end of the month."

Chapter Fifty-four

Rather than let the small ranch house go into foreclosure, Shelly and Dean White agreed to rent it out to the young woman from the District, who, along with her three children, would move into the Hillcrest Heights, Maryland home before winter set in. They were initially leery of renting their second "fixer-upper" home to someone apparently seeking to escape the trials of life in the far Southeast section of the city, particularly a young, black single mother. But the elderly couple, having long since moved well away from the city into a still rural part of Southern Maryland, met with the young mother and agreed that she seemed, well, if not a preferred Christian, at least a non-drinking, non-drugging and caring mother. They had their lawyer draft a one-year lease for Shirley Thurman, and were there providing "guidance" when the family moved in, though in truth, the homeowners were simply being nosey, believing they were able to gauge the prospects of renters' ability to maintain their property by observing the furniture, the accoutrements, even the car, that the renters bought into their home or used in their move to the suburbs.

Miss Thurman and her three children met with their approval when they made the move in late October. But one of the men assisting in the move, the brother with the wide head bordering on deformity and introduced as Miss Thurman's younger brother, did cause the White's to give the family a more critical overview.

The real estate market had been in decline precariously over the past five years, the Whites were acutely aware of this. And the Hillcrest Heights home, long in the family, was collateral for yet a third home equity loan, moneys needed by the Whites for the very upkeep of their Southern Maryland property. The Hillcrest Heights home was now valued at less than the value of the loan, and rather than have the bank take it for the delinquency currently existing, they decided the best thing to do was to rent it out, at a considerably high monthly rate, if they were even to keep the "investment property." Miss Thurman came forth readily with the $4000.00, which included the first and last month's rent, and the Whites took that as a reassurance that the black woman could well afford and maintain their investment property.

The man Dean White had overheard being called "Block," however, for some reason caused to White's to belatedly second guess themselves.

Assured by some of their remaining historic (and white) neighbors in the Hillcrest Heights neighborhood that they would keep an eye on the newcomers, the Whites returned to their primary residence hard on the Chesapeake Bay, financially comforted by the rental dollars and set to wile away their remaining years as absentee landlords and, for Dean, as a part-time waterman, setting out and retrieving pots which captured bundles of the Bay's blue crabs cherished by both Marylanders and city dwellers. They would have been shocked when, as winter set in, the black woman and her children were joined in the home by a gang of black youths, some in their teens, a few a bit older, and motor traffic around the house increased so dramatically that the historic residents were themselves hurrying to find homes in other quarters of Prince George's County.

Moving over from a two-bedroom apartment in nearby Indian Head, Maryland, Mumbles felt that the comfortable home was well suited to their needs, and "clean" where any law enforcement officials were concerned. Shortly after Shirley Thurman had been given $10,000 by her brother and Mumbles to secure the home, she and her children graciously returned to a small home brother Block, through a female friend, had acquired in the Southeast section of D.C. These familiar grounds were much more appealing to

Shirley and her children, and the sister asked no questions when a number of SUVs arrived at the Maryland home one Saturday morning, along with a rental van, full of young men from the city ready to move her back to D.C., and at the same time move Mumbles, Block and some of their underlings in.

They had erased their path out of Shelter Road, although business still boomed there for them. And having secured the services of Tondra, Mumble's now favored head nurse, to look after the infant child of Ellis's they still held on to as insurance, the Shelter Road Crew felt it had established itself as a major player in the D.C. region's drug distribution game. Block and Mumbles continued getting their key supply through the NYC pipeline, but little did they know that, as another holiday season approached, arrangements were being made to completely eradicate the current Shelter Road Crew, the posse in Kenilworth supplied by Block, and most all present connections between D.C., Dominique and Rachelle.

Chapter Fifty-five

Under vehement protest by the accused, all charges were dropped against Ellis, even though he'd languished in confinement and under extensive judicial pressure for well over a month. Now he was back into his rental unit with Donna, still in contact with Shantelle over their missing son, but quite fearful of taking to the streets of Southeast in search of information which might lead him to the abducted Marquis. Mumbles and Block had spoken to him briefly, but even through those cold conversations, Ellis was now quite unsure that he could even trust his childhood friends. He was quite afraid, and without the influx of narcodollars, even his present arrangement with Donna and his daughter Lauren was growing questionable. He languished in the apartment, afraid to venture out, and not sure who might eventually venture in.

Rachelle knew exactly where Ellis was located. She knew also of the Hillcrest Heights home Block, Mumbles, Lil' Melvin and their crew presumed was a safe, secret and secure location. In the guise of a corporate executive in the city on extended business,

Rachelle came into the District and took up residence in the Capitol Hill Grand Regency Hotel, an expensive, boutique facility just a few blocks from the U.S. Capitol building which offered suites, complete with kitchenettes and full living quarters, for $1700.00 weekly.   She booked a suite for a week, quite sure that she'd have completed her diverse tasks and be on the Amtrak Acela back to New York City well before the Thanksgiving holiday.

For reasons not fully understood by either Rachelle or Dominique, Ellis was to be spared. She'd argued in defense of him, reasoning that she'd seen something in the tall young man on a few of his visits to New York which somehow convinced her that his considerably young life could be spared, redirected, and at no threat to either the New York connection nor their confederates further south. And admittedly his three children had played into the equation, in Rachelle's mind. She was very upset at those who'd taken his new baby in an attempt to weigh some kind of leverage in the drug distribution fiasco that was D.C.'s current situation, and Rachelle was first and foremost going to deliver a deadly, agonizing blow to those who still held the baby boy as some cruel sort of bargaining chip.

With little effort, she located the Hillcrest Heights home being used by the Shelter Road Crew, the apartment where Block lived with his main lady friend and the one where Ellis and Donna stayed. But her plan called for an erasure from the bottom up, eliminating quickly and efficiently the mid-level dealers along Shelter Road, Mississippi Avenue, in the Barry Farm and Kenilworth neighborhoods, all recipients of their cocaine packages from the Block/Mumbles confederation.

A contact in Alexandria, Virginia, an illegal resident with documentation which would have passed the muster of Homeland Security officials, rented her a fine, luxury sedan. She'd use this the entirety of her operation, without having to have any concerns about the car being even returned to the rental agency. It would be burned after use, completely eradicating any fiber evidence she might have carelessly left in it and probably chalked up by officials as stolen by some unknown culprit.

Secondly, she had another contact from the Adams Morgan section of Washington acquire for her a perfectly fitting uniform from one of the region's cable television companies, and two laminated, magnetic logos from the same cable business, which would be used later, affixed to the sides of the rental car. She'd brought no weapons with her from New York to D.C., and this critical need was met by a long retired intelligence agent with close ties to her family.

She secured all of the weapons and explosive ordnance she'd need from him, motoring casually out to his farm deep in the pristine acreage of horse country in Loudoun County, Virginia.

She was ready to undertake her mission less than 24-hours after taking up temporary residence in the Capitol Hill hotel.

At the same time, Detectives Perry and Ortiz were being redirected away from the Shelter Road Crew, and their intense pursuit of Mumbles. Crime was soaring through the roof as the District's unemployment rate surpassed 17 percent, with the far Southeast and Northeast regions suffering under the weight of nearly half the young black men between the age of 16 and 40 idled, with little prospects on the horizon. Those who had jobs faced extremely high rates for automobile and property insurance, the insurers making no secret that rates in these regions were nearly double those in Georgetown and the upper Northwest communities specifically because SE and NE autos and properties were twice as likely to be vandalized or stolen.

The search for baby Marquis Bridgefield was experiencing little success either and, to be sure, the black baby of a reported drug dealer was not generating Amber Alert lookout notices around the region. The drug market was even suffering intensely under the economic crisis, nationwide, and more violence was associated with the waning drug trade as dealers, with drugs by now their only sources of income, waging combat over the same increasingly meager dollars.

This was of little concern to Rachelle. She had always been quite astute at investing her extensive earnings, her retired parents often facilitating her purchase of properties, stocks, bonds, and a wealth of mineral investments, with more than a few safety deposit boxes in New York, Florida, California and Texas weighed down with gold bullion, platinum investments, and the deeds to an array of properties. An avid motorcyclist and owner of a ranch which boasted valued thoroughbred horses, Rachelle spent what could be considered her vacation times either on the back of a horse, or astride a custom Harley-Davidson.

"I always enjoy something big and powerful between my legs," she'd often joke to the few people she counted as friends. "There's nothing in the world like a fine ride."

On the second day into her D.C. mission, she felt that everything was in place, and every target's location surveilled and mapped out with precision.

On the second night, she donned the uniform of the cable company, affixed the cable television company Magnacards to the side of her "loaned" vehicle, cruised across the Anacostia River and rolled slowly into the deepest part of Southeast Washington.

Chapter Fifty-six

It was Lil' Melvin's job now to oversee sales on Shelter Road. His mother still lived there, along with his siblings. But he was "rolling" now, in his pea-brained assessment of his financial wherewithal. He had a nice car, and for the most part, was in residence full-time at the Hillcrest Heights home he and his superiors had acquired. But the business required him to make deliveries and collections in his old neighborhood, a task considered quite menial now to his bosses, Mumbles and Block.

With a precision even some real telephone and cable employees might have admired, the assassin attached a pair of tree- and pole-climbing spikes around her lower legs, just above the ankles, and professional mounting cleats. The method had long been put aside by true cable and phone men, who quite some time ago adapted the more expedient, and safer, use of a truck mounted bucket or, at minimum, an extension ladder. But her mission wouldn't allow for such frivolities; she secured the spike and cleats professionally, was atop the pole in twenty seconds.

To the throng of drug dealers, the cable lady up on the telephone pole seemed to be undertaking a task that should have been done during daylight. The boys along The Road at first expressed suspicions that she was Five-O. But upon closer perusal, the uniformed woman was much too attractive to have been anything close to a police. Indeed, she was so striking, with the long, flowing hair cascading from below the brim of the uniform hat, that quite a few of Lil' Melvin's minions couldn't help but stand below her, surrounding the telephone pole and shouting various and assorted come-ons up to her.

Lil' Melvin, pointing out the string of cars idling along the street with windows down, admonished his minions to take care of their business, and within fifteen minutes of the cable woman's arrival, he was the sole person looking up to the woman, a wide grin on his face and a string of uttered, somewhat unintelligible diatribe spilling from him in an effort to engage the woman.

She had on protective gloves, and advised the young man below her to step away, be cautious; she was about to work with some live wires.

"You don't want to be under me when I cut this cable and lower it down to carry it over to the next connection," she said, guessing correctly that the unreasonable move she was describing would make little sense to the young man.

He stepped back into the street, still looking up to her, as she clipped an electrical wire, sending a few sparks flying. She looked into the windows of some nearby buildings, reassuring herself that she'd only disconnected a line providing secondary power to the apartment units. Still securing the cut wire, she slowly descended the pole, smiling to the young man, who was the only one close to her current station midblock. Both ends of the street remained filled with activity, cars with passengers and drivers making exchanges with young men, young women standing outside their car windows. Few were even aware of the quiet exchange occurring between the "cable woman" and Lil' Melvin.

Carefully maneuvering the wire, she stepped curbside, wire in hand, towards the next telephone pole, about thirty-yards away. Lil' Melvin trailed her, spouting tracts which still made little sense to Rachelle. She suddenly paused half way to the second pole, bent forward as if examining something on the ground before her.

"Hey, young man," she said, motioning for Lil' Melvin to come closer to her. "Is this part of what all the activity is around here?"

He looked into the small patch of dirt and grass to where the woman was pointing, saw what appeared to be a sandwich bag, sealed and burgeoning with a white powder.

"Oh, snap!" he blurted out, bent and retrieved the baggie.

With a swiftness that didn't even allow Lil' Melvin chance to formulate in his addled mind what was occurring, Rachelle whipped the insulated part of the cable around his neck three times, adeptly pulled it tight and shoved the cable's end, flush with a bundle of exposed wires, deep into his mouth, down into his throat. Sparks danced from about his teeth, his skin blackened then sizzled a charcoal grey, his eyes bulged then began bleeding from around the sockets, the pupils swelling with bulbous welts then themselves leaking a mixture of blood and white ooze.

Gently, she lay him curbside, close to a parked car. She placed the baggie of cocaine, one of her many operational tools, into the breast pocket of Lil' Melvin's oversized shirt. It would be a little while before anyone noticed the dead body lying there, and when law enforcement officials examined the body for possible identification, finding the package of cocaine would more than likely distract any keen minds among them momentarily away from the gruesome method in which the young man had died.

Rachelle cruised out of the neighborhood with little notice, figuring quite correctly that this first elimination would not raise any alarm before she had time to complete the entire mission.

Chapter Fifty-seven

While she was at it, Rachelle saw no reason not to earn an additional $200,000 by taking on a contractual request of the Miami Boys. They had a problem in D.C. they needed erased, and after taking out Lil' Melvin, it was only a short distance to the camp of a notorious heroin dealer, a flamboyant man known by the name of Lucky Frog. So proud of his narcotically-underwritten achievements, Lucky was well known throughout the Woodside Terrace public housing project a few miles from Shelter Road, arriving on those depressing streets in a maroon convertible Bentley apparently to rub his financial success in the faces of those enslaved by his drugs. He wasn't a complete idiot, however: Lucky never carried narcotics in his personal ride, but was always followed by a ramshackle Toyota, whose occupants worked for him and were paid handsomely for merely ferrying his heroin packages into the poor communities.

Police were certainly well aware of Lucky. If the presence of his Bentley and colorful entourage in the projects weren't enough, the announcement of his coming was without fail preceded by the Jamaican rhythms blasting from an enhanced sound system which one might have mistaken for the approach of a marching band. And he not only served the heroin addicts in Woodside, but was the prime merchant of death in three other D.C. neighborhoods, a pocket of poverty in close-in Maryland, and a depressing string of public housing units in Northern Virginia.

His purchases from the Miami Boys was a major portion of their millions of dollars in annual sells. But it was certain that Lucky Frog would eventually be leapt upon by D.C. officials under federal pressure to do something about the city's narcotics problem, and even a casual assessment of Lucky's personal profile gave indication that he was not one who could face the prospects of a lengthy prison sentence if an alternative was offered. And that alternative of late had been federal and local teams offering lesser sentences if a corralled local dealer informed on their international source. The flamboyant Jamaican's time was quickly approaching, the Miami Boys had determined. While undertaking her own business in D.C., Rachelle was also to take out Lucky Frog with fatal efficiency.

She removed the Magnacards from the rental car after leaving Shelter Road, parked in the deserted lot of a decrepit housing complex and changed out of the cable company uniform, donning her black gear, a uniform not unlike that worn by law enforcement SWAT teams, but without the boisterous yellow logo. She assembled a weapon from her arsenal which, even then, brought a smile to her face: The high-powered sniper rifle, with scope, was so precise that, as she so often reminded herself, she could shoot a gnat off of a mosquito's ass at 500 meters.

Lucky Frog lived in a luxurious community just outside Southeast D.C. His Fort Washington home, where such luminaries as a retired professional boxer, a noted jazz musician, and high-ranking African-American government officials also lived, was a spectacle in and of itself. Sited on five acres on a bluff overlooking a southern bend in the Potomac River, Lucky owned the home out right. His wife, Gloria Manchester-Armstrong, was a popular reggae artist in her native Kingston, Jamaica. The two had been together since both were little more than "ragamuffins," poor, undernourished urchins begging for scraps in Trenchtown.

The two blossomed though, each in their own right, Gloria quite vocally, and quite legally, while "Dennard Regale," Lucky's given name which he'd always hated, worked his way up through the illicit drug trade. He was fortunate in having Gloria by his side all along the way; she facilitated an easy entrance for her eventual husband into the United States, both gaining permanent residency status, and also provided the legal income which justified their ability to acquire property and wealth many of their fellow countrymen only dreamed of.

Rachelle had the layout of their home down pat, and was also well aware of Lucky's habits, down to the hour, and was correct in predicting that he would be at his palatial home this evening, probably setting on the wrap-around, glass-enclosed patio to the rear of his mansion, dining or sipping drinks while peering out upon the dark Potomac waters a few yards off the rear of his property.

From a mile upriver, in a cove favored by local fishermen, Rachelle found the small watercraft exactly where she'd been told it would be moored. The moon, just entering its first quarter over the region, provided little light in the tree lined alcove; she had to move mostly by instincts, the beam of a flashlight too chancy, maybe catching the eyes of curious residents whose expensive homes sat all along this stretch of the river. She wouldn't use a motor either, her expertise with oars paying off well now, as she ensured the beloved marksman's rifle was secure in the watercraft, freed it and took to the considerably rapid currents.

She'd previously mapped out the complete contours of the river from her taking off point to the bend in the river a quarter mile beyond Lucky's home. She passed right by him, could actually make out his figure on the glass-enclosed balcony, took to struggling with the oars to direct the watercraft to the shore less than 100 feet down river from her target. After a brief fight with the currents, she managed to wrestle the boat into a small cove, was wet from foot to knees upon debarking, but secured the small vessel and moved stealthily. Taking the sniper's rifle and ensuring it stayed well above the waters, she waded up a small stream pouring into the Potomac, found the trail local fishermen had worn along the shoreline and moved towards her target.

Directly behind the home, she peered up a slight incline, reasoned correctly that a clean, effective shot from this angle was at best iffy. A few hundred yards from the rear balcony, a spacing of massive oaks sat majestically a short distance from the shoreline, and just far enough away from the home to provide a lush, protective canopy above the home's spacious back yard. Rachelle wished now she still had the cleats and spikes which had easily allowed her to scale the telephone pole earlier; a perch in the lower branches of one of the oaks would place her near perfectly horizontal to her target. She did however still have on leather gloves, and these might afford her purchase, a reasonable grip in combination with her lithe acrobatic skills to mount one of the trees. Slinging the rifle over a shoulder, she took to the base of an oak, gripped and shimmied her way with considerable effort until she reached a lower branch and was able to fix herself on a perch comfortable enough to allow her a clean shot or two.

She sited herself, freed the rifle from her shoulder, adjusted it and turned to a clear view of the balcony.

Lucky Frog was no longer there.

Chapter Fifty-eight

"It's always wit your mother!" Lucky Frog complained in his heavy Jamaican accent. "Always wit de fuckin' mwah!"

He was trailing his wife out the front door, lambasting her as he did with regularity when she answered the call of her mother, who lived in a comfortable condominium abutting Georgetown in the Northwest section of Washington.

"Always!" he continued. "De bitch call to you, you run like a rat to her! Always wit de fuckin' mwah!"

He stood in the ornate doorway, watching as his wife pinned him with a glare and climbed into the seat of her Lincoln Navigator. He remained there until she'd backed out of the driveway before the garage, still steaming. Watching also, from a low crouch to the far side of the house, the black-clad figure had a clear view of the front doorway. When Lucky Frog retreated within, Rachelle crept slowly back alongside the house and returned to the massive oak.

Back aloft, she looked through the telescopic scope of the rifle, could see activity on the second floor of the home; two children, apparently, bounded about on a bed in what was surely a rear bedroom. In seconds a young woman, appearing little more than a teenager, entered the children's room. She had on the blue uniform of a domestic, and the thick braids in her hair made her appear even younger. She appeared to chastise the children, who ceased their bounding and appeared to retire.

Through the scope, Rachelle focused back in on the lower rear balcony. Lucky Frog had returned there, pouring himself a drink and seeming to shout out to his rear, head bent upwards. In seconds the uniformed young lady appeared to his rear. She seemed a bit anxious, antsy, as Lucky Frog, standing and motioning with a hand, apparently issued instructions. Rachelle felt a measure of disgust as Lucky Frog took a big swig from a large goblet, planted himself in a lounge chair and undid his fly, leaned back and pulled penis from pants. Administering a few strokes unto himself, he motioned for the young lady to come forth, nodding at his midsection to the hesitant uniformed figure.

Slowly, she took to her knees before him, took him into an obviously unwilling mouth, began servicing him. Rachelle undid the Velcro which secured a black tab over the luminous dial of a watch, checked the time and realized she was at least an hour behind her planned schedule. She resecured the patch over the watch, wrapped a hand into the belt of the rifle and shouldered it, sighting in on the thrown back head of Lucky Frog. The silencer on the end of the high-powered rifle only allowed a little "puff" when she squeezed off the first round. A second round was directed at his head a millisecond later.

Dennard "Lucky Frog" Regale's *heads* exploded. Yes, plurally. Semen spattered into the domestic's mouth at the same time that dual sprays of blood, bone and brain erupted from his destroyed head, and the young lady, unaware of the gruesome activity occurring north of her kneeling position, thought that her boss had been especially pleased this time, the globule of semen nearly choking her. By the time he relaxed, slumped and unmoving, she realized the tinkling she'd heard was not the ringing in her ears she'd often experienced when "The Madam" was away and "Mr. Regale" had forced himself upon her. She looked around to see that a mid portion of the glass enclosure had been shattered, looked up to inform her boss. But the mass of destroyed flesh upon his shoulders was barely recognizable.

Rachelle heard the young lady's piercing scream just as she eased down the embankment towards her watercraft. She gave thought to the method in which Lucky Frog had just died, chuckled lightly. But she only gave thought to the unexpected confluence of his "coming and going" but for a few seconds. The night was still young, and she still had the bulk of her mission to accomplish.

Chapter Fifty-nine

Mumbles received word of Lil' Melvin's death by cell phone just before midnight. He was seated in the basement of the Hillcrest Heights home playing video games with a younger member of his crew, and one thing about the method of Lil' Melvin's death made something plain to Mumbles: This was certainly not the work of the Congress Park Boys.

He went to check on Tondra and the baby; little Marquis was surely taken out of necessity, presumably to ensure that his father didn't snitch to investigators. But that was perhaps behind them now, and although Block and others had argued that the child be "disposed of," Mumbles had taken to the baby as if it were his own, and was seriously considering keeping it as such.

Tondra complained that the cable was out upstairs. Returning to the basement, he motioned to the youngster Leon to hand him the television remote device, deactivated the game they were playing and was greeted by a screen of static and snow on the channel which should have been blazoned with some cable channel.

"Shh…..sh….sh…shit!"

"Cable out?" Leon asked.

"Wh….wh…wh…what……the……the…f…f…fuck….i…i…it……look like?"

Mumbles didn't abide questions he believed had a clear and obvious answer. It was enough that he often had to struggle to present a simple "No."

"Shit," Leon said. "I was gonna watch this movie later tonight."

That was the moment that they received the call.

Yes, their cable was inoperative. Sure, there would be somebody at the home when a repair person called at 8 the next morning. Tondra assured the woman caller that they'd be expecting her, informed Mumbles, Leon, and Block, who'd arrived home later. The men played games into the early morning hour, Tondra saw to the baby, and by four in the morning, the house was quiet. Additional members of the crew had come in during the predawn hours and joined the others. Within minutes, the house was totally silent, the occupants sound asleep.

In the rental car three blocks from the Hillcrest Heights home, the woman who'd called the house and promised early morning repair service decided to get a little shut-eye herself. Rachelle set her wrist alarm for 7 a.m., though only for added security reasons. She was almost certain that her precise internal clock would awaken her at the appointed hour. She eased into the back seat of the car, pulled a blanket over her and eased into a light sleep.

Never a heavy sleeper himself, Mumbles awakened just after sunrise to the cries of the baby Marquis down the hall from his own bedroom. He pulled on a pair of sweatpants, moved to the room where the baby slept alongside Tondra. The crack head woman was snoring with the roar of a 747 engine, mouth agape, with the small baby almost tucked under her frail form, appearing to Mumbles as if afraid of the roaring creature beside him. Shaking his head, Mumbles moved over to the bed and hoisted the baby to a shoulder, patting it gently on the back and cooing to it softly.

"B…b…b…bu…bu…baby. Sh…sh…shhhhhh. Sh….sh….shhhhhh."

Everyone else in the house remained abed, and would remain so well towards the noon hour, which was common among the residents, and those who frequently visited well into the next day and wound up camped out on the living room sofa, the living room floor, or on either the sofa or chairs in the basement.

Having watched Tondra prepare the baby's formula over the past few months, Mumbles was quite adept at preparing the baby's bottle. He moved about the kitchen with Marquis still embraced in one arm, head on his shoulder. He checked the time on the face of the microwave oven: 7:47 a.m. He switched on the portable television on a kitchen countertop. The snowy image reminded him of the cable outage. He flicked the unit off, moved to the stove to test the progress of the bottle heating in water in a saucepan.

A few blocks away at the same time, Rachelle was again donning the cable company uniform. She checked again the tool bag she was to carry, ensuring that the weapons were loaded, the silencers in place, initial rounds chambered.

"Seven fifty-five," she uttered the time, climbed out of the rear of the car and slid into the driver's seat.

Seemed that most residents in the sleepy community were heading out, taking the small streets towards a main thoroughfare which led further towards the Capital Beltway, to the city and expansive suburban business locations. Rachelle drove against the traffic, a few smiling neighborhood faces waving a cordial hand at the "cable woman," her car again sporting the Magnacards of the company. At exactly 8:00 a.m., she pulled before the ranch style home, its small driveway before a two-car garage still occupied by a late-model luxury car and an equally new SUV. She grabbed her bag, a clipboard fixed with a ream of official looking papers, took the walkway up to the front door.

"Y...y..yo!" the man who answered with the baby on his shoulder said. "C...c...cable?"

"Yes, sir," the attractive woman said. "From our headquarters, there appears to be nothing wrong with the external lines leading to the house. Can I come in and check on your internal connections?"

He stepped aside, still holding open the storm door.

"C...c....come," he motioned with his head.

She smiled, stepped into the warm home. Mumbles. She knew this was the one she'd heard so much about, but had never met. She looked around, seeing no others in the living room, or in the kitchen and dining room, visible from the main entrance.

"I...have....t....t...to...f...f...feed....b.....baby," he said, moving back towards the kitchen.

"Go ahead. I'll find my way around to the connections I need to check. The basement that way?" she pointed to a closed door.

"Y...y...yeah."

She presented a final smile to him as he disappeared into the kitchen. She eased the basement door open, unleashed the clasp on her bag, palmed the silenced 9mm and descended. A dim table light illuminated a scene straight out of a 1970's fraternity flick: Young men, from teen to young adult, sprawled about on the carpeted floor, in a lounge chair, one stretched out on the leather sofa. Silently and efficiently, without arousing a soul, Rachelle moved to each individual, placed the 9 flush against a temple, and squeezed off two rounds. Four souls engaged in a final ascension even as their facilitator placed the 9 in her satchel and climbed back up to the main floor.

Just next to the main entrance, a stairway led to the upper floor. There, in three bedrooms, those deemed key residents of the home maintained bedrooms. Mumbles had his, one was set aside for Tondra and the baby, the third belonging to Block, when he spent the night and wanted to "freak" Tondra instead the girlfriend he lived with in the city. Unfortunately for him, Block had an express desire for Tondra's practiced tongue the previous night, had come, been served, and gone to his room to sleep away the morning.

With an uncommon urge to be torturous, Rachelle eased the bedroom door open and recognized Block, a frequent visitor to her New York residence and secondary in importance on this list of those she'd been dispatched to, well, dispatch.

He was sleeping soundly. She crept up to his bedside, retrieved a nearby chair and took a seat just a foot from his spacious head. With a wry smile, she rested a second, fully loaded 9mm on one thigh, pointed directly at the man's head. With her free hand, she gently shook him awake, put the index finger on the same hand before her lush lips, demanding silence as the confused eyes eased open, then grew wide with recognition and cold blooded fear.

"Hi baby," Rachelle smiled. "Just wanted to wish you a good morning before giving you a final goodnight. You and your boys really messed up, Block. Goodnight, darling."

Effortlessly, not even moving the gun from her thigh, she squeezed off four rounds, in groups of twos, and it was virtually impossible for any of the rounds to not carve a critical path through the oversized cranium. The eyes still bulged out in total shock as last breath escaped the body and, still with the slight smile, Rachelle arose and stepped silently out of the room, closing the door behind her.

She moved down the hall, peered into a room where a skeletal women's rumbling snore seemed to send a breeze skirting through Rachelle's flowing locks. The woman was obviously a victim of the Shelter Road Crew, and Rachelle saw no need to disturb her sleep. She'd more than likely be awaken most viciously later, so Rachelle allowed her to sleep on, closed the door and headed back to the stairway.

It seemed that, without fail in his considerably short but violent lifetime, Mumbles had been provided with something of a sixth sense when it came to danger. As if to make up for his lack of a gifted, or even general tongue, he seemed to have been granted an ability to sense when things were going wrong, or when danger was near. Even as his friend Block issued last breath upstairs, Mumbles settled the baby on an amassment of pillows on the sofa, placed the bottle so that the infant could feed, then eased to the top of the stairs. Peeping around the corner down the hallway, he saw the "cable woman," gun in hand, peering into the room from which Tondra's growling echoed. He needed one of his guns, seriously. But they were down the hall, in his bedroom, just past the armed woman.

Just as she turned, Mumbles considered that he had little choice, that the woman was evidently a professional. He immediately connected her to the report he'd received of how his minion Lil' Melvin had been brutally slain the previous night, took only a second to grab a coat, head for the back door behind the kitchen, and tear off on foot into the woods to the rear of the house.

Chapter Sixty

She checked the house over again. Thoroughly. Mumbles had evidently become aware of what awaited him and high-tailed it out of there. Both vehicles remained in the driveway, so she rightly assumed that he had escaped on foot.

"Man!" she said to a house all but empty of life. "I thought you were supposed to be a true terror."

She then saw the baby on the sofa, knew it had to be the kidnapped infant belonging to her one-time business associate Ellis, and had her second uncommon idea on a mission gone pretty smoothly thus far. On the coffee table before the baby was a cellular phone. She retrieved it, pressed a few buttons and accessed the device's phone book. Her mind formulating plans rapidly, she wrapped the baby securely in the blanket it lay on, took him in her arms and returned to her car.

She put the baby on the floor behind the passenger's seat, ensured it didn't move much by packing her satchel and a few of her soft travel bags around it. She scrolled again through the retrieved cellular, wrote down every number in its address book. Then she made a 9-1-1 call from the cellular she was by now sure belonged to Mumbles, sobbed into the unit in a performance worthy of an Emmy.

"He's killed them all!" she wept. "It's that crazy man they call Mumbles!"

She gave the address of the home, tossed the telephone out the car window onto the home's lawn, its 9-1-1 connectivity still active. She then drove apace towards the nearest road leading onto the Capital Beltway.

Well aware of where Ellis, her last "contact," was located, she had plenty of time to give thought to the adjusted plans she had in mind. The rush-hour traffic in the Washington region was among the worst in the nation, and she had plenty of time creeping along heading to the apartment where Ellis was probably alone with his daughter Lauren. Her skills as an investigator rivaled those of many law enforcement and intelligence agencies, and she was well aware that his girlfriend Donna had been recently employed by a temporary agency. As a new hire, she was surely heading to work to meet her 9 a.m. appointed starting hour by now.

In traffic that crawled at times, she made her way to the apartment building, a high rise unit in Southeast which seemed out of place, surrounded by nice, single-family homes to one side, seedy, two-story rentals to the other. She checked on the baby, retrieved a large gym bag from the rear seat and fitted the child comfortably in it. She left the car, moved around it to retrieve the child/bag, stepped into the complex, made the call to Ellis. He answered on the third ring.

"Hello Ellis," she said, the sensual voice unmistakable. "I'm in your city on business, got a hold of your location, down in the lobby and would like to meet with you. Can I come up?"

Ellis had been watching the morning local news since Donna arose at 5:30 and turned it on as she prepared for work. Only vague reports were being aired about a few murders in the city overnight, but a camera shot of Shelter Road had caught his attention. No name of the murdered youth was given, but Ellis figured he knew everyone out upon that location, and became edgy even hearing the report.

A second one, about what appeared to be the professional assassination of a notorious heroin dealer in his Fort Washington home, was chalked up by Ellis to just another sordid part of the expansive D.C. drug game, not associated with him whatsoever.

"Dern, Miss Lady," he replied, still watching the news but muting the volume, "You're in *my* building? How you know where I live? I just moved here not long ago."

Something wasn't right, and although he'd long trusted Rachelle, her presence here didn't sit quite well with him.

"I have a package for you," she said sweetly. "And, no, it's not what you generally receive from me. Come on, baby. I have business to take care of. Don't have but a few minutes and I'm *sure* you'll just love this little gift I have for you."

With a measure of caution, he relented. He made sure that the 9mm was loaded, setting on a chair shoved under the dinette table. Another weapon, a smaller, .32 revolver, was under the cushion of the living room sofa.

"If you're by yourself, come on up. Apartment 701," he instructed, but the phone was dead and someone was tapping lightly on the door.

He looked out the peephole, its convex structure providing a near full-body view of the voluptuous woman and the immediate hallway about her. Cautiously, he eased the door open.

"Hi baby," she said, placing a free arm around his shoulder, planting a kiss on a cheek while appearing to struggle with the weight of the gym bag she held.

She lifted the bag, held it forth to Ellis.

"I believe this belongs to you," she said.

Ever cautious, he took the bag, which was partially opened, nearly shoved it back to her when a whimpering sound filtered from within the satchel. Easing it to the floor, he opened it fully, kneeling, looked with wide, confused eyes down upon his baby.

"Damn! Marquis!" He carefully lifted the boy out of the bag. "What....? How the...? Damn!"

He pulled the baby to him, gently, kissed a chubby cheek, put it to his shoulder and looked up to a smiling Rachelle.

"How the *hell* did you get my boy?"

"Business, Ellis. A lot you don't know, son."

She looked around the well appointed apartment, to the living room flush with expensive furnishing, to the balcony beyond the sofa, a view of the U.S. Capitol, downtown Washington in the distance.

"Can we sit for a minute?" she asked.

He cuddled Marquis before him, looked down upon the child then back to her, confused. He motioned towards the living room sofa.

"Sure."

She took a seat, stern, serious, watched him closely until he was seated with the baby directly across from her.

"Ellis, you really never knew me," she began, leaning into the conversation. "Beyond what you saw of me and Dominique, and the product we provided you and your crew with, there's a whole other arena I operate in, which is an integral part of our international enterprise. An arena you and your boys here were never really a part of."

He remained silent, eyes dancing between the baby and the woman across from him he no longer felt comfortable with.

"Your drug distribution days are over," she continued. "Well, either *they* are over, or, to put it bluntly, your life is. You do have a choice in the matter."

Her tone was chilling, and not the pleasant, sensual one he'd heard dancing through the rooms on Adam Clayton Powell Boulevard. She even appeared, if not chilling, then cold, lacking the warmth her beauty and smile had reflected in past meetings.

"Your friend Block is no more," she went on, eyes now haunting, piercing, "and I'm responsible for that, Ellis. I've been sent to erase any links between your...*crews,* here in the D.C. region, and our extended operations out of New York and Florida and further south. To tell you the truth, we never really considered you guys to be much a part of our extensive network; sure, you brought us a few million over the years, but in the grander scheme of things, that was but a pittance. And with the federal authorities determined to accomplish a major public relations ploy with the arrest of some they determine to be large-scale dealers, well Ellis, it has been determined that your little organization has got to be eliminated."

He looked to his child, closed his eyes momentarily and leaned back, as if in deep thought.

"That...that *thing* I heard on the news this morning, about a dude killed on Shelter Road last night?"

"The one you called Lil' Melvin."

"Aw, snap! That was Lil' Melvin? He dead?"

"Cooked, as a matter of fact. Roasted. Nice little piece of work, if I must say so myself. Made a powerful statement to his friends over there."

"Aw damn! And you know who did that shit, huh Rachelle?"

"I did." She was smiling now. "And your friend Block, just a little while ago. Four of his...how you say...*posse,* in the basement of the Maryland home they thought no one knew of. Your friend Mumbles? I would think before another sunrise, he'll no longer be with us."

"Man! Rachelle, you're crazy! What the fuck?"

She just smiled, leaving him a moment to ponder his own fate. In a few moments, he did apparently, pulled Marquis tighter to him.

"You ain't here to take me out, are you?"

"Like I was saying moments ago," she said, the warm smile returning, "your drug distribution days are over. And remember the caveat I added: Either that's over, or your life is. Doesn't seem like so hard a choice to make."

Ellis was crumbling under the pressure, indecisive and not sure of just what to do. He'd never been one to engage in violence, and the .38, just inches behind him under the sofa cushion, was a considered option at the moment. He eased a hand away from around Marquis, to his lap, then to the creases between the sofa cushion.

"Don't be a fool, Ellis," she said, again the cold eyes unfamiliar. "Think about Marquis there, and…little Lauren. And your other daughter, Michelle. By the way, is Lauren in her bedroom, watching her morning cartoons, videos?"

Ellis returned the hand to around his son, shook his head.

"We got her in daycare just this week," Ellis said.

Rachelle gritted, mentally lambasting herself for the matter, no matter how small, of having not already known this about the little girl.

"Well, I'm going to take your silence as an agreement that you and the drug game are no longer in the same venue, as it were," she said, arising.

"Ellis, I'm going to get right to the point, because I still have your friend Mumbles to contend with. *If* we ever get word that you are even attempting to recop, from *anywhere*, and start back up with your considerably juvenile drug distribution game, we will have to consider that, eventually, you're going to wind up back in the hands of authorities, and truthfully, we may not be at the same location in NY that you are familiar with, but we will *not* take any chances on you sitting down with officials and identifying either myself, Dominique, or any of our other associates you might have come into contact with. Ellis, get you a job; I know you're kind of short on funds right now, but that's not my problem. Get you a job, settle down with either this lady friend, Shantelle, Linda, whomever, raise your children. And you can thank your children, especially that little cute one you're holding there, for your very life. It was only after knowing of the situation with his being kidnapped, then finding him at Mumbles' and Block's house, that I reconsidered my order to eliminate you too, along with your confederates."

She moved towards the door, retrieved her gym bag, turned with the warm smile he was more accustomed to.

"Goodbye, Ellis. Remember, if I ever see you again, if I ever *have* to see you again, believe one thing: You will not see me."

Chapter Sixty-one

He knew he was headed in the right direction, and the sun began burning away a light fog which had clung to the lower level of underbrush in the woods. Ahead was a clearing, a dip in the terrain, a valley. Far ahead on a hillside, he could make out the archaic brick form of Garfield Elementary School. The old neighborhood. Home.

It would be at great a risk if he even went near Shelter Road. But he didn't have a dime in his pocket, or a morsel of crack or powder. His car keys, guns and a rack of money had been left in the room just past the gunman he'd seen standing outside Block's room. He wasn't going back their either. Nothing of value remained at Miss Charlene's, but in his mind at the moment her apartment seemed the only place he could head to get out of the public, to give some thought to his situation and, yes, bang her out with such a heated drive that at least he might gain a moment of relief from the situation which he presently found himself in.

"Sh….sh….sh…..shit!" he murmured, fought through the thick foliage and made his way towards the clearing.

By now reports of the Hillcrest Heights "mass murder," and their apparent ties to a couple of other regional slayings in the past 24-hours, was making both local and national news. Few on ground level had heard about the slayings or connections though, most not of the mind to keep abreast of news items. Mumbles, of course, was completely in the dark, and as he stood on a hillside surveying the scene around Miss Charlene's apartment for a possible police presence, he was still not sure exactly what had happened in the Hillcrest Heights home. And surely, he had no idea as to who was responsible.

Rachelle was also surveying the scene around Miss Charlene's, but from a different vantage point. She had the location on a list of possible locations used by "Delano Johnson" even before coming to the city, and having almost connected with him at the Maryland locale earlier didn't sway her in the least: She was sure to complete the entirety of her mission before too long, and was even now giving thought to the culmination of her mission. She wanted to ensure that Johnson, aka Mumbles, went out with a splash.

There he was! Dashing across the street and into the building as if a lion was on his tail! Same clothes as he'd worn when she went to solve the "cable problem" at the Maryland home. Same simian-like stride and features. She'd correctly guessed that he'd seek solace at the crack woman's unit where he'd reportedly spent the previous summer. She was also sure that, once in there, he'd not be leaving for a good while.

Rachelle returned to her car, a short distance away, took inventory. The "flash/bang" grenade would be used to shake her target from his cave. There were children in the unit, she knew, and they'd evacuate also when the device was deployed, but would not face any danger. The flash/bang was often used by law enforcement officials, and sometimes by military forces in combat situations: An explosive which did little damage but momentarily interrupted the mental faculties and temporarily blinded those unexpectedly exposed to it.

The sniper rifle was useless in the take-down she planned. She'd wield the Uzi submachine gun, silenced; carry the 9mm as back up in case something unexpected occurred. She really didn't believe Mumbles had any weapons left in the apartment where he currently took shelter, but Rachelle was not one to chance anything.

She looked to her watch, took her time donning a completely black outfit. Nightfall was a few hours off. She picked up a book she kept just for such moments, to avoid boredom, and read passages from Machiavelli's "The Prince."

Even before moving to the rear of the unit to surprise Miss Charlene by knocking unexpectedly, Mumbles moved to a unit known to be occupied by crack head squatters. Sure enough, the bedraggled men who had taken over the empty unit lounged around inside, one fingering the residual contents of some cigarette butts into a fold of rolling paper, creating an emergency smoke. They acknowledge Mumbles, two seeming to even lighten up at his unexpected entrance, until he shook his head, an indication that he didn't have any drugs.

"Sc....sc....screwdriver," Mumbles asked, looking around the dirty space.

One man reached behind a mattress pushed against one wall, pulled a screwdriver out and handed it up to Mumbles.

"B...b...be right....bb.....b....back."

Quickly, he moved to the metal mailboxes just inside the apartment entrance, pried open the slot to his old unit upstairs, reached into the rear and smiled, pleased to find that his secreted pistol was still there. He returned the screwdriver, went to Miss Charlene's unit.

Miss Charlene was flabbergasted to see him, his usual poise and confidence melted away. He appeared frightened, and Mumbles feared no one. Or so she and most of his associates had long thought. Kanisha, Michael, Ricky and Patrania didn't notice anything but that he was bearing no gifts, yet still ran to him excitedly, embracing him around the waist and thighs.

"Mr. Mumbles!" they cried, while their mother stood by the secured door, sensing that this was one time when she'd be sorry that her previous lover and drug enabler had come calling.

"H…h…hey….y…y…y'all," he said, so soft it was all but a whisper, another sign to Miss Charlene that something wasn't right with the man.

He stumbled through an explanation of his plight, quite torturous to the woman who was still battling her addiction and equally to the four children, who were still battling hunger. Listening to all this through a stethoscope-like device flush against an outside window was Rachelle. Her plan was ready to be put into motion, but out of consideration for the kids, she'd not use the flash/bang, but a simple smoke grenade, which would most assuredly have every occupant of the place fleeing outdoors, unharmed.

She moved stealthily in the darkness along the lower rear edge of the building, to a set of windows lighted and barely covered. She peered through the kitchen to Mumbles and the woman seated at the dining room table, moved to another smaller window which was most certainly the bathroom. She attached a suction device to a lower pane, quietly used a tool to etch a circle around it and easily popped out an opening. She pulled the pin on a smoke grenade, tossed it through the opening and, not awaiting its effect, dashed back to a previously surveilled spot in underbrush to the front and side of the building.

"Wh...wh...what the...f....f....fuck?"

The children let out piercing screams while their mother embraced the youngest, arose and attempted to peer into the bathroom. Thick white smoke poured from the small room, and no knowing its source added to the confusion. Kanisha was already wrenching open the front door and, followed by her siblings, racing out of the unit, down the hallway and out the building, all still emitting piercing screams. Mumbles was still trying to fix his mind around what had happened, but always cautious of the law and familiar with many law enforcement tactics, he believed the police had tossed a smoking device into the unit and lay wait for him to exit. But there was little choice. The smoke quickly permeated the unit, and, securing the pistol in his waistband, he tore out of the apartment behind Miss Charlene.

The mother stood with the children grouped around her, and Mumbles' confusion grew further as the outdoors was all but deserted. No police. No SWAT team descending on him. But he knew *something* had been put in place for him, not Miss Charlene and the children. Someone had thrown the smoke device into the unit after seeing *him* enter the building. And he wasn't about to wait around to find out just who it was that was stalking him.

He looked to Miss Charlene, who remained huddled with the children, a confused look on her face. There wasn't need or time for an exchange of words. Mumbles tore off across the street, to a row of identical apartments in the complex, with the sparse woods backing these from which he'd surfaced upon arrival.

Right into the sights of Rachelle, who lay there with a measure of patience, so that her burst of gunfire would not unintentionally tear into the woman and children who remained in the immediate background.

He was just 50 feet away from her now, moving directly towards the position she'd taken, unseen in the underbrush. She released a small burst of rounds from the submachine gun, raking the burst expertly across his legs, kneecap level. Shocked and immediately hobbled, Mumbles fell to the ground between two apartment buildings, feet from the woods, from the hidden assailant. He wrenched around in pain to one side, the shattered kneecaps completely disabling him. He was able to retrieve his pistol, cut loose two rounds into the woods, rounds which spit past Rachelle harmlessly.

"Sh...sh....shit!" he cried, now determined to at least level damage himself upon the unknown assailant.

He dragged himself towards the woods just as spits of dirt apparently from directed gunfire torn up from the ground before him, descended to him, ripped into a shoulder.

"M...M...Mother...f....f...fuck!"

He now had a clearer target, a clearer direction, though only thick foliage lay before him. He'd seen flares from the weapon in the woods, directed the .25 there, sent off five rapid rounds.

"K…K….Kill……………... M….M…Mumbles! K…K….Kill!"

He tried again to raise himself, managed a more upright crawl.

Singles shots. Spat! Spat! Silenced. But the impact was great. One round tore into a bicep, another into his abdomen. But Mumbles was only further infuriated, dragged himself closer to the gunfire on his good arm, directed the .25 into the darkness with the other.

"K….K…Kill,…………….. M…M…Mumbles! K….K….Kill!"

Three more rounds into the woods from his pistol, and then the chamber locked rearward, an indication that the clip was empty, all bullets expended.

He tossed the gun aside, looked about for a rock, a branch, anything that he might wield, determined to continue an offense, inching further towards the woods.

"M….M….Mumbles…Mu….Mu…Mumbles…. .r…..*ready* t…t….to….die! M..M..Mumbles….tired!"

He reached the edge of the woods, and the black clad figure who emerged just before him only further served to enrage him.

"A…m….mother…f….f…fuckin'…..*bitch*!" he cried out, looking up to the woman, quite attractive but for the submachine gun she leveled directly at his head.

"Yeah, Mumbles," the assassin said with a slight smile. "I'll be your bitch."

With the machinegun still at waist level, seemingly relaxed in her grip, she squeezed off a burst of four rounds. They peppered his face almost symmetrically, ripping a pattern up his face dead center. Only fragmentary bone and cartilage kept the head from separating entirely, and even the last breath of Delano "Mumbles" Johnson had to bubble up through destroyed sinuses and escape in a wet globule of blood-string trailings and crimson snot.

"So long, son," Rachelle said, breathing a sigh of relief that this latest mission was at last concluded.

She returned to the car, her bags already packed. A block away, the Southern Avenue Metro station marked the first over ground rail yard for the city subway system after it rose through Southeast and sped into Prince Georges County. Her plans had already been made, with precision. She left a series of electronically-delayed incendiary devices in the car, in the vehicle's trunk, passenger compartment, and under the hood. One device, timed to detonate 1.5 minutes after the first three, was securely attached to the car's gas tank. She had made sure to fill it much earlier.

Rachelle left the weapons, extra ordnance, maps, the cable uniform, the Magnacards, in the vehicle. She carried only an overnight bag bearing lingerie and cosmetics, travel items suitable for the beautiful, well-suited and adorned woman who left the vehicle for the short walk to the subway station. It was fifteen minutes before a train from Maryland headed to downtown Washington would arrive. She heard the distant explosion, smiled slightly, then reread her Amtrak Acela ticket and checked her watch.

The subway, after a single transfer, would put her at Union Station in plenty of time.

She boarded the arriving Metro train, all but empty at this hour heading in the direction of downtown. She took out her copy of "The Prince," relaxed and headed back to New York City.

Epilogue

At 35, Ellis Davidson was still struggling to gain his footing in the general workplace. He'd spent his teenaged years and most of his twenties marketing drugs, did quite well at that for a while, but when he was given the option of either living or continuing, however briefly, in the drug trade, he chose life, but was quite unskilled at pursuing it. With three children at the end of his narcotics escapade, five now, he had responsibilities many gainfully employed people found a struggle. Taking his initial steps into the legal workforce at the age of 28, he found the luxuries previously afforded, let alone his judicially reinforced responsibility to support his children, almost impossible on a minimum wage salary.

Adding to the financial calamity, the world had finally been made aware that the global sources of fossil fuels, crude oil which fueled major segments of world economies, were in shorter, non-replinishable supply than previously disclosed. When this fact became widely known, gas, home heating oil and electricity prices quadrupled. Americans, used to paying then $3.00 per gallon for gas, were abandoning cars by the lot full, unable to keep up with costs averaging $7.79 per gallon and, making matters even worse, a near cutting of gas station locales nationally by 60 percent.

This was of little concern to Ellis; he'd long since found that even insurance for his SUV had been unaffordable, and anyway he had been forced to sell off his ride to satisfy the judgment of the courts in the case of child support for Marquis, later for Michelle, his daughter by his old Barry Farm flame Linda, while still maintaining a household with Donna, Lauren and their latest child, Evan. To make matters worse, Ellis, never quite as hardcore and streetwise as he'd made himself out to be, had been robbed on two occasions, completely debasing him and additionally dissuading him for even a considered attempt at acting as a middleman for some drug deal for a quick profit.

The price of gas was not the only thing that weighed most heavily on the lower-income communities of D.C. which Ellis was now a solid part of. National and international efforts at combating drug distribution nearly completely wiped out the sales of cocaine of any form, particularly the cheaper crack form, on the streets of the inner cities. And just like Ellis, teens and young adults who'd spent their youths wallowing in unaccustomed wealth from dealing drugs were now scraping by on a pittance, unskilled and with a work history which could not be cited by potential employers as references.

After working a series of day jobs for a meager paycheck, Ellis was finally afforded a full-time, permanent job with city's Department of Public Works, the unit responsible for, among other things, picking up citizens' trash. Oddly enough, he was able to get the position through the inside efforts of Shantelle, by now a seasoned DPW employee. She had years ago written him off as a potential husband, had pawned the $4000.00 engagement ring for $300.00, and failed to retrieve it before the time limit and lost if for that small "loan."

Shantelle was also well aware that Ellis had taken up what seemed to be permanent residency with Donna and their now two children, but had dual purposes in helping him find gainful employment: She still had feelings for the father of her son Marquis and, secondarily, his having a job ensured that his child support payments were made regularly without her having to again petition the courts.

For her part, Donna maintained work as a secretary, but with their two children, and his years of day work before gaining the DPW job, the family was forced to move out of the considerably middle-class apartment building they'd initially occupied when first cohabitating and, to her dismay, move into one of the few communities in the city affordable to them: the Shelter Road Apartment Complex. Ellis had a most sordid history there, but after ten years out of the drug trade, and with most of his prior underlings on Shelter Road long dead or doing extensive prison time, he was little recognized upon his return there.

That is, except for by a team of juvenile stick-up boys at one time, who, seeing a shopworn worker in DPW soiled overalls, reasoned that the trash man was probably coming home with a least a few dollars in his pocket.

Now well into his thirties, Ellis spent little time outside the home, didn't drink or smoke, and had little in the way of entertainment at hand other than watching television end on end and, on occasion, revisiting one of the last persons with whom he could reflect on the past, on his considerably short span of prosperity, and uncertain prospects for the future.

Most warm summer evenings and especially on a Saturday night, his old friend in the wheelchair, Big Mack, still held court by the Shipley Terrace Liquor Store. After a most torturous day riding on the back of a city trash truck, he went home, showered and dressed in the best jeans, the newest tennis shoes, and the most stylish and colorful dress shirt available from his modest wardrobe, walked the seven blocks to the liquor store and greeted Big Mack with an appreciative hug.

"So, young blood, here you are back at square one," the finely dressed paraplegic said, peering up from under the Kango cap rakishly pulled down upon an Afro hairstyle, puffed and teased out into 1970s-era splendor.

"I hear ya, Big Mack," Ellis said, smiling slightly.

"Been a while," Big Mack continued. "Not a lot of your crew from your hustling days still around, huh man?"

"Not many…"

"Remember your boy Mumbles. That was one cold-blooded mother fucker," Big Mack said, staring at the throng filtering in and out of the liquor store. "From what I hear, hit came out of New York on his ass. Real professional shit. Never did catch the people did him in, did they?"

"Naw. Say it was the same ones hit Block and them out there at the house in Hillcrest Heights. And Lil' Melvin down on Shelter. And a couple of other mother fuckers. All in about twenty-four hours. Them was some bad mother fuckers."

An image of Rachelle played through his mind, but ever since their last meeting, when she'd issued him the ultimatum, he still couldn't believe that the exotic beauty was behind the string of killings.

"Bad mother fuckers," Big Mack allowed. "Bad, bad sons of bitches."

They were silent for a minute or two, watching the joyous children run in and out of the Korean market, the drinkers pour their last dollars into the liquor store, the single mothers, even at this evening hour, toiling carts of spoiled clothing into the Laundromat adjoining the storefronts. The oversaturated, already drunk with a stomach calling out for relief, stumbling into the Chinese carry-out for, more than likely, fried chicken wings.

"So, they tell me your with DPW," Big Mack said. "You was lucky to get on there: Lot of the dudes pulling trash fresh out from doing time. DPW one of the few joints hire ex-cons."

"Yeah. Everybody else on my route did time a while back, or just recently."

Big Mack took off his dark shades, the sun disappearing behind the few trees and crumbing edifices to their west.

"I always told you, young buck, while you were rolling in the dough, to put it to use wisely." He looked up to see if Ellis was paying attention, peered back across to the storefronts and waved at a familiar drunk. "At one time I remember you were telling me you had to find somewhere to stash a few hundred-thousand dollars. A few hundred-*thousand!*"

He paused, looked up and nodded, as if for emphasis, but also in a gesture of chastisement.

"Now look at you," he continued. "You hardly got a pot to piss in or a window to throw it out."

This statement somewhat shamed Ellis, and Big Mack could sense it, wishing he'd not been so cold, so blunt.

"I don't mean no harm, young buck," he said, smiling. "But you know the truth hurts. All you young'uns, thought you was all that, selling coke a hundred miles an hour, riding around in Escalades and Navigators, Mercedes, Lexuses. Going down Constitution Hall to all the shows. Clubbing. Living it up. Well, young buck, at least you came out of it in one piece. And you're still considerably a young'un, comparatively. I told you you'd be right if you kept two things in mind: Don't let your dick make a bum out of you, and don't be hustling backwards. I guess you thought an old fool like me, shot and crippled before I hardly got to your age, was just talking loud, saying nothing."

"Naw, Mack. I always did take you seriously. You know that."

"Yeah. But the shit went in one ear and out the other, evidently."

The street grew even more active, seemingly correspondingly with the arriving of darkness. As Ellis and Big Mack loitered there, taking in the scene, five young ladies, appearing in their late teens, early twenties, walked by. One paused, looked to Ellis as if gauging his potential for...something. Dressed in sagging jeans and tan Timberwolf hiking boots, she appeared quite masculine, and to be sure, was the leader of a gang of female marijuana dealers familiar in the area and reputed to despise men.

"You want some of this good weed, slim," the young lady said, looking directly to Ellis.

"Naw babe," he said. "I don't fuck around."
"Cool," she said, then moved off to her posse.

"Man, these young girls something else," Ellis said, shaking his head and grinning broadly. "She looks like this little girl used to be around the way long time ago. Probably is her."

Big Mack looked to the retreating posse, quite familiar with this particular group, and well versed in the backgrounds of most who were presently in the community, new to the community, or grew up in the community.

"Yeah, young blood," he said, again focusing on the hectic goings-on across the street. "That's that little girl got a lesbian posse, be selling weed and, if that ain't enough, be running around with guns sticking up dudes and shit. I done seen that one whip up on a girl thought she was Miss Fine till we had to call an ambulance. Her name's Kanisha. Some people call her KK. You might have known her mother, old broad used to be a crack head, your boy Mumbles used to mess with sometimes I hear. Her mother been dead about four, five years now. Was in the Laundromat bathroom giving head for crack one night, got on the wrong side of somebody or tried to steal one of them dude's drug stash, shot her cold dead. Think they used to call the girl's mama Miss Charlene. Or some shit."

"Damn!" Ellis said, recalling the women once a favorite companion of his old buddy Mumbles. "That's the oldest girl of Miss Charlene's: Kanisha. Wonder what happened to her other children after their mother got killed?"

"The boys are already in jail, so I hear," Big Mack said knowingly. "Other girl, I think, out whoring. Still a child basically, teenager, but working the streets uptown. Nobody know how to hustle no more, young buck. If it ain't legal, it ain't about nothing in the long run, better bet it. The old hustlers are all mostly dead, my man. Deader than a mother fucker. Deader than most of the mother fuckers gonna be eventually out here today who call themselves hustlers. Two things you don't see out on the streets today, young buck: Old dope fiends, and old hustlers. Neither one of them joints conducive to longevity, know what I'm saying?"

Ellis merely nodded, stood silently for a moment reflecting on his own past, the wasted years and, to be sure, the seriously wasted volumes of energy and countless mounds of money.

"Sure you're right, Big Mack. Sure you're right," he said finally, bent to deliver a respectful hug to the man then headed back to his family's small Shelter Road apartment. He walked the bustling few blocks alone, unrecognized, unacknowledged, in thoughts of a future more clearer now than ever but certainly one lacking of any of the grand expectations he'd long held for himself, for his family, and for his now all but nonexistent circle of true friends.

The End

Made in the USA
Charleston, SC
06 December 2014